# HOME WHERE SHE BELONGS

### Abbott Island Series

## Penny Frost McGinnis

M ✠ Zion Ridge Press LLC

Mt Zion Ridge Press LLC
295 Gum Springs Rd, NW
Georgetown, TN 37366

https://www.mtzionridgepress.com

ISBN 13: 978-1-955838-16-0

Published in the United States of America
Publication Date: May 1, 2022

Editor-In-Chief: Michelle Levigne
Executive Editor: Tamera Lynn Kraft

Cover art design by Tamera Lynn Kraft
Cover Art Copyright by Mt Zion Ridge Press LLC © 2021

## Dedication:

For my husband, Tim, who helped me follow my dream. You are my love and my protector.

*Trust in the Lord with all your heart*
*and lean not on your own understanding;*
*in all your ways submit to Him,*
*and He will make your paths straight.*
--Proverbs 3:5-6

## Acknowledgements:

Writing is a journey, and I'm so thankful to the folks who traveled with me, encouraged me, and made me a better writer.

First and foremost, I thank God for His mercy and grace and for the opportunity and huge nudge He gave me that inspired me to write Sadie and Joel's story. Through much prayer and preparation (and lots of learning), God has helped me grow as a writer and a person. I'm so thankful for the hope I have in Him.

Just as Sadie has a hero in her story, so do I. My husband, Tim has loved, sacrificed, encouraged, brainstormed, and listened. Most of all, he has believed in me. I'm so grateful to take this journey with him.

Thank you to my wonderful children who encircled me with love and support, along with their spouses and my grandchildren. I so appreciate your encouragement.

Thank you, Mom, for teaching me how important it is to read and for instilling in me a love of books. I appreciate your interest in my writing and your continued encouragement. And thank you to my dad, for teaching me to work hard and not give up. To my siblings--thanks for being proud of your little sister.

A huge thank you goes to my publisher, Mt. Zion Ridge Press. Thank you, Tamera Kraft for reading my story and giving me the opportunity to publish with you and for creating a beautiful cover. Thank you, Michelle Levigne for your expert editing and making my story better.

Special thanks to my critique partner Kathleen. Your editing and encouragement meant the world to me. Thank you to my beta readers Bev, Jody, and Linda for taking the time to read through *Home Where She Belongs* and giving me honest feedback.

I believe God places people in my path to encourage and push me forward. I appreciate each and every one.

# CHAPTER ONE

Sharp breaths escaped Sadie Stewart's lungs. Her legs wobbled like cooked spaghetti as she pushed to reclaim her routine and run the rest of the route. Confidence surged through her as her running shoes crunched dried leaves and pounded Abbott Island's hard dirt trail. Rosie, her beloved canine companion, kept rhythm with each step.

Aged maples decked in orange and scarlet bent across the trail and shaped a golden canopy. The pungent scent of wood smoke hung in the air. Rosie's red flag of a tail slapped the calves of Sadie's legs as she bounded alongside her. Her dog never judged her or caused her pain. Not like the man who had ripped her emotions to shreds.

A chill wind from Lake Erie rushed at their backs and pushed them toward the only place where Sadie found peace, her grandparents' home. Every summer for twelve years, she'd lived in the warmth and comfort of their care, played with her friends, and helped her Gram clean the rental cottages. Grandpa had deeded the property to Sadie, but she'd neglected the place for three years. Now, she depended on the island rentals to rescue her from a life of regret and hurt.

Around the curve, she pushed her legs harder. A daily run helped clear her mind and build her strength. "Run, run, run." She panted. Run, run, run... from him.

Fear dogged every step as she raced toward freedom from the man who shattered her heart. The memory of Bryce Shaw's screams and accusations played akin to a recording in her head. She prayed he'd give up and not track her to the island.

His constant text messages and incessant calls obliterated the peace she sought. Three months and the man refused to give up his game of superiority over her. She'd changed her phone number once, but he must have dragged it out of her father. Or Dad offered her information without hesitation. At least the island's spotty cell service might delay the next threat to tranquility.

Tomorrow she'd drive Coop, her Mini-Cooper, onto the ferry and search for the closest place to trade in her number. This time she'd keep it to herself, except for the handful of people familiar with her story. She'd enlist the folks at the phone store to help her block the two people who tormented her. Two birds with one stone, as Gram used to say. Her father, who had never loved her, yet forced her to work for him, and Bryce, the man who had destroyed her trust, both fueled her determination to start over. As she ran, sorrow swallowed her heart. The hurt and humiliation weighed heavy as an anchor.

Her legs carried her to the edge of her yard. The sanctuary where she'd spent summers, she now embraced as home. Across the road, waves splashed against the shore and invited her to stay. Her grandparents' voices echoed in her head as if they called to her. "Sadie girl, we miss you."

Many hot, muggy days she'd rested by the lake's edge, feet dipped in the water as the sun shone. She'd begged to understand why God saddled her with parents whose hard veneer kept her at arm's length. Her mom had resented Gram and Grandpa's kindness. Her dad resented everything. Sadie lived for her grandparents' gentle ways. Now she longed for the calm she'd experienced during those sun-filled seasons she'd stayed on the island. She'd sprinted the last few yards of her run, determined to build on Gram's rental business and live a life of peace.

The sagging porch floor stretched across the front of the snug cabin she would call home from now on; the one Grandpa had built. Sadie dismissed the loose boards and chipped paint, as her heart relished the love those two precious people had wrapped around her. She'd lost them both, but they'd left her a place to start over, hope of a new beginning.

She paced across the yard to the guest cottages, two quaint bungalows she planned to rent to Abbott Island tourists. With a little elbow grease, she'd make them gleam. Hands on her hips, Sadie treaded back to her house and stretched her weary legs on the weathered step, one foot at a time. The run energized her, but she sensed pain in her future. When her muscles stopped screaming, she climbed the steps to the wooden, paint-chipped rocker where her grandpa used to whittle. She ran her hand over the rough wood and longed to rest beside the one man who took the time to listen. He had loved her without strings or conditions. She'd tucked years of fond memories in her heart. No one could steal those.

After she conquered the dirt in the cottages, she'd refinish the rockers. She'd search for a how-to video and attempt to follow the instructions. Sadie's head fogged with the challenges of resurrecting her Gram's business. Maybe she'd taken on more than she could handle, but when she prayed for guidance, she sensed peace in this sanctuary she loved.

Sadie showered, then rambled room to room and penned a list of to-dos for the house. Paint the loft, the space she'd adored and made hers every summer. Add new backsplash behind the sink and stove, scrub the cabinets, and cover the crayon drawing she'd decorated the living room wall with as a blooming five-year-old artist. Gram never covered her handiwork. She said it brought a smile to her each day. Sadie sighed, sweet memories. She folded the list of repairs and pressed it into her fixer-upper folder, with her checklist for the cottages. The old homestead needed a facelift, but today she'd bask in the glow of her grandparents' gift.

On the porch, Rosie curled between the rockers and settled into a red-haired fur ball. Sadie petted the dog's soft coat.

"Thanks for running with me, girl. I don't know what I'd do without you."

The Golden Retriever lifted her head and gave her master a lopsided grin. Sadie smiled and rocked. The rhythmic click-clack soothed her soul.

Her gaze followed sailboats as they bobbed across the choppy water, beyond the small beach and the dock her grandpa installed. The folks who sailed in October showed dedication and determination. Like Joel, the boy who stole her heart the summer she turned eighteen. The one she'd let go of eight years ago. Where had he landed? He'd talked about travel or college. He might still live on Abbott Island. If she ran into him, would it be awkward? Maybe she'd duck and run.

Memories of Joel warmed her heart, even as the brisk air chilled her. Sadie scurried inside and dragged one of Gram's quilts off the couch, wrapped herself in a cocoon, and settled in the rocker. Gram had blessed more than a hundred people with her intricate handiwork. Her creations enveloped folks in comfort. If only Gram's quilts had protected her from Bryce, the man who had tried to destroy her.

The purple bruise on her arm from three months ago had faded, but the sting of betrayal remained. Sadie had made the mistake of confronting Bryce in his apartment, instead of a public place. He had grabbed her when she moved toward the door, then thrown her on the couch, like a rag doll. He hovered over her. His hot, nasty breath washed over her face. She jerked her head away when he tried to dominate her with rough, unwelcome kisses. Disgusted by his anger and demands, she had grabbed his Tiffany lamp, smacked him on the head, and ran.

Sadie tightened the quilt around her shoulders. Her heart raced. *Breathe.* She focused on the waves as they lapped the shore. Their rhythm calmed her nerves. Her counselor's voice echoed in her head. "Center your thoughts on God's peace."

*How?*

# CHAPTER TWO

Sadie swung open the door to the Ohio Cellular store. She dreaded the paperwork and the time it would take to update her number, but she needed the number changed. One customer chatted with the salesperson. Sadie signed in on the wait list, then wandered to the electronics tethered to the walls. Sleek gadgets pressed against glass shelves invited customers to keep in touch, yet she craved disconnection.

Five days ago, her cell pinged ten times in the first thirty minutes of her drive from Dublin, Ohio, to the island. Bryce demanded attention. She'd silenced the menacing ringtone. Her dad joined the chaos and recorded ten messages. He demanded she return to work. She'd punched the delete button. Why hadn't she left Bryce and Dad sooner? She had a home on the island, but fear had frozen her in place.

"Hi, I'm Jim. How can I help you?"

The voice jolted Sadie. She closed her eyes to regain her poise, then opened them and stepped toward a young man. Dressed in khakis and a purple polo shirt, he looked like a television commercial. His aftershave drifted to her before she reached the counter. She smothered a sneeze.

"Hey, Jim." She drew closer. "Wait ... Jimmy? Little Jimmy Grayson?" A chuckle escaped. Her shoulders eased as she recognized the young man.

"Yeah?" He furrowed his brow. "It's Jim, now." From the desk chair, the six-foot-tall, lanky young man rose to his full height.

"Maybe you don't remember me." Sadie grinned at the handsome fellow who reminded her of Zach Efron. "I'm Sadie. I'm friends with your cousins, Lucy and Joel. You used to come visit them in the summer."

"Wow, yeah. I remember you. Island Girl." He gave her the once-over. "I guess we've both grown up."

"You must be about twenty, now." Sadie shook her head. "You were what, twelve the last time I saw you?"

"Yeah, I guess. Do you live around here? Speaking of my cousins, Lucy and Joel still live on the island. He's a police officer, and she manages a store." A smirk crossed Jim's face. "Didn't you and Joel have a thing back in the day?"

Heat crept up Sadie's neck. "Not a thing. We hung out and worked together." Her memories of Joel had filled her dreams too often over the years. The one who got away. On a tiny island she'd bump into him. For all she knew, he'd married a gorgeous model. What did it matter? She had no interest in tangling with a man again. Not even a man she once had deemed a friend.

5

Jim's voice cut into her thoughts. "He's still single."

Her lips formed an "O." *Of course he is.* She fumbled with her purse, retrieved her phone and waved it at him. "I came to get my number changed." No point reminiscing about the past. Bryce had soured her on men. She refused to allow Joel's sweet disposition to drop her guard. "Do you need to see my phone?"

Jim opened his palm, and she dropped the cell in his hand. He tapped through several screens, gathering information.

"Let's see. According to our records, you changed it three months ago." His fingers clicked across the computer's keyboard. "Are you positive you want to do that again, so soon?" He twisted his mouth and looked annoyed.

"Positive." Sadie scowled. She hoped it bore a resemblance to her mother's glare back when she was in high school, and Mom had insisted she attend dinners with Dad's clients. Sadie had perfected the look with her dad's patrons when they pushed their interest in her too far. "Can you put my number on a private list of some kind? I heard you have an unpublished list I can sign up for.

"We do have an unpublished list. I'll add you." He looked at her phone again, then checked the computer screen. "Let's see what I can do."

"I appreciate it, Jimmy ... I mean Jim." She perused the phone covers displayed on the wall that screamed *Buy Me*. Her old case bore a scrape across the corner, the result of Bryce's anger. He'd thrown the cell when she had answered a call and interrupted their date.

A purple cover with sparkles caught her attention. Perfect, a new life and a brand-new glittery cell cover to remind her to shine like the stars.

"Sadie," Jim called her to the service desk. "Is there a number you'd like to permanently block?"

"You can do that?"

"Sure can."

She jotted Bryce's number on a notepad, but hesitated to block her father, on the off chance he would need her as a daughter.

After a few clicks, he set the phone on the desk. "All set."

"Thanks so much." She waved the phone cover in front of him. "I want to buy this, too." Sadie pulled the old cover off, snugged the new case over the phone, and admired the bling.

"Great choice." Just a few minutes later, the exchange was made. "Here you go." Jim handed her a bag with the old case and packaging. "Good to see you again."

"Thanks, Jim. You, too." She waltzed out of the store, with her phone in hand and a new lease on life.

Down the street, Sadie spied The Great Lakes Popcorn Company. The salty smell drifted from the open door. She almost tasted the spicy Wild Walleye flavor and the Island Mix of white cheddar and caramel corn as she ambled along the sidewalk. She and her mom had stopped at the little shop with the red and white striped awning every summer. One of the few indulgences her mom had allowed when she dropped her at Gram and Grandpa's.

Ever since Sadie's fifth birthday, Mom had rushed up the highway to drop her off on the island. She'd spend an hour or two with Gram and Grandpa and then make her excuses to leave. Sadie would stand in the driveway and wave goodbye. She figured her mom hurried away because she couldn't wait to leave her. After Mom died, Dad had let the truth slip. She'd never wanted to be pregnant. When she asked why, he had said, "I suppose she didn't want to ruin her figure."

No wonder she'd treated Sadie more like a Barbie doll than a child. Mom had demanded the perfection from her she'd never achieved.

Inside the popcorn shop, Sadie sampled the black cherry and blueberry flavors. Both proved a bit too sweet. She plucked her favorite, the Island Mix, off the shelf of bagged treats. A light warmth from the fresh popcorn met her touch. She closed her eyes and dragged in a breath.

"This store smells like childhood."

"Yeah, that's what all the old people say."

Sadie raised her eyebrows at the teenage girl and passed her a debit card.

"Sorry, Ma'am." The young lady ducked her head.

*Old* and *ma'am*. Good grief.

Outside, she carried the bag of goodness across the street and eased onto a bench. She buttoned the top of her coat and settled into the breezy day. Fishing and leisure boats bobbed in the cove. Waves lapped along the pier. A white egret ducked its head in the lake and fished for dinner. She snatched a handful of popcorn. The taste of caramel and white cheddar burst in her mouth, like fireworks on the Fourth of July.

As a teen, Sadie and her friends had planted blankets on the beach and applauded the sprays of light and color displayed to celebrate the nation's birthday. She longed for the bond she'd shared with her friends, neglected since she'd left them behind. They might embrace her now or not, but she'd open herself to the possibilities.

Over the last three months, she'd broken the chains Bryce had wrapped around her mental and physical health. Although anxiety still reared its ugly head, she'd calmed enough to sleep through the night.

The languid splash of the lake along the shore boosted her desire to pursue a life filled with peace and joy. Unlike the busy city streets of Dublin and Upper Arlington, the lake offered a tranquil environment. She'd tired of the constant traffic, horns honking, and people complaining. Wise old Grandpa Ben had understood her heart and knew she'd need the island.

After another handful of popcorn, she twisted the top of the plastic bag closed and walked to the car. When she got home, she planned to curl up on the couch with the salty and sweet deliciousness and watch *You've Got*

*Mail.* Maybe she'd meet her Tom Hanks someday.

For now, she'd wait to find the man who made her heart sing. Her friend Ann had repeated several times, "Sadie, you need to heal. That awful man did a number on you. Let yourself rest and seek peace. God loves you, my friend."

Uncertain anyone loved her, she kicked around the idea of God and His supposed care. Her gram and grandpa had attended church on Sundays. Both of them had read their Bibles and bowed their heads in prayer. Her mother scoffed at the idea of a God who loved His children. She claimed loudly and proudly she didn't need Jesus or the church. Once in a while, Sadie threw a few prayers God's way, then doubt popped up and mocked her.

From the ferry, Sadie heard the waves clap against the boat. The wind whipped her hair. A small child who rested in his dad's arms reminded her of the island church's Vacation Bible School. She'd attended since her sixth birthday, then as teens she and Lucy had acted out Bible stories with puppets. She'd loved the creation story, how God made the world. From the tiny ant to the elephant, God's hands fashioned the entire universe. Even her.

The teachers recited every year how God created each person with purpose and worth. How could an abused, abandoned woman find worth? How could her battered life give value to others?

The peace she'd gained from updating her phone number escaped her. The pain of insignificance stabbed her heart. She ached even as she hoped for a new beginning.

# CHAPTER THREE

From the shopping bags piled on the kitchen island, Sadie plucked bananas, blueberries, and carrots.

"One thing I learned from Gram was to stock up on fresh produce when I ferried to the mainland. Not that you care, Rosie." She stashed potatoes in a lower cabinet. "However, you might want to know I picked up your dog food. Scoot over, girl."

She bumped against the dog's midsection as she opened the cupboard where her grandmother once stored baking powder, vanilla, and salt. She hoisted bags of flour and sugar onto the empty shelves. On many a summer morning, the tantalizing smell of banana, blueberry, or her favorite cranberry muffins greeted her at breakfast. Gram had whipped them up without a peek at her recipes.

Sadie's first attempts at baking had required measuring every ingredient she'd read from Gram's worn, stained recipe cards. She planned to practice baking chocolate chip and oatmeal butterscotch cookies along with muffins, as gifts for the folks who would rent her cottages. If anyone bothered to make reservations.

A pang of homesickness for her gram shot through her as she leaned to grab another bag. Rosie scurried around the side of the counter. Sadie tripped and flew over top of the dog and landed in a tangled mess of arms and legs.

"Rosie, what are you doing? I about dropped the eggs." She pushed herself from the floor and rubbed her hand over the dog's head. How did life get woven into a snarled mess? Thank goodness a few things stayed stable: her dog and her grandparents' home.

After Sadie tucked the eggs and milk in the refrigerator, she squatted in front of her pet. "What do you say we check the cottages? I'm guessing the insides are in worse shape than this house."

In the few days she'd stayed on the island, she had avoided the tiny cottages for fear she'd discover a rat's nest or a snake. She worried her plans to open by spring could send her into a tailspin of anxiety, but she knuckled down and drew on her determination to be independent and confident.

"This could be an adventure, Rosie." The dog ambled behind her, out the door, and down the steps as she traipsed across the driveway. Grandma Julia's rental business had thrived. She had leased the tiny homes to folks who vacationed on the island. Sadie had met people from all over the country those summers when she visited, plus a few from Canada.

A sweet older couple from Toronto holidayed for a week every year.

9

Her mouth watered at the memory of the maple leaf-shaped candy they brought her. The woman and Gram wrote letters back and forth for years. Gram loved her Canadian pen pal. Sadie hoped to make a few new friends and give visitors a place of refuge, like the island now gave her.

"Here goes, girl." Sadie turned the key. The door squeaked open. Dust motes floated in the light rays that shimmered as they filtered through the mucky windows. A musty odor swirled around her nose. The shadow of a bed filled the corner. The door gaped open on a small refrigerator. Sadie flipped on the lights. How many times in the summers had she scrubbed the cottages? Joel and Lucy had insisted on helping. The sooner she finished, the sooner they'd swim and explore the island. Within an hour, Lucy had gotten antsy and excused herself to go home. Joel had stayed, always by her side. Then he'd faded from her life.

Sadie craved the summers. Her body had melted into the sand as the sunshine and waves calmed and replaced the stress her parents poured on her to achieve high marks in high school. Today, she threw the stress behind and faced the challenge.

With no sign of a snake, she relaxed and ran her finger through the dust covering the old sink's surface. She promised herself she would polish the porcelain to a satisfying gleam. After her mom died her senior year, their housekeeper taught her to clean. Her mother would have been mortified, but Sadie's desire to be more self-sufficient would pay off on the cottages.

She peeked under the sink. Other than remnants of the mice who visited, she didn't find any left-over supplies. She grabbed the notepad she'd brought and jotted Mr. Clean and Lysol along with a few other cleaners. Excitement bubbled in her. Her feet danced. She'd do this.

Outside, she clicked the wooden door closed and sucked in fresh air.

"I've got a boat load of work to do." She and Rosie tramped around the buildings. Green and brown sprouts peppered with leaves shot out of the gutters. "Guess I should start there." She patted Rosie's head as she glared at the unwanted vegetation.

~~~~~

Rosie raced circles around the ladder as Sadie climbed, then she dropped to the ground for a snooze. The gutters dripped with leaves and gunk from years of neglect. In long sleeves and her gram's flowered garden gloves, Sadie dug sludge out and flung the nasty mess to an old tarp she had found in the shed. After an hour, her arm ached like a throbbing tooth. She rubbed her neck. Maybe she'd lift weights along with her running. She'd need the strength to survive.

Last time she had helped Grandpa with yard work, Sadie had tumbled into a pile of wet leaves and grass. Gram and Grandpa had both laughed after they checked to see she wasn't hurt. Her bottom stung, but she had giggled with them. Her physical prowess needed help.

For two hours, she repositioned the rickety wooden ladder every few feet, then clambered to the eaves to clean. She'd stripped off her long sleeves and donned a Cleveland Indians t-shirt she'd found in Grandpa's closet. Her nose twitched from the earthy smell. "Achoo." She wiped away sweat with the back of her hand and smeared dead leaves across her cheek. Her face must look a mess. *Ugh.*

She'd skipped supper to clear as much as she could before nightfall. Her stomach's growls matched the rumble of an engine whining on the road. With no time to turn to see who passed by, she tugged a rooted plant from the gutter.

"Excuse me." A man's deep voice made her jump.

She grabbed the rung in front of her, steadied herself, and took a deep breath. She hadn't heard the vehicle stop.

"Sorry. I didn't mean to startle you," he said.

Sadie twisted to find the person with the commanding voice.

A man in uniform had parked his golf cart in her driveway and advanced in her direction.

Even with an official cap pulled down, she recognized her friend, Joel. Jimmy told her he had joined the police force. She appreciated the way the uniform gave him an air of authority. He'd grown from a scrawny teenage boy into a man with muscular biceps and a commanding stride. However, she told herself his looks didn't matter, any more than the tug at her heart. She'd not heard from him for years, no letter, no call, and no email.

With no desire to chat with him, Sadie descended the ladder one heavy footstep after the other. Her throat tightened, her heart sped, and her palms perspired.

*Breathe. He's an old friend. Nothing more.*

Once on the ground, she turned toward him. She sucked in a breath and checked him out, top to bottom. Her sweet Joel stood in front of her. Muscles bulged under his uniform, his face soft but angled and much more handsome. He plucked off his hat. His hair had darkened, but the golden streaks still gleamed. His mouth, set in a straight line, struck her as all business. She studied his face as his blue eyes locked on hers. For a moment she froze, then her feet propelled toward him as if a magnetic force tugged her.

~~~~~

"Ma'am, I keep an eye on Ben's property. Who are you and what are you doing here?" Joel stepped in front of the woman walking stiffly toward him. He eyed the tarp full of rotten leaves, visible evidence of her work.

The Golden Retriever accompanying the woman sniffed the cuffs of his pants. She circled him and plopped at his feet.

He sensed the woman's stare as he knelt beside the dog and rubbed her fur. She licked his hand. "You look familiar. Aren't you Ben's dog?"

"She might not answer you, but I will." The woman stepped closer to him and seized the dog's collar. "Grandpa gave her to me when he got too sick to take care of her." She backed away.

Joel stood. His gaze lifted to her face. "Sadie?" The girl who haunted his dreams stood close enough for him to touch. He resisted the urge to hug her. She'd thrown up a wall with her ramrod straight stance and her shoulders held high. She tossed an "I dare you" stare at him.

"Yep, it's me." She gave a terse nod and wiped at her cheek.

"Wow. I haven't seen you in what, eight years? Not that I was counting." He blinked as if a mirage had come to life. "I can't believe you're back." He drank in the sight of those gorgeous green eyes. She'd blossomed into the woman he'd dreamed about. Her beauty enchanted him. The dirt on her face didn't detract from her gorgeousness or those kissable lips. He'd leaned into her eight years ago and stolen a sweet kiss, his most embarrassing moment. He'd fumbled with the hug and they both tumbled into the sand. She'd laughed, but his face had burned like fire, as he wished the beach would swallow him. Kind of what he wanted to happen now.

The last person he expected to run into stood in front of him. He'd longed to see her, talk to her, but too much had changed for him. He carried too much baggage from the one dark blot on his life.

# CHAPTER FOUR

With assurance, Sadie released Rosie, straightened her spine, and held her head high. Her counselor's voice sounded in her mind. "Stand with confidence." Over the years, she'd formed the habit of slumping to protect herself. Not anymore. She and Joel had shared a past filled with friendship and fun, but she didn't know him now. Had he changed? Was the kindhearted boy buried inside this attractive man? She'd lift her guard enough to be cordial, but she refused to melt into a puddle of cowardice.

"It's been a long time." She put her hands on her hips. "Why weren't you at Grandpa Ben's funeral?" she blurted, voicing the hurt she'd carried. She'd looked for him that day, searched the crowd of islanders who loved her granddad. Disappointment had flooded her when she didn't find Joel.

Now he stood about a foot away. Rosie rested at his feet. Betrayed by her dog.

"I'm sorry I missed the service. I wanted to come, but I was training at the police academy." He stared at his shiny, black leather shoes, then lifted his face to peer at Sadie. "As you can see, I'm one of the island's finest." A small smile crossed his lips.

"I don't remember you wanting to be a police officer." Her memory of the island boy she had climbed trees with, worked beside at the store, and sat under the stars with jogged through her mind. He'd talked about an architecture or construction management degree. Something where he'd build and use his hands. Never a police officer. She shook her head.

"I didn't until Mom got hurt. I don't know if you heard, but she got hit by a drunk driver. Left her in a wheelchair." Joel's lips flattened into a grim line, and his gaze dropped to the ground. He rubbed the toe of his shoe in the dirt.

"I had no idea. I'm so sorry." Sadie's shoulders sank, as if someone poked her with a straight pin and all her air escaped. "Is she still here? On the island?" Joel's parents had poured love over her when she had stayed with her grandparents. His mom had knelt with her in the garden and showed her how to tend flowers. They would pull weeds, talk about weather, and laugh about everything. Then she would embrace Sadie in a huge bear hug. Joel's mom epitomized kindness.

"They moved to the mainland. Bought a one-story in Lakeside." He lifted his face and captured her gaze with his aqua blue stare. "Lucy and I live in Mom and Dad's old house. The rent helps them out. Luce manages the General Store."

"She loved that place even as a kid. I'm not surprised she's still there."

13

Sadie pushed her hair away from her face. "I'll have to stop and see her. I've missed her all these years." Once upon a time, she'd written Lucy once a month, then work monopolized her life. She'd failed to answer Lucy's emails and letters. Sadie had loved her. They had laughed at everything and found joy in the smallest accomplishment. She hoped for a chance to rekindle their friendship, someone to confide in, but how much of her past did she want to share?

Sadie tiptoed with baby steps to rebuild her trust in people. She wanted to forgive herself but didn't know how. She had fallen for Bryce's charm and attention. The struggle to forgive Bryce and move forward overwhelmed her. She wanted to fall in step with her friends, like old times. Fear gripped her. What if she let herself believe her friends wanted the best for her? She'd be duped, again.

"She told me you stopped answering her emails." Joel stood with his feet apart, arms crossed.

Intimidation crept up Sadie's spine. She gazed at the ground as if the grass might dash away. He cleared his throat. She lifted her face to meet his stare. "I spent my time trying to please my father. After college, I worked for him at the company."

He raised his eyebrows at the mention of her dad. "Your dad, huh? Must have been tough."

"More than you can imagine." Dad remained hard as nails. He demanded respect and struck fear in his employees, Sadie included. No more. She refused to return to Columbus or his company. The day she'd spilled her personal experience with Bryce across her dad's desk still haunted her. Dad had tossed the accusations aside.

"He's my right-hand man. Seems he treats you okay, to me." He trusted the man to run the finance company.

"I resigned over three months ago. He was pretty upset with me."

Her father's lack of respect convinced her to dig in her heels. Without her dad, she'd establish herself on the island and resurrect her gram's business.

"I'm sorry you went through that, but it's good to see you." Joel rubbed his chin and stepped closer. "So, are you staying here or selling out?"

~~~~~

Joel scrubbed his hand down his face. Could he be any blunter? He had missed Sadie. The calendars he'd marked off from September to May, from eighth grade through high school, lay buried in his desk drawer.

The months of police training had kept him busy, but in his free time he'd prayed for Sadie. He had dared to hope she'd return. After his life turned upside down, what did he have to offer? A broken heart he couldn't mend.

"Sorry for blurting that out. You arrived here, what, a week or so ago?"

She lifted her chin. "Yeah. How'd you know?"

He pointed to the badge on his belt. "Comes with the territory, and I saw a car I didn't recognize in the driveway, last week. To be clear, Ben and I made a deal before he died. If you didn't come back right away, I'd keep an eye on the place."

She lowered her eyes. "Oh well, I guess that makes sense."

"I have a key, too. Want it?"

"No. Keep it for now. Being you're a police officer, it might be good for you to hold on to it. As a spare. If you don't mind."

"No problem."

~~~~~

Sadie twisted away from Joel and repositioned the ladder against the eaves. She quelled the urge to spill her story as she grabbed her gloves, tugged them on, and wished Joel away. After all, she decided not to trust another man. He'd find out whether she stayed in due time. If she left, he'd have a key to manage the place again.

She clutched the sides of the ladder, but her memories cemented her to the ground. Eight years ago, she and Joel had shared an awkward kiss. They'd spent three precious weeks together before she left for college, then nothing. No letters, no phone calls, no emails. Nothing.

"Sadie?" Joel stood so close, he brushed against her arm. In kangaroo fashion, she leaped then fell flat on her bottom into the pile of gutter gunk. Rotten leaves flew in the air and fell like slimy glitter.

"Ugh." She let out a grunt. Dirt dappled her face, her hair hung in a rat's nest, and liquid soaked her backside as a sewer-like smell attacked her nose. Her hand slid in the slime as she tried to get up.

He grabbed her arm and helped her stand. "I'm sorry. I didn't mean to startle you." He stared at her. "Wow, what a mess."

She reached around to her backside and swiped off leaves and goop. "You think?" Sarcasm spilled off her words.

She jerked away from Joel and held her palms out toward her old friend. "Not your fault. Look, I'm going to get this off me. Change my clothes. You know." She trudged to the porch steps.

"I'd be happy to come by and help clean the eaves tomorrow." He trailed her, then paused. "I'll be off duty. In fact, I am now, just heading home." He held his cap and fingered the brim.

"No. That's okay. I've got this." She marched into the house and let the screen door slam.

Why had she collided with Joel her first week home? Of course he wanted to help. His kind heart had drawn her to him before. Regardless of his caring way, she planned to accomplish her goals on her own, without his help. She couldn't tolerate another man who wanted to orchestrate her life.

~~~~~

After a shower, Sadie towel dried her hair, then ran a brush through

15

the long, dark brown waves. She'd embarrassed herself in front of him, again. Instead of the peace and calm she sought, she'd achieved frustration and humiliation. She dressed in her pink flowered pajamas and piled her hair on her head, then plopped on the bed to think.

Over the next few weeks, she'd employ a scrub brush and bleach and clean the cottages while she sorted the remnants of brokenness in her heart. She'd wipe out the fear she'd developed and replace it with courage. Like the lion in *The Wizard of Oz*, she'd discover her bravery. Or fail trying. She recalled a verse about being strong and courageous. Ann's preacher spoke about a man named Joshua who found courage. If he could, perhaps she could too.

The shower had eased the aches and pains she'd earned from clearing the gutters, but the muscles between her shoulder blades screamed for the heating pad.

Those three months she'd burrowed in Ann's apartment left her out of shape. Pity parties on the couch. Locked behind her friend's door, she'd waited and planned her escape. Twice Bryce had slammed his fists on Ann's front door as he screamed obscenities for the neighbors to hear. The restraining order hung in oblivion, as if he had never received the thin piece of paper mandated to protect her. A shiver clutched Sadie's spine as she cringed at the damage she'd suffered from her ex-boyfriend, the narcissist.

Downstairs, she poured milk over cereal in one of Gram's antique Belford bowls and steeped a cup of Earl Grey. Comfort filled Sadie as she wrapped her hands around the flowered china Gram's British aunts gave her for her wedding. She carried her snack to the living room and curled into the well-worn recliner. Through the window, she watched the sun sink on the horizon. Yellow and pink light filtered around the ball of orange. A golden ribbon sailed across the waves and reflected the delicious color. Peace flowed on the island. The tranquility she longed to capture. She had experienced calm during the summers of her young life. Then she had returned home to constant turmoil and bickering.

The sun sank into the large-as-an-ocean lake. Sadie clinked her spoon in her empty bowl, and a lonesome sound echoed. Enough of the self-pity. Time to look up instead of at her feet. She padded to the kitchen and set the dishes in the sink. A thump sounded at the side of the house. *What on earth?* She peered out through the curtain.

Joel stood on the ladder along the cottage and tossed leaves onto the tarp. He'd changed from his uniform into jeans and a t-shirt. With every movement, the muscles in his arms rippled. He'd grown from cute boy to handsome man.

Sadie covered her heart with her hand, as if to protect it from more heartbreak. She appreciated her old friend's efforts to help her. In spite of his attempt to help, she'd prefer he left her alone.

16

# CHAPTER FIVE

Sadie donned her robe and tied the belt around her narrow waist. She trudged outside in her teddy bear slippers, hands on hips, and planted herself on the porch. The chill nipped her cheeks. "Joel, what are you doing?"

He angled his body back to see where the voice came from. The top of the ladder jerked into midair, then landed on the eaves with a plop. "Are you trying to give me a heart attack?" He pulled a handkerchief from his pocket and wiped dirt from his hands.

"I asked what you think you're doing." Sadie crossed her arms and glared at him. Her foot tapped against the wooden floor.

He descended the ladder and landed both feet on the ground. "I'm helping a friend who's too stubborn to ask for help." He brushed leaves off his pants.

"It's dark, and you might get hurt. Besides, you scared me." She tightened her belt and shoved a damp curl out of her face. "If you insist on helping, do it in the daytime."

"I tried..." He approached the porch. The light shone on his handsome face. Her stance eased, and she rubbed her forehead.

She rejected the temptation to gaze at his perfect features, his dimple and those gorgeous eyes. No. Not happening. Sadie pointed a finger at him. "I know you tried to tell me." She threw her arms in the air. "You are as stubborn as ever, you know."

Joel stuffed a piece of gum in his mouth and chewed. "Yep. I am." His face split into a grin. The smell of peppermint floated through the air. His smile pierced her heart.

"Go home. I'm going to bed."

She'd protected herself from hurt for three months. Why did he have to come along and tempt her to drop her guard? Her grandparents' gift had offered escape, and she'd fled here to heal. They'd ensured her protection and a way to make a living. The property commanded top dollar, since the land rested near the water. They could have sold to the highest bidder. Yet, they'd saved the place for her. She'd socked away enough money to tide her over for a while, but she needed to sink money into improvements if she planned to rent the cottages in the spring.

"Sadie."

"What?" She barked louder than Rosie.

"Where'd you go? Zone out?"

Sadie stared into Joel's blue eyes. "Sorry. Guess I'm tired. Not used to so much physical labor." Her legs ached and her back throbbed.

He retreated to the golf cart. "'Night. I'll swing by tomorrow and finish what I started." With a nod, he reversed the cart and drove into the night.

"Whatever you want to do." She lifted her achy legs up the steps one by one, stepped inside and closed the door. She squatted in front of her dog and patted her head. "Rosie, I can't let that man get to me."

~~~~~

The metallic taste of the nails he held in his mouth pushed Joel to finish the job. He hammered the nails into the eaves to secure them against the island's unpredictable weather. From the top of the ladder, he surveyed the home Ben had built for Sadie's grandma, Julia. Humble but beautiful. The stone columns on the porch, reminiscent of the work at the limestone mines, represented the history of the island. The days when industry kept them alive, instead of tourism.

As an officer, he put in longer hours in the summer. In the off season, life slowed down. He relished the quiet. Fewer people meant less crime. Not that the island experienced much criminal activity. He loved his job, but this winter included an unexpected obstacle: Sadie. As soon as he recognized her, his heartbeat sped. Even covered in leaves and dirt, she looked beautiful. No longer the girl he swam or climbed rocks with, she had grown into a woman, mature and flat out gorgeous. He suspected she had no idea of her loveliness.

He'd never encountered another woman who compared to his Sadie. Except she never was his. He had mourned, at least that was what Lucy said, for months after she had left. Fear of rejection had stilled his hand every time he tried to write a letter or email. He'd let her go, but not the memories. Those played like movies in his head, every day. He would rewind and hit play and pray for his best friend. Last night she had flooded his dreams. He had awakened in a state of confusion and uncertainty.

Her spell clung to him even now. Teenage puppy love wagged its tail whenever she'd stayed on the island. From age thirteen to eighteen, Joel's hormones responded. For the last eight years, he'd heard no word from her, except a few letters to Lucy. The most beautiful girl he had ever met had left him behind. When she didn't return, he had stuffed the sadness into his pocket and moved on. He'd dated here and there, yet nothing permanent. The women he associated with lacked the joy of his childhood friend. Now sadness and weariness exuded from the Sadie he saw last night. She had put up a good front until she landed on the ground. Then her shoulders slumped like she'd been defeated in battle.

What brought Sadie back? She'd left the buildings to rot. If he hadn't been vigilant about mowing and tending to the flower beds, the island council would have tracked Sadie down and demanded she take care of the property. He had promised Ben he'd keep the place tidy. Her grandpa had expected her to neglect the cottages, not even appreciate the gift. Ben told him, "I want my granddaughter to have the opportunity to live here if she wants to. She's not happy working for her dad. Breaks my heart."

Ben's wife, Julia, had built a thriving business, renting out the cottages all summer. Would Sadie apply her business sense and make a go of it? Or would she disappear again? Joel shook his head. He'd promised Ben, not her, he'd care for the place. He valued the gift of a promise, so he would not disappoint his old friend, despite Sadie's rebuff.

Had she planted herself on the island or was she visiting? The property could command a pretty penny. The acreage spread across a couple lots on the west coast of the small island. Sunsets every night, when the fog hadn't rolled in. The lake lapped against the pier. Two small cottages and a main house meant good income potential. He'd consider buying the property himself, to supplement his police paycheck. Thirty-hour work weeks and picking up odd jobs and extra shifts helped him get by, but a steady flow of extra cash sounded appealing.

Joel toted the ladder to the second cottage. His stomach grumbled. Past noon and no Sadie. Did she pack her bags and dog and hightail it home? She'd fled the island before and left his broken heart behind. He looked around. No, her car sat in the driveway.

Should he knock on her door, take her to lunch, invite her to visit his sister, Lucy, or leave her alone?

~~~~~

Self-control flew out the window, as Sadie pushed the lace curtains aside. Joel's muscles rippled with every leaf he tugged from the gutters. The man must work out. Her midsection tingled and her heart fluttered. She enjoyed the show a little too much. Hadn't she run to the island to forget one man? She didn't need to tangle with another one.

Why did he want to help? She didn't deserve kindness from her old friend. She'd left him behind and trudged into her work life, where she'd kept her head down until Bryce had enticed her with his charm.

Hands on her hips, she paced. Grandpa had taught her how to do yard work. He'd encouraged her to do whatever she wanted. She was capable. Or maybe not. Bryce had called her a useless, whiny girl. Dad, too. Mom had claimed she lacked ambition or talent. They were wrong, and she'd prove it.

The counselor had taught her not to let the negative talk win. God loved and valued her. Yet, her brain refused to process her worth. Too many negative layers covered the intelligence and beauty underneath. Like a salmon, she struggled upstream against the roaring water.

When she peeked at Joel again, he tossed gunk from the last cottage's eaves. He deserved a thank you. Instead, she cowered in the house. If only he didn't make her feel seventeen again. The best summer of her life, she had climbed across every crevice of the island with Joel and Lucy and worked with them at the General Store. Their laughter echoed in her head.

Grandpa had encouraged her to enjoy her island time before she dragged herself off to college. He had cheered her and loved her like no other.

That summer remained her last memories of love and joy.

After Sadie had quit her job and moved in with Ann, her friend tried to get her to have a little fun.

"You can't stay cooped up in here forever."

She'd urged her to join church activities. Sadie had played games at a singles night, then viewed a couple new movies with friends. Each time she ventured from Ann's apartment, her hands trembled with fear she might run into Bryce. Even though her heart calmed at Sunday church, she had prayed he would not discover where she attended. Yet she feared he'd see the congregation as one more group of vulnerable people. His greed and lack of discretion invited him to target anyone he could sink his teeth into, even at church. He'd hook his claws in, then control his victim's finances.

Ann had poured kindness over Sadie as she had assured her God loved her. Years ago on the island, Sadie had walked to church with her grandparents. She had mouthed the pleasant hymns and listened to the preacher, but she had never dug her feet into living a life for God. Snuggled between her grandparents in the wooden pew, she had embraced the comfort, but never understood how much Jesus loved her. Not until Bryce had ground her self-esteem into a worthless pile of dust did Sadie search for someone or something to redeem her, to acknowledge her as a person. She had reached from the pit of despair and sought the possibility of peace.

Ann's church family had gathered around her and prayed. Their words of comfort spurred her to move to the island and start over. A new life free of Bryce.

A knock at the door startled her out of her memories.

20

# CHAPTER SIX

Certain Joel had knocked on the door, Sadie straightened her posture and tucked a loose wave of hair behind her ear. She tugged the hem of her Avett Brothers t-shirt to pull out any wrinkles, then she opened the door.

"Oh my goodness." Sadie's hand flew to her mouth. "Marigold."

"How's my girl?" Marigold wrapped Sadie in one of her bear hugs. She stood five feet ten. Her plumpness invited a comfortable embrace. Warmth radiated through Sadie. Marigold stepped back and gave her the look a mama might give a child who came home from a week of camp. "Have you been eating enough? You're looking scrawny, kiddo."

A chuckle escaped Sadie's lips. "It's so good to see you." She gestured from her head to her toes. "Yes, I'm eating." She clasped her hands and bounced on both feet. "It's so good to see you. Come in."

"I'd love to." Marigold nodded and strolled into Sadie's living room, the place she first met her grandmother's close friend. Her long flowered skirt flowed behind her. The beads around her neck tinkled together, and her long white braid swayed as she moved. She slipped off her Uggs at the door, then perched on the long red couch.

Sadie rubbed her nose at the smell of patchouli, Marigold's favorite fragrance. "How'd you know I was here?" She settled beside her friend.

"The island news chain. You know rumors fly through faster than Facebook." Marigold waved her hands in the air.

"Of course. Joel told you, didn't he? He never could keep a secret."

Marigold flipped her hair over her shoulder. The roped braid dangled an inch above her waist. "Our boy's excited you're here. He's missed you, you know." Her eyes rounded as if to say, *Listen to me because I'm right.*

Sadie shook her head. "I don't think so. I haven't heard from him since I left the island." She had written him letters, but never received acknowledgment. Her heart cracked a little each time she checked the mail and didn't see any envelopes with his return address. Not even a reply to email.

She rose from the couch. "How about coffee or tea? I have cookies, too."

"Coffee and cookies sound good."

She popped a coffee pod in her machine.

"You've got one of those fancy coffee makers." Marigold propped her hands on the counter.

"Not fancy, convenient and practical for just me." She retrieved creamer from the refrigerator and set it beside the sugar on the kitchen table. "Have a seat."

Marigold and Sadie settled in the old oak kitchen chairs her gram had refinished.

Eight years ago, Marigold, Gram, and Grandpa had nestled around this table, while Sadie cried about going to college. Even though she relished the freedom of campus life, she had dreaded a major in finance. Dad didn't bend. Finance or nothing. He was paying for the degree, so he had control. Sadie had dreamed of being an art major. Dad laughed at the idea. Mom didn't help matters. She stood by Dad no matter what. If she didn't, he'd cut off her precious allowance.

"I bet I know where your mind has wandered. To your last summer here. I remember sitting here, holding your hand and talking to you about your future." Marigold sipped her black coffee and munched on a chocolate chip cookie.

"How do you always know what I'm thinking?" Sadie grabbed the biggest cookie from the jar and stuck it in her mouth. With a stuffed mouth, she'd keep quiet about Bryce and the anxiety and fears he caused.

"Sadie, girl, you know I can read you. I've had years of practice."

She giggled like the fourteen-year-old she was when she used to talk to her about boys. "You always knew."

That dripping hot summer day, when naive, pig-tailed Sadie and her best friend, Joel, rented a kayak from Marigold, she had guessed about her crush on him. Her friend didn't know the hurt she held in her heart now. At least Sadie hoped not. Too much had happened between then and today, years of agony and pain brought on by her dad, her mom, and her own stupidity.

In a manner of months, Bryce had worked his way to the top in her dad's company. By the time Sadie had joined the firm, he worked as her father's number one assistant. His charm enchanted her when they'd met. The gaze from his dark eyes had held her captive. He complimented her and welcomed her into her father's business. After a few dates, he insisted she wear the designer dresses and heels he purchased for her. Like a Barbie doll, he showed her off at elegant restaurants and business gatherings.

"Sadie, you still with me?" Marigold patted her arm with a gentle touch.

"I'm sorry. Guess I was daydreaming." Or reliving a nightmare. She posed a half-grin.

"Anything you want to talk about? Maybe the young man out there pulling junk out of your eave spouts?"

"No, not Joel or anyone else of the male species." Sadie rose from the table and hiked to the window. She thrust the lace curtain aside and searched around the cottages. "I think he's gone." Good thing, too. She didn't want to talk to him or about him. She didn't trust herself not to sob on his shoulder or Marigold's. She'd take care of herself. Sure, Joel jumped in and helped at the first opportunity. As an officer, he leaped to defend and take care of people. He embodied the type of guy a girl relied on, but she didn't plan on falling for the knight in the police uniform.

Marigold joined her at the window. "If you say so." After a quick hug, she opened the door. "Good to see you, sweet girl. I've got to get home and work on my macramé."

"Stocking up for the winter fair on the mainland?"

"You bet." She nodded. "We'll talk soon, sweetie. So good to see you." She jogged down the steps. Sadie watched her round the curve, then she pushed the door closed.

She leaned on the door and shut her eyes. Should she pour her story out to Marigold about her pitiful life with an arrogant jerk? Or hide the wounds under her bruised ego? Every summer on Abbott Island, she had worked hard at the General Store and built her confidence. In the fall, she had circled home to have her ego squashed and her self-esteem deflated. She refused to go there again. The island stood for independence and peace. She'd lasso both, no matter what it took.

~~~~~

October's wind rushed across the lake. The maple trees' bare branches rattled. The sun's rays cut through the clouds, yet warmth didn't reach Sadie. She grew chilled and drew her wool coat tight around her neck as she climbed the church steps. The last time she'd attended a service there, her grandfather's coffin had rested at the front of the sanctuary. Dread enveloped her as she entered the tiny chapel.

In the aisle, she stopped and perused the mahogany woodwork, pews, and pulpit. They emanated warmth against the gray-green walls. She let go of the breath she'd held. Stained glass windows let in a rainbow of sunlight to brighten the otherwise chilly autumn day. The addition of deep purple seat cushions enhanced the church's comfort she'd embraced as a teenager. Marigold occupied her front row pew. Sadie admired the hand-crocheted hat her friend no doubt had made, and the dangling silver earrings.

A voice half-whispered in Sadie's ear. "Hey girl, long time no see."

She spun a one-eighty. "Lucy." She spoke in a stage whisper to keep from shouting. The two old friends flung their arms around each other.

"I can't believe you're here. Joel told me, but I was on the mainland with Mom and Dad. I got back last night." Lucy grasped her hands. "We've got to catch up."

Sadie nodded. "We do." Except how much story should she spill? She loved Lucy and sensed she could trust her, but so many years had passed. Should she be honest? Or wait and see if the friendship remained solid?

"Let's sit with Miss Marigold." Lucy linked her arm with Sadie's and tugged her down the short aisle.

~~~~~

As notes of *Blest Be the Tie* drifted across the sanctuary, Sadie and Lucy ambled outside with Marigold. The sun warmed the air as rays passed through golden leaves.

Joel stepped to Sadie's right in full uniform. She gave a small gasp. Why did he startle her every time she saw him?

"Ladies, how about lunch?" His spicy aftershave tickled her nose, and the uniform clung to his muscled body. She cast a glance to her feet, so as not to get too enthralled.

Sadie cleared her throat, then met him eye-to-eye. "Aren't you working?"

"I will be, at two o'clock. So we've got time." He lifted the cap off his head and ran his hand through his hair.

Lucy rocked on her toes and heels, then winked at Sadie. "I'm game, if you all are."

Sadie's chest tightened and her breath caught. Her heart desired a simple life. One without confusion and pressure. A lunch with friends shouldn't make her feel awkward. Had she removed herself so far from these people, she'd made herself inaccessible? Did her MBA shove a layer of her parents' haughty lifestyle between them? Or did the damage Bryce had pounded into her leave her hopeless? She shook her head to clear out the cobwebs. She lived in a safe place now, with people she trusted. At least she hoped so.

"I'd love to, let's go." Sadie sauntered to the parking lot.

Lucy and Marigold piled into Sadie's car.

Sadie turned to Marigold. "Where are we going?"

Lucy piped up. "How about Johnny's?"

Marigold and Sadie spoke at the same time. "Sounds good."

Lucy waved her phone from the back seat. "I'll send Joel a text to let him know where to meet us."

With the Mini-Cooper in gear, she drove on to the road, and caught Lucy's gaze from the back seat in the rearview mirror. "What's the wink for?"

A grin split her friend's face. "I think you know. Don't you remember all the burgers you and my brother shared over the summers? You and Joel used to split fries, a burger, and a shake. Kind of romantic, don't you think."

"No." Sadie glared in the mirror. "We were trying to save money." She parked in the restaurant's lot and they climbed out of the car.

Sadie inhaled the fragrance of hamburgers and fries. *Heaven on a bun.* They met Joel, and he led them to the restaurant with the neon sign blinking "Johnny's."

"Still enjoy a good burger, Sadie?"

"I still love cheeseburgers. I haven't had one as good as Johnny's since I left the island." Inside, 50s music blasted from the jukebox. Customers, seated on tall stools, surrounded the fake marble counter. Formica tables and vinyl chairs in shades of red and aqua filled every other corner of the room. Plastic-covered menus, salt and pepper shakers, and silver napkin holders filled one end of each table. The place smelled of comfort.

They pulled out chairs and sat at a table at the rear of the restaurant. Lucy browsed the menu as if she'd order something new. Marigold fanned herself with the printed sheet of listed burger selections and Greek specialties. Sadie's taste buds tingled over a bacon burger she hadn't seen before, not to mention so many shake flavors. Her mouth watered over the berry swirl. Yep, she'd order a cheeseburger with pickles and ketchup and a berry swirl shake.

A teenager approached the table. "What'll you have?"

Marigold pointed to the menu. "I'll have the spanakopita and the big Greek platter to share with my friends."

The waitress jotted their orders. Sadie's gaze followed the young lady until she disappeared into the kitchen. "I missed this place. Can't wait to taste everything."

Lucy stacked the menus on the end of the table. "I love the pita bread and feta cheese. Thanks, Marigold."

"Sounds delicious. I'm guessing we'll be stuffed like the grape leaves when we're done." Sadie folded her hands in front of her and took in the people seated nearby. "How many kids live here now?"

Lucy held out her fingers and counted. "This time of year we have six younger school-age kids plus four teens who ferry over to the high school near Lakeside. There might be a few babies and toddlers. A young couple moved here over the summer and decided to stay. He works from home, a consulting business. They have five kids."

"Seems like more young people work from home these days. Any chance some will stay?" Sadie spread her napkin on her lap.

Marigold scanned the place as if she searched for someone. "I doubt it. Seems they want to leave and not look back. Johnny had a time finding enough workers to help for the winter."

Joel's face split into a grin. "So Marigold, how are things going with Johnny these days?"

# CHAPTER SEVEN

*Rock Around the Clock* crooned from the jukebox. Sadie's mouth formed an "O" as she turned to her friend.

Marigold's cheeks pinked, and she batted her eyelashes. "I don't know why you're asking me about Johnny."

Joel raised an eyebrow. "When I was on patrol, I saw the two of you walking the beach together the other night. You looked pretty cozy."

Still a beauty at fifty-something, she wrapped her braid through her hands. "You see too much. We're friends who take walks. Nothing more." She raised her chin and pursed her lips.

Sadie patted her friend's shoulder. Marigold never blushed. She kept her emotions in check and imparted a calm demeanor. "Joel, stop with the teasing."

Lucy gave a toothy grin, then chimed in. "I can smell the cheese melting off the burgers."

As if she'd conjured the sandwiches, Johnny appeared with a tray piled with burgers, fries, and shakes. "Hello friends." Cheese dripped off the sides of the burger he served to Lucy. He tucked in Marigold's Greek sampler, then gave her a quick wink no one missed. Joel, Lucy, and Sadie smiled at one another.

"And for our Sadie." He presented her berry shake and burger in front of her. "Good to see you."

"Hi, Johnny, I can't wait to bite into one of your burgers. They're the best."

Perspiration glistened on Johnny's bald head. "Thank you, sweet lady." He made a living fattening people up, yet he cut a decent figure. The island nicknamed him The Runner because he jogged five miles a day after his shift at the restaurant, no matter what time he finished. Sadie's gaze shifted from Johnny to Marigold. They made a cute couple. Maybe Joel's guess of a blossoming romance wasn't off the mark. She hid the revelation in her heart. She'd never embarrass her sweet friend.

"Enjoy your food, and welcome home." Johnny clasped his hands in front of himself and gave a quick bow, then he sauntered into the kitchen.

Home sounded great. Could she stay?

The group lingered over lunch. Sadie relished the juicy sandwich and the sharp cheese. Lucy launched into how she came to manage the General Store.

"When Chuck decided to retire, he asked me to take over management duties. He still owns it, but I ... "

Sadie's thoughts drifted. As much as she loved the sound of the island being home, she needed to turn the rentals into a livable income and keep Bryce from destroying her dream. She planned to update the vacation rentals and advertise, all while praying he would stay away. The worries niggled at her confidence. She caught herself twisting her napkin into shreds.

"You okay, Sadie?" Joel touched her arm, and she jumped.

"Yep." She shoved the napkin bits under the edge of her plate. "Time to head home. Lucy, I'll be by the store soon." Joel pulled out her chair as she stood. "Thanks, Joel. Can I take you girls home?"

Lucy and Marigold said in unison, "No, I'll walk."

"Okay, I'll see you all later." Sadie waved and hurried to her car.

~~~~~

At home with a cup of tea, she retrieved a pad of paper and pencil from Grandpa's roll top desk. Lucy had reminded her the General Store carried cleaning supplies. She added Windex, paper towels, and plastic gloves, plus a few more necessities to the list she'd started. Guests could arrive as soon as March, or they might book a cottage for the 5K run in November. She'd at least paint and buy new linens by then.

She slipped another paper out of her notepad. Rosie needed dog food, and she wanted to make oatmeal butterscotch cookies. As she scribbled on the pad, her spirits lifted. She had waited three years to return to Abbott Island. Maybe she'd discover her niche and be a businesswoman like Gram.

~~~~~

Monday morning, the sun shone through the early morning fog. The azure sky reflected a soft navy on the waves. Light glinted off the water and looked as if God sprinkled glitter on the lake. The temperature measured fifty, not bad for October. Sadie picked a good day to ferry over. At the Sandusky home improvement store, she'd choose the paint. Gram had kept the inside of the cottages a neutral beige. Sadie pictured one with light blue walls, the other gray-blue, both with white trim. Cherry red, a hint of green, and crisp white accents created a fun lake palette to play with. She'd attract folks who wanted more vacation experience rather than the anglers. Many of the island rentals offered fish cleaning stations. Not Sadie's cottages. Instead, she planned to attract families or people who wanted to get away from life and relax. She longed to host a women's weekend or artist's retreat.

Sadie had invested the money Grandpa left with the property. Thankfully, her dad found no interest in the island. He had never wanted to return. Since he paid her a fair salary, she'd socked away enough to implement needed upgrades to the place. The outside updates depended on the weather, but for now she'd conquer the inside.

At the store, Sadie fanned out several paint chips. On the counter she alternated a lighter shade of blue-gray with a darker blue-gray. Perfect for the wall the headboard snugged against. She'd splatter-paint the light over the dark, then finish the other walls with the lighter shade.

As she sorted through the light blue swatches for the other cottage, a deep voice bellowed behind her. Her heart thumped. Sweat beaded on her forehead. She glanced sideways, then let out the breath she'd held. Not Bryce. The man's voice shared the same confidence and timber of the man who had torn her heart out. Except this man smiled when he spoke. The jolt left Sadie's hands shaking.

Scars of fear and anxiety burrowed in her soul. Her legs held her as she leaned on the counter. *Breathe.* She closed her eyes and imagined her grandmother's flower garden. The zinnias splayed with deep pink and yellow blooms. The fragrant memory of the lilac bush calmed. With a push off the counter, she steadied herself. Spine straight, head erect, she focused on the display of paint chips.

Sadie plucked a pink swatch, bright enough to energize her new sanctuary, the loft. She'd surround herself with Gram's quilts, Grandpa's Bibles and books, Rosie, and pink, lots of pink.

Lunch with Joel, Lucy, and Marigold had ignited hope in her future. Yet, her heart waved a caution flag with regard to Joel. She counted herself as damaged goods. He deserved better.

~~~~~

Tuesday morning, Sadie let Rosie out to run in the yard and do her business, while she lugged the paint cans to the porch of the house. Yesterday evening, after she unpacked groceries, she'd swept the leaves off the slatted wood and pushed the debris into a trash bag. She'd dragged the two red rockers to one side and created a cozy space with a rattan table she'd found in the garage. An old tarp made the perfect drop cloth for the other side of the porch, where she'd staged the work supplies.

After she'd hauled the last can of paint and plopped it on the tarp, Sadie stood and stretched. Another run might help loosen her muscles and strengthen her core. Locked to a desk ten hours a day, then hiding at Ann's had depleted her of physical strength. She'd rebuild her stamina and use her newfound strength to tackle her chores, and lessen the aches and pains of hard work.

In cobalt running shoes, an old Cleveland Browns t-shirt, and black cotton capris, she coaxed Rosie along the trail. A golden glow from the sun shining through the orange and red-leafed canopy fueled her with energy. The mossy smell of autumn calmed her.

Home to a state park, the center of the island offered beautiful East Quarry Trail. About halfway into the forest, she and Rosie stopped and listened to the birds chirping and the sound of leaves rustling in the trees. Unaccustomed to the quiet of the forest, Sadie stopped. She lowered herself to a large rock and closed her eyes. In Columbus, highways cut through the city, cars honked, mufflers backfired, people shouted. Quiet never happened.

In the midst of the forest, she bent her head back. Birds tweeted, leaves rustled, peace settled. Until a snap broke the silence. Rosie raised a low growl. She opened her eyes and focused on a scrubby bush. A brown bunny hopped out and hightailed it across the path.

"Rosie, we heard a rabbit." Sadie shook her head and laughed at herself. She fidgeted and checked her surroundings so often, she'd forgotten she rested in a woods, on an island, in the middle of an enormous lake. Maybe she'd found a safe haven at last, or maybe not.

~~~~~

Sadie carted the bucket of cleaning supplies and a broom to the small front porch of the second cottage. The new lock she had installed shimmered as the sun peeked around a few dark clouds. With the turn of the key, she let herself into the tiny place.

A musty smell hit her nose. She shoved the windows open to air out the small bungalow. With a swing of the broom, she annihilated cobwebs and dusted the walls. At one point the spider's sticky silk caught in her hair. "Yuck." She batted her hands and brushed the threads out.

She'd obliterated the webs in the cottage. Not the ones stuck in every corner of her mind that pushed her to the edge. On her runs, every snap of a branch or thud in the woods made her jump. Bryce held on to her, regardless of what she did to forget him. He'd wormed his way into her life. *"You're so beautiful." "I couldn't have found a more intelligent woman." "Where have you been all my life?"* She'd fallen for his compliments, hook, line, and sinker, as Grandpa used to say.

He'd sucked her into his game. Made her feel beautiful and needed. He'd convinced her he'd die without her. Months later, he raged and tossed out insults whenever he wanted. Memories of her dad surfaced. Except Dad never gave compliments. Bryce's voice raged in her head. *"You're so stupid." "Why do you think you can make anything of yourself?" "Your dress looks hideous." "You know your dad is on my side."*

Sadie blew out a deep breath. She squared her stance and worked off her angst. Years of dirt disappeared as she scrubbed away crud along with her fear. She admired her work. The cottage's lemony-clean smell filled her with the essence of hope. Yet, a sense of dread overshadowed her.

She beat the broom against the outside wall. Dust fell out, cobwebs untangled to the ground as dark clouds loomed overhead. She swung the broom in the air and slammed it against the wall one last time to try to dislodge her regret. The force knocked her legs from under her, and she fell into a heap on the ground. Drops of rain fell on her and mixed with long-held-back tears. Why had she opened herself to Bryce's wrath? Sobs echoed through the air. A drizzle at first, then the rain poured, and she didn't care. She let the icy rain drench her.

# CHAPTER EIGHT

The thunder pounded. Sadie heaved herself off the ground and stood with her arms outstretched and head back. She shivered in the downpour. Lightning streaked the black sky. With arms wrapped around her middle, she sloshed across the yard and trudged inside.

She climbed to the second floor and dripped all the way to the shower. Soon, warm water washed over her. By the time steady rivulets rinsed lavender-scented shampoo from her hair, her shaking ceased as the steamy bathroom warmed her.

A flash of lightning lit the sky. From her bedroom window, she witnessed the waves smacking the shore. In flannel pajamas and a pink terrycloth robe, she padded down the stairs to the kitchen to make some tea.

Soon, steam feathered from the Earl Grey in her cup. She spread butter and raspberry jam on toast.

"Rosie, come curl up by the couch." The Golden Retriever trotted behind her.

Sadie nibbled on her toast. The sweet jam didn't take away the bitter taste Bryce had left in her life. She tossed the bread on the saucer and stared out the window at the storm. Anger seethed in her. She'd let him worm his way into her life.

He had craved the number one spot. He'd squash anybody who got in his way. Dad had searched for six months for a vice president. He'd appointed Bryce a few weeks before she joined the firm. Sadie would rather sort mail than work with Bryce or her father. Thank goodness she had spent most of her days at the company working in her office and not under Dad's watchful eye. As for Bryce, he demanded attention from anyone who could help him scale the corporate ladder. With the stealth of a venomous snake, he'd sunk his fangs into her, and Dad let him bite. She'd discovered, too late, Bryce played her as a pawn in his game to garner power in the business. He would cozy up to the boss's daughter, then push to marry her, become a member of the family, and gain a permanent position in the family business. Dad wore blinders. As long as Bryce brought in revenue, he paid no attention to anything else he did.

*Oh, Dad. Such a workaholic. Never around. Hard-as-nails shell and unbearable attitude. Ugh.* Sadie didn't like her dad, but she loved him as his daughter, with some modicum of respect. She shifted the tea to the coffee table then bowed her head. A low growl rose from Rosie's throat. "Hold on, girl." Sadie patted the dog's head, then closed her eyes. *God help me forgive my dad for not loving me, for using me for his gain. I know he provided for me, yet he never gave me his love. My heart breaks for him and his selfish ways. Please forgive me for my anger. Help me as I ...*

Rosie's angry bark halted Sadie's prayer. The dog howled at the door.

"What's going on, girl?" She pushed the curtain aside and peered out the window. Lightning brightened the dark sky. A shadowy figure rushed across the yard and dropped something. A glimpse of the nearest cottage gave her pause.

She flipped on the porch light, then scurried down the slippery steps.

"No!" An unfinished skull-and-crossbones glared at her from the cottage wall. "Ugh." She drew her hands into fists. "They've ruined my cottage. Why would someone do this?"

Who painted over the beautiful shaker shingles?

Rosie panted beside her.

"Come on, girl. We need to get in the house. No telling who's out here."

Light rain pattered on the roof as she scrambled to the porch. Once back inside, Sadie plopped on the couch and ducked her head into her hands. Her shoulders shook as tears pricked her eyes. Tired of crying, she counted to ten to regain her composure. She'd chosen the island as a transition to peace and quiet. Did she make a mistake? The evil symbols freaked her out. The calm she'd funneled from the lake seeped out of her.

Her heart ached for a tranquil refuge, a comfortable home with no drama. Instead of relaxing in peace, she punched the couch cushion with frustration and fear.

~~~~~

Joel clicked the computer keys and recorded details of island incidents from the day. He hit save, then he dug out the office calendar to double check next week's work hours. Whether Sadie would accept his help on his days off or not, he planned to make himself available, in case she called him. The phone jangled as he tucked the calendar into the desk drawer.

"Island Police, how can I help you?"

"Joel? It's Sadie."

His heart hammered when he heard the rush in her voice. She sounded distressed. Not good.

He stood and slid on his holster. "What's wrong?"

"Can you come over? My cottage ... it's been vandalized." The tears in her voice tugged at him.

"I'll be right over." He grabbed his hat. "Come on, Griff." Joel loaded the German shepherd into the squad car.

He'd worked with his buddy for more than a year. The two of them had broken up a small drug ring about a month ago. Griff's nose distinguished any whiff of a clue from the fishy scent of the island. He'd trained him to ascertain the odor of narcotics, even when the smell of grilled steak hung in the air.

Minutes later, Joel spun the squad car into Sadie's driveway. As she stepped off the porch with Rosie, he released the door and jumped out. "What happened?"

"Look at the cottage. I hope the shingles aren't ruined." Sadie flapped her arm toward the nearest rental. "They must have seen me look out the window." She closed her eyes for a few seconds, then opened them and locked on Joel. "I think ..." She paused as if to slow her words. "I think he dropped something when he ran off. I didn't want to check until you got here."

"Okay. We'll take a look." Joel opened the rear door of the car and signaled for Griff to get out. "Let's go buddy."

"Who's that?" She wrapped her fingers around Rosie's leash.

"Meet Griff. He's the unit's K-9. He's got a good nose and knows his way around the island." He and Griff launched toward the cottage. Sadie traipsed behind with Rosie.

A glimmer of silver reflected in the last light of day. "Over there, see it?" Sadie pointed to the corner of the cottage.

Joel reached for her arm. "Don't touch it." She jerked away then stepped back. *Go easy, she's spooked.* "It's possible evidence."

Her eyes widened. "I know. I had no intention of touching it." She locked her arms together in front of her. Her hardened gaze pierced him. The lips he'd once kissed pressed together in a straight line.

"Okay. No problem." Joel stretched gloves over his hands and bagged the can.

~~~~~

Her cheeks flamed. Fear ripped at her core. No man had touched her since Bryce, the monster who had destroyed her confidence and broken her spirit. Mr. Ultra-Professional left bruises where no one else noticed. He'd grab her arm, then let go before he left marks that showed his anger. His pinches near her ribs and smacks on the back of the head left painful memories of his abuse. Even though she'd survived the physical assaults, the emotional ones still haunted her.

Joel gave her no reason to believe he'd evolved into an ogre. His mom taught him to be a gentleman. He'd never hurt her or played rough. She needed to get a grip.

From the porch, a safe distance away, she trained her eyes on Joel and Griff. Gentle waves lapped the water's edge. A steady rhythm of calm met the shore, the opposite of the anxiety that screamed through her head. The sun dipped into the lake. Purple and red streaks fingered across the sky after the storm. For a moment, she soaked in the beauty. God's creation outshone her circumstances. Her heart calmed for a brief moment.

She'd fled to the island for the promise of safety and security. She had never dreamed she'd have to worry about vandals. Why mess with her? Maybe a bored kid dared another one to spray the graffiti. The place sat empty for a few years, a perfect target for delinquents. But what if Bryce had found her? She settled on the porch step and rested her head on her arms. Rosie curled around her feet.

"Sadie." Joel's voice cut into her thoughts. "The silver glimmer you saw is a spray paint can. Found footprints, too. I took photos."

She stared at the officer, her friend. "Now what?" With a groan, she pushed herself from the step. He reached out to take her by the elbow, but she pulled away. She cast a bare smile his way.

"Griff got a good whiff of the area, so we'll do tracking with him. In the meantime, we'll check for fingerprints and see what else we can find. If you don't mind, you'll have to wait a couple of days before you clean off the paint. Plus, I'll need your statement."

"Of course, no problem." Sadie grabbed hold of the porch's rail. She willed herself not to collapse. *What if Bryce had found her?*

From the bottom of the steps, Joel spoke in quiet tones. "I can help you on Thursday, my day off."

"You don't have to keep helping me. I'm capable of doing it myself." With a wave, she backed toward the door and reached for the knob, shoved it open, and retreated inside.

~~~~~

The lock on the door clicked. Joel knelt beside his dog.

"Griff, I don't know what's up with Sadie, but she's a mess about something. She's sure not herself." He rose and gave Griff the command to get in the car. "Maybe she'll talk to Lucy. 'Cause she isn't talking to me."

At the station, he created a file for the vandalism. No one had destroyed property on the island for a few years. Most of the kids respected the place, but he'd not met a few of the young adults he'd spotted around the island. He'd check with the ferry line for any strangers they'd noticed recently. With the storm, he suspected the vandal lived there, or at least visited the island frequently. He slid open his desk drawer and pulled out a notebook. He flipped to the back. Tucked in behind a few newspaper clippings, an old photo reminded him why he needed to help his friend. Sadie stood between him and Lucy, her arms draped around their shoulders on the last day of summer. Sadie's eyes shimmered with unshed tears of joy and sorrow. They'd reminisced about the memories they'd all shared, swimming in the lake, kayaking around the cove, and working at the store. He knew Sadie had feared the path her dad set for her.

"I don't know if I'll get to come back to the island. You know how Dad is," Sadie had said.

Joel knew. Her dad hinted to him not to keep in touch. Which he'd planned to ignore, yet out of fear of rejection he had complied after all.

He had asked Marigold to help him make Sadie a bracelet, in hopes she'd remember him and the good times they'd shared. When he gave her the beaded, braided threads, she'd hugged him and slipped the blue and green wristlet on her arm. "Joel, I love it. I'll never take it off."

Did she keep the goofy attempt he'd made at letting her know he cared? Or did she toss it away as soon as she left? He drew a wrinkled photo of her from his wallet. One he'd kept to himself and stashed in his billfold all through police training. Sadie stood on the beach, with her hair tossed by the wind. They'd been swimming, and she'd fixed a picnic lunch, a perfect end to the summer. Since then, his daily prayers had begged God to rescue her from the life she'd hated. Maybe God had heard him, after all these years. Even if He had, did he dare share the one thing that he regretted with her?

# CHAPTER NINE

Shoulders back and head high, Sadie marched across the lawn Tuesday morning and threw open the door to the second cottage. Musty air floated out. She stopped a sneeze. Armed with a bucket, lemon cleaner and a mop, she attacked the dirt in every crevice. By noon, a pile of trash rested on the curb, ready for pickup. She stood with her hands on her hips and nodded. One more goal accomplished.

Sadie refused to succumb to the worry that crept into her thoughts after last night's antics. After lunch, she thrust the windows open in her house. Ownership of her home, not Gram and Grandpa's, excited her. She'd waited too long to accept their generous gift.

Without consideration of her own needs, she'd focused on the cottages and neglected the house. Other than a wipe down of the bathroom, she'd lived with the years of life her grandparents had created. Their scent lingered. Mint and fresh cut wood comforted her as she slept on the couch. She'd avoided her room in the loft, even though she planned to update the space. Ghosts of her past life lingered where she'd left her journals and books to the dust bunnies.

Sadie scanned the living room. Gram's sewing basket caught her eye. She'd tried multiple times to teach her to sew. Most of the time, Sadie's fingers fumbled with the needle. She'd stuck herself and sucked the blood from her finger too many times. She stitched a hole in her sweater once and attached a loose button. She'd attempted to sew a pair of shorts, but she lacked Gram's skill set, yet she'd love to learn. She cherished the quilts and embroidered pieces her Gram gave her. She'd tucked them into her hope chest at the end of the bed in her old room.

"Rosie, I forgot about my quilts." Sadie sprinted upstairs two steps at a time. The dog trotted at her heels. The books she'd read summers ago spilled over on the chest. A thick layer of dust reminded her of the neglect and years she'd stayed away. Why had she ignored the cottages and her home? Her dad had thrown guilt at her, that was why. He'd tossed the obligation to the family business in her lap.

She brushed the dust aside, stacked the books on the floor, then creaked open the chest. On top a beautiful wedding ring quilt rested, the last one Gram had quilted. Each tiny stitch, sewn with meticulous precision, wove through the layers. Sadie ran her fingers over the interlocking rings of fanciful fabrics. She loved how they contrasted with the white background. This beautiful piece of handiwork reminded her of a summer day.

Sadie had once dreamed of marriage. Her tenth summer, she had played with Joel and Lucy at the beach. They'd built a huge sandcastle. Joel pretended to be the handsome prince and Sadie the princess. Later in her room, she'd drawn a picture of her prince and herself holding hands, dressed in a suit and gown. She'd shoved the silliness of childhood behind when Bryce squashed her dream of a man committed to kindness and love. Just as well. She needed to live in reality. Happily-ever-after stories belonged in fairy tales.

As Sadie lifted the quilt from the chest, a card tumbled from the folds. She tugged a note from the aged envelope.

*Dear Sadie,*

*I pray this finds you well. If you are reading this, then you've made your way back to the island at last.*
*I'd hoped we'd have spent more time together, but the good Lord will call me home soon. Just so you know, I'm okay with dying. I can't wait to see my sweet Julia again.*
*Anyway, I want you to know no matter what life throws at you, you always have a home here.*
*I want you to make this place your refuge. More important, I want you to remember the only refuge you'll ever need. God loves you, Sadie-girl. He's your protector. He puts good people in your life. Trust them.*
*Trust Joel and Lucy, and Marigold, if she's still kicking.*
*Live the life you want to live.*

*I love you, girl,*
*Grandpa Ben*

Tears stung Sadie's eyes. She blinked away the hot liquid, then closed her eyes. She pictured Grandpa in the rocker on the porch. His white hair and beard fluttered in the breeze. A pocketknife and a piece of wood in his hand. He had loved to whittle as much as he had loved to fish.

Gram and Grandpa had repeated every summer, "Live the life you want to live." She hoped her dream of peace and quiet existed on Abbott Island. Could a life with less stress and a business to make some money exist for her?

Sadie tucked the wedding ring quilt into the chest, placed the letter on top, and shut the lid. She hauled herself from the floor and perched on the wooden box. Grandpa gifted her a safe place to live. He and Gram had watched Sadie's life unfold, and had witnessed her parents pressuring her to compete. When she'd stressed over high school and ended up in the hospital with ulcers, Gram had insisted she recover on the island.

She moved to the window and opened the blinds. "Rosie, I'm going to make this place mine." The dog whined. "Okay, yours too, girl."

After she dusted, changed the sheets on the bed, emptied the drawers and filled them with her clothes, Sadie ambled downstairs. She gathered a well-worn quilt from the recliner, then wandered outside.

Orange and purple streaks draped the darkened sky. She snuggled into the pinwheel quilt and cozied into Grandpa's rocker. Rosie rested her head on her paws. The sun disappeared into the lake while the gulls perched on the dock. She soaked in the evening's tranquility. Grandpa spoke of God as her shelter. She wanted to trust, even as her heart nagged with doubt. He'd said to trust Joel, too.

The wash of the waves on the shore quieted her. She bowed her head. Maybe Grandpa's God would listen to her prayers for the strength to start over.

~~~~~

Thursday morning, the landline on the wall chirped. Sunlight flooded the kitchen. She settled plates on the counter with a clatter in a move to answer the phone.

"Hello." The wall phone didn't have caller I.D.

"Hey, Sadie."

Her heart skipped a beat at the voice on the other end. "Hi, Joel." Her voice raised an octave, and she wanted to kick herself for her reaction.

"Any leads on the artwork on my cottage?" *Please don't discover a connection to Bryce.* If Joel tracked him down, he'd find out about her wretched past.

"You weren't the only one. The Browns and Kaufmans have damage, too. Same paint color and design." He sighed into the phone. His voice sounded tired. "We're waiting to see if they do it again. My guess is kids, but it's hard to tell. All the damage occurred on the same side of the island."

"Oh, man. I'm sorry they got damaged, too." Sadie viewed the lake out her window. "I guess I can clean it off now?" The question hung in the air.

"Yeah, you can." He cleared his throat. "My offer still stands. I've got cleaner and scrapers to take the paint off."

Sadie rubbed her temple. Joel wanted to help her as a friend. Grandpa had trusted him. "Sure. Okay. Come over in half an hour."

"I'll be there."

~~~~~

In the daylight, the skull and crossbones glared at Sadie. A tingle ran up her spine as if someone peered at her in her own yard. She gripped the tiny bit of comfort that other islanders found graffiti, too. Somehow their misfortune calmed her.

The crunching of tires sounded from her driveway. Joel steered his golf cart into her yard and parked out of the way. He toted a bucket with a bottle of yellow cleaner, a scraper and several rags sticking out.

"Hey, how you doing?" He dropped his load by the marred wall.

"I'm good." With a small nod, Sadie lied. *Good* did not define her today. She tried to shake the feeling somebody lurked in the shadows. Her mind had played tricks on her ever since Bryce's deceit. On their first date he had admired her as if she reigned as princess. By the last date, he snarled at her and accused her of using him. He'd broken her trust. She pushed herself to shake off the self-doubt he'd planted in her mind. The damage she had internalized had ripped a hole in her stomach. Any hope to forgive him faded.

Sadie glanced at Joel. Opposite of Bryce in so many ways. He cared and protected. Maybe he could be her friend again. Maybe.

"You ready to tackle this mess? I brought gloves. I figured if this stuff took off paint, it might remove skin, too." Joel sprayed graffiti remover on two worn dish towels.

"Good thinking. Thanks." Her hands swam in the plastic covers, but they'd work. Sadie wrinkled her nose. "That stuff stinks."

He capped the cleaner's lid. "Yeah, it's potent, and it'll do the job."

Both of them scrubbed at the paint. Little by little, the ugly marks disappeared. They swiped the towels in small circles on the cedar shakes and made gradual progress. Sadie straightened her sore back and checked the work. After an hour, they'd expunged the crossbones and half of the skull.

"What do you think? Another hour?"

"Maybe a half-an-hour or so." Joel stepped away and drew off his gloves. "Were you planning to repaint the cedar shakes?"

"I'll give them a fresh coat in the spring." She tugged off her gloves, then shoved a strand of hair from her face. "You ready for a break? We've worked up a sweat in October." She admired him and his muscled arms as he scrubbed at the paint. The same attraction pulled her to him now that she had experienced as a teenager. She should avoid him, not spend too much time with him. Then again, she needed a friend. "I made iced tea and chocolate chip oatmeal cookies. Want some?"

"Seriously, you made my favorite cookie? You remembered?" Joel beamed.

"Maybe. Don't go thinking I'm aiming to please you." Sadie tapped his arm.

"No worries. I'd never stop you from making my favorite cookies." He tagged behind her to the porch. "Mind if we sit out here and cool off? Cleaning is hard work."

"You bet it is. I'll be right back."

Minutes later, with cookies and tea balanced on a tray, Sadie nudged the front door open. "What do you think about a red door on each cottage?"

"You asking my opinion?" He grabbed the tray and placed it on a side table.

"Yeah." She sidled into a chair. "I'm trying to keep my focus on my project. The more I think about the damage, the more I get the willies."

"The willies, huh? My grandma used to call my fear of the monster under the bed the willies." In a high voice, Joel said, "Boy, you've got the willies." He took a bite of the cinnamon-spiced cookie.

Sadie chuckled. "Yeah. Grandpa said willies, too. Now, I've got to get my mind off the vandalism and move on." She lifted her tea glass as if to click it with his. "I trust you'll figure out who did it. I need to leave it in your hands."

Joel drew his brows together. A worry line creased his forehead. "You seem pretty shook up about a little graffiti. Is there something else I need to know, Sadie?"

# CHAPTER TEN

The next morning, Sadie's mind whirled over Joel's question. She'd stopped herself from spilling the truth about Bryce, then blamed her stress on all the work she needed to do, and the shock of something so ugly happening on the island. While she harbored the truth, her heart ached over the lie she'd told Joel. Sharing her past with him required trust. He seemed like her friend, however, as an officer he might nose around in her business and stir a hornet's nest with her ex.

As her childhood friend, he embodied kindness, but he'd light a fire under any man who caused her pain. He'd punched a guy when they were teenagers because the idiot flung his arm around her, then drew her into an unwanted hug. He'd erupt, if he found out the emotional and physical abuse she'd suffered from Bryce.

Sadie dragged her old bike out of the shed. She chuckled at the wide lavender fenders with the hot pink seat. Gram and Grandpa gave it to her on her twelfth birthday, and the old girl still rolled. Sadie found the tire pump in the garage and attached the nozzle to the valve stem. She pumped the inner tube full of fresh air. The perfect tread and the bright white logo told her Grandpa had taken care of her, again. He must have traded the ancient tires for new ones before he had passed away.

As she cycled to the walking beach, she waved to some folks sitting on their porch. Everett and Peggy, now in their seventies, owned the prettiest house on the island. Not the biggest or the oldest, but the most unique. The pristine gingerbread edging the eaves and posts lent the three porches a Victorian flair. The vertical wooden slats on the main porch added an interesting twist. They'd already secured the yellow shutters on the second floor, as they prepared for rough winter weather.

Gram and Sadie had baked cookies with Peggy. Gram's friend had encouraged her to move to the island. "There's not enough young people here. Wish some of you would stay." She'd have packed and moved in a heartbeat, but Mom and Dad had disapproved. Perhaps she'd stop and see her old friends. Or not. They'd question her about what she'd been doing. Why attract attention?

Sadie propped her bike against a maple tree, then stepped onto the packed sand. Driftwood littered the shore. She and Grandpa had combed the little beach every summer. They'd tote buckets and shovels early in the morning and scavenge for treasures.

She held out her right hand and admired the jewelry on her ring finger. A piece of aqua blue lake glass, set in a silver braid, reflected the color of the waves. Gram and Grandpa had commissioned one of the artists on the island to create a one-of-a-kind ring for her sixteenth birthday. When Sadie showed her mom, she had sneered. "Throw that piece of junk away. Someday, you'll inherit all the expensive jewelry your dad gifted me. Why humiliate yourself by wearing a piece of garbage on your finger? Picked out of a lake, no less."

Sadie had walked away from her mom's expensive baubles. The aqua glass she'd worn since her sixteenth birthday meant more to her than all the rubies and diamonds her mother had owned.

She picked her way across the beach. The sense someone might be nearby prickled her skin. Off to the right, a great blue heron posed. She held her beak out, head back, her neck curved like a sink pipe, the wide wings tucked into her sides.

Sadie whispered. "Esther."

She tiptoed toward the bird. Gram had named her after Esther in the Bible, a queen who stood tall and saved her people. Sadie estimated Esther's age at about twelve. She still had a few more years. Unlike the other herons who inhabited the island, black feathers speckled her left wing. She'd fly south soon. Maybe she contemplated her journey as she stood on the sand and stared into the water. Sadie snapped a photo with her phone.

"Such a beauty."

Esther might travel to warmer climates, while Sadie intended to avoid any place south of Sandusky. She made no plans to expose herself to a run-in with her dad or Bryce. She'd refurbish the cottages and invite travelers to experience the tranquility and adventure with nature. The life she longed for.

Esther turned her head and looked at Sadie. With a nod, she spread her wings and soared above the water. Planted on the sand, Sadie appreciated the graceful stretch and flight of her friend. She longed for the courage to spread her wings and fly like Esther.

~~~~~

Once she lost sight of the bird, Sadie spread a small blanket across the sand. She sat, then folded her arms over her knees and rested her head on top. The ebb and flow of the waves mesmerized her. She longed for a steady flow in her life. Sadie dreamed of a give and take with people who loved her for herself.

Before she had left Columbus, she'd listened as Ann talked about Jesus as a rock and a second chance. She wanted to believe in the Jesus her grandparents loved, but depression dogged her. She couldn't shake the sorrow. Let alone commit to a deity she didn't understand.

Bryce's cruel words still echoed in her mind. Utterances she'd never repeat. Yet they played like a movie in her head. How stupid was she to believe his lies? She'd earned the highest honors and grades in college. Then she fell for Bryce's charms and got caught in his games. The first six months, he had lavished her with compliments, and praise. He acted as a gentleman and opened her door, then he changed. The dates to fancy restaurants ended with him berating her manners, her clothes, and her hair style. She'd try harder on every date, with hopes of a new ending. No matter what she had drawn from her closet to wear, he reprimanded her for trying to embarrass him. No matter how sweetly or politely she treated his clients, he accused her of rudeness.

The next day, he'd send her flowers or leave chocolates on her desk. He'd stop in to say hello as if nothing happened. Then he'd whisper in her ear, "You're a fat and ugly embarrassment." For over a year, Sadie tolerated him. Every day she hoped for change. When he offered kindness, she embraced the day. Then a dark shadow overtook him and transformed him into a more evil version of himself. The last straw came when the physical abuse claimed her sanity. He left marks, but didn't hit. He pinched and poked and grabbed her too hard, and tried to convince her she enjoyed the roughness.

One day she'd had enough. Sadie marched into her dad's office and closed the door.

"Want something?" Her dad stared at the computer's monitor.

"Dad, I need to talk to you." She had plopped into his client chair. No response except clacking on the keyboard and the smell of his nasty cigar.

"What do you want?"

"I want you to look at me so I can talk to you." She stood and paced in front of him.

Frank wrenched his glasses from his face and plunked them on the ornate cherry desk. "What's on your mind?" He stared at Sadie and drummed his fingers.

She had eased into the chair. "It's Bryce. He's hurt me."

"Hurt you, how?" A frown crossed her dad's face.

"He pinches and leaves bruises. He makes fun of me and belittles me." Sadie wrung her hands.

Dad stared out the window, then turned his head to meet her eye to eye. "Bryce is the best VP I've ever had. If whatever he's doing doesn't interfere with business, I don't see how it's any business of mine. This is personal. You're a big girl. Fix it yourself, just don't impact the business."

"Dad, can't you talk to him?"

"I can, but I'm not going to. End of story. You're excused." He tapped his glasses onto the bridge of his nose and started plinking the keys.

In the hall, Sadie had stomped her high heel as tears dripped on her cheeks. She stepped across the corridor with her arms cradling her roiling stomach. Then she eased into her office and closed the door.

~~~~~

Sadie's hair whipped across her face. In the sand she spied a cobalt blue piece of lake glass, the size of a quarter. On her knees, she picked the beauty out of the sand. She and Grandpa had searched for this color for years. She brushed the grit off and rolled the gem between her fingers. The piece wore the sanded down sheen of glass tumbled by the waves. Sadie loved this little island. As she held the blue sea glass, she raised her hand and declared Abbott Island as her forever home. She'd find a way to stay and live at peace.

Footsteps pounded behind Sadie.

She tucked the lake glass into her pocket and pushed herself from the sand.

Lucy jogged toward her with arms open. "Good morning."

"Hi." After a quick hug, Sadie stepped back and looked at her childhood friend. Her blue eyes sparkled with the charm she remembered.

"It's good to see you. I've wanted to catch up with you, but I've been cleaning." A laugh escaped Sadie's lips. "I haven't had such chapped skin since I helped Grandpa clean fish, then scrubbed my hands raw."

"I remember. You wanted him to think you were a brave twelve-year-old. The odor clung to you, and you smelled fishy for days." Lucy giggled.

Sadie lifted her hands to her face and sniffed. "My new fragrance this week is bleach."

Lucy scrunched her nose. "I'm glad we're outside. I'd rather smell the beach than the bleach."

"Want to join me? I'm watching the lake come to life this morning." Sadie dropped to the sand and patted a spot beside her.

Years ago, the two friends descended on the small beach every morning to plan their day. They hiked in the woods, rode bikes all over the island, and swam at the park beach. In their mid-teens, their days changed. Hours of retail at the General Store ended with evening campfires, s'mores, and Joel. Lucy had kept all her childhood secrets. Sadie had cried on her shoulder over her parents' neglect. When Mom died, Lucy had listened to her moan about college and her dad's control over her life.

Lucy leaned in. "So you're living on the island."

"Yep. I am." Should she spill to Lucy? She used to pour her heart out to her sweet friend, but this time she wanted to bury her secrets in the sand.

Lucy scooped a handful of sand and sifted the grains through her fingers. "How's it going? Have you had to do much work at your grandparents' place?"

Sadie nodded. "Yes, there's so much to clean and repair. I'm working on the cottages and hoping to rent them out, come spring."

"That's so exciting. Now you'll be one of the 115 year-long residents. Make that 116." Lucy clapped her hands. "I've missed you so much. The island lacks in people our age. There aren't many of us."

"I remember you talking about how small your class was in school."

Her friend still bubbled over with joy. Maybe Lucy's positive spirit would infuse her life.

Lucy bit her lower lip. "Joel told me someone damaged your cottage."

"Yeah. They used their artistic skills to decorate."

"Pretty bad, huh?"

"Joel helped me get most of it off. I plan to paint them in the spring, anyway." Sadie fingered her ring.

"Any idea who'd do such a thing?"

"I wish, but then it wouldn't matter." Sadie shrugged. Even if Joel found the culprit, her peace of mind was shaken.

"They at least owe you an apology."

"I guess. I just hope they leave me alone, now."

"Me too. Hey, why don't you come to the corn maze with me?" Lucy pointed to the northeast part of the island.

"You have a corn maze?"

"Mr. Green made one this year. He's the last working farm on the island." Lucy scrunched her face. "You can get a pumpkin there, too. If you like."

Sadie nodded. "Okay. I need something fun. When are you going?"

"Saturday night, in the dark with flashlights." Her friend wiggled her eyebrows.

"Flashlights? Sure, why not." She tilted her head. "Who all is going?"

"Joel and me and a couple of our friends." Lucy stood and brushed the sand off her pants. "I'm off to the store. We're working on inventory and preparing for winter. The year-rounders depend on me and the grocery to supply food and toilet paper."

Sadie stood. "No doubt."

The creases around her lips showed as she smiled. "So you've seen Joel a few times?"

"Yep." Warmth flushed Sadie's cheeks. "He helped me get the paint off the cottage and clean the gutters. Even though I didn't want him to."

"Joel and his good deeds. He's still trying to make up for ... never mind." Lucy waved. "Gotta go. See you Saturday."

From the beach, Sadie watched her friend roll off on her bike. *What does Joel need to make up for?*

# CHAPTER ELEVEN

Saturday evening, the corn reached over Joel and Sadie's heads as they trekked into the opening of the maze. He led the way, with her close behind. A musty, earthy smell floated in the breeze as the friends waved flashlights into the stalks.

Joel held his phone in the air. "I'm not convinced this app they gave us will help us find our way through the maze. The signal out here is terrible." He shined his light on Sadie, Lucy, and their friends.

Sadie pressed her cell button. "I don't have much signal either. I guess we'll have to wing it."

Lucy held her flashlight under chin and made her face glow in the dark. "The maze can't be that big, can it?"

"Luce, are you ever going to grow up?" Joel shook his head.

"Nope. I'm not." The light reflected on her teeth and her eerie grin.

"Let's give it--" Sadie paused when corn stalks grabbed her hair. "Ugh." Joel untangled her waves. "It's just the corn grabbing you."

Lucy waved her light. "How about we split up and see who gets out first? Joel, you take Sadie. The rest of us will head out together."

Joel brushed Sadie's arm with his. "I'm game if you are."

She frowned at Lucy, then looked at Joel. "Okay."

He held out his hand. "Let's go this way."

She hesitated, then clasped his hand.

~~~~~

Warmth flowed from Sadie's fingers to her shoulder. Joel's calluses rubbed her soft skin. More than one person lately had bragged on Joel and how he helped whoever needed him. Mrs. Garrett had gushed about him replacing her roof. Mr. Henesy had told everyone at the cafe how Joel raked his leaves. When did he find the time to help all the people and work?

Joel's voice broke into her thoughts. "Which way should we go?"

Sadie eyed the path they walked. Two trails led away from the entrance while another moved parallel. "How about the one that's parallel? It lines up with the front. Do you think it's a spiral?"

"Let's go." He kept a hold of her hand.

After two false starts, they progressed along a route that wound past several rows.

"This might be it." Joel pulled her along. "By the looks of the corn, we're at the back of the field. I can see the barn through those stalks." He let go of Sadie and dragged the stalks apart.

In place of the warmth from his touch, a chill embraced her fingers. She missed his tender touch. Before she let herself get swept away by the moment, she stuffed her hand in her pocket.

Joel turned to her. Before she could stop herself, she bumped into him, so close his minty breath tickled her nose. She froze, and her heart thumped.

"You okay?" He ran his hands over her arms.

"Sure. I'm fine." Her hands begged to touch his face, or run her fingers through his hair. His lips invited her to kiss them. *Control yourself. Breathe.* She backed away and turned toward the path. "Let's go."

"Okay. I'm right behind you."

Sadie listened as his boots crunched the leaves. Soon they were free of the maze.

"Hey, you two. We beat you." Lucy waved from the bales of hay she sat on by the exit.

Sadie headed toward their friends. "By how much?"

"About two minutes." She giggled. "Let's get a bite to eat."

"Sounds good," Sadie and Joel responded in unison.

She rushed to Lucy's side and linked her arm with her friend, anything to create space between her and Joel. Old feelings had crept in, so she would squash the tingles and thumps of her heart. She'd focus on the rentals and leave romance on the sideline.

~~~~~

Rosie barked from inside the house. Too tired to let her canine companion out, Sadie rocked on the porch and stared at the cottages. For two weeks she had scrubbed and painted. She held out her hands and cringed at her broken fingernails and dry skin. The odor of lemon cleaner clung to her.

The temptation to quit hounded her with every swirl of the scrub brush and swoosh of the broom. *Not good enough*, echoed in her head. Why did she think she could create a peaceful ambiance when a quieted heart eluded her? The fear of failure dogged her. What if her dreams crashed?

Had she jumped in with both feet before she researched the reality of running a rental business? She had lugged paint and cleaning supplies across the lake and onto the ferry. Her hands ached after she scoured every corner and sanitized all the surfaces. The cottages sparkled. Yet unease seeped into her soul.

She fingered the flier someone left on her door. Abbott Island's Fall Fest splayed across the top of the orange paper. The advertisement touted best pumpkin pie contest and a chili cook-off. Plus games and craft booths, Saturday from 2 to 6 at the park. Chili sounded good, and she needed to acquaint herself with the community. Many of the older people remembered Gram and Grandpa. If she wanted to succeed in her business, she had to mingle. She'd rather hide under a rock, but she'd make herself go.

In the house, she stuck the flier to the refrigerator with a magnet.

The wall phone's ring startled her. She lifted the receiver to her ear. Lucy's peppy voice jumped through the line. "Hey Sadie, how are the cottages coming along?"

She wrapped the cord of Grandma's old landline around her hand. "Hi, Lucy. The inspector came by yesterday and okayed me for business. Why?"

"The community hosts a 5K and 10K race the beginning of November. My friends are coming here to run. I offered for them to stay with me, but they asked if there were any cottages open where they'd get a feel for the island. I think they plan to stick around for four or five days, to hang out and relax. Think you can be ready?"

"Wow. Less than a month." She paced across the kitchen. "I think I can pull one together. It won't be the final product, but I'll make it work."

Lucy's voice rose an octave. "Yes. We can call it a soft opening."

"Sounds good. Have your friend call me, and I'll set up their reservation." Sadie hung up and eyed the old sky-blue rotary telephone her grandparents had installed for Gram's business. She adored the vintage look. With the spotty cell service, she'd need the solid connection. The old contraption reminded her to emulate her gram's business sense and be professional.

*Gram, I'm going to do this.*

Sadie fist bumped the air. "Rosie, we'll have our first guests soon. Do I put them in the rustic, woodsy, lake life cottage or the English cottage?"

She danced around the kitchen. "We can do this girl." She stopped and took a breath. "At least I hope so."

~~~~~

Spicy aromas floated in the air at Fall Fest. The sun broke through the clouds and warmed the cool day, as people milled around. Joel bobbed between the pie tent and the chili. He indulged in the excellent cooking every year, as he judged and helped the committee decide on the best entry. He loved this job perk. Who didn't like pie? The rest of the time, he patrolled on foot and walked off the festival calories.

A young boy crashed into Joel.

"Whoa, Scottie. Slow down and look where you're going."

The blond-haired boy's eyes grew round. "Sorry, Policeman Joel."

Joel patted his back. "It's okay, bud, just be careful."

In the craft area, Joel spotted Sadie. She wrapped a long hand-crocheted scarf, like his grandmother used to make, around her neck. The splash of pink highlighted her fair skin. She twisted her long waves over her shoulder.

*She's stunning.*

He sidled next to her. "Find something you want?"

Her smile warmed him. "I did. Isn't this gorgeous?"

He fingered the soft threads. "Almost as beautiful as the woman wearing it."

A faint blush colored her cheeks. "Thank you."

"What do you think of our festival?" They meandered along the walkway. "You were never here in the fall."

She shoved her hands in her pockets. "It's fun. I love all the booths with the handmade items. They remind me of Gram."

"Have you eaten anything yet?" He nodded at the food tent. "We have chili, hot dogs, and pie. I got to taste the pumpkin pie and help decide who has the best recipe. That was after I tasted ten different kinds of chili." He patted his stomach. "We announce the winners in a few minutes, then everyone can eat." He crooked his elbow. "Care to join me?"

She tucked her hand into his arm. "Sure." A hint of the Sadie he remembered peeked through. The gold flecks in her green eyes sparkled in the sun. Those lovely eyes had taken over his dreams. Now they gazed at him and warmed his heart.

~~~~~

A local band played everything from country to rock-n-roll. Couples danced in the street. Children raced one another in potato sacks. Sadie's mood lightened and her shoulders relaxed as folks celebrated her favorite season. She adored the small-town feel. People said "hi" and smiled. She longed to fit in and garner the trust of the town.

"Here goes." Joel nudged her. "I'm announcing the winners." He hopped up onto the tiny wooden stage. "Good afternoon. It's my pleasure to award our amazing cooks with well-deserved ribbons." He picked up the winners' prizes. "Miss Mercer, you've done it again. For the tenth year in a row, you won the blue ribbon and a gift card to our local General Store for your delicious pie." He clapped, hugged the white-haired lady, and offered her the prize.

"If you don't know, Miss Mercer makes all the pies for the Sail Away Inn on Main Street."

"Now for the winner of the chili cook-off. Jason Holder, come to the stage. You've won, for the first time, with your spicy white bean chili." Jason took the ribbon and held it in the air. "If you want chili to warm you to your toes, try Jason's." The crowd laughed. "Thanks to all of you who entered this year. It was tough to pick a winner, everything tasted so good." Joel pointed at the food tent. "Now, you guys go enjoy the festival."

He caught up with Sadie standing near the stage. "Which chili do you want?"

"The winner, of course."

"You sure? It's spicy."

She raised her chin. "I can handle it."

"Okay, Jason's chili coming up."

She secured them a place at the closest picnic table, while Joel grabbed the food.

Folks milled around the tables and tents. She admired the islanders' choice to live in semi-isolation through the winter. Her grandparents had regaled her with stories about the colder months. The ice floes from the lake crumpled piers. The wind wailed and promised brutal sweeps of ice and lake effect snow. Ferry transportation stopped when ice threatened the lake. A small plane carried the mail and supplies, as they flew high school students back and forth to the mainland. Was she made for island life? She planned to find out.

Joel placed a steaming bowl of spicy chili in front of her. "Pie?"

"Not right now, thanks."

He sank onto the bench beside her.

"This tastes delicious." She scooped another mouthful. "Mmm ... spicy." She dropped the spoon in her bowl and waved her hand in front of her mouth.

"Here, drink this milk." He picked up the carton he had snagged on his way to the table, anticipating just this reaction from her.

She downed the carton. "Much better. Thanks." She pushed the bowl aside. "Maybe I better eat pie."

Joel gulped a bite of her chili. "I love the heat."

"You enjoy burning your mouth." She lifted her chin and peered at the dessert table. "Do they have pie other than pumpkin?"

He swallowed another scoop. "About any kind you want. You liked cherry, right?"

"You remember?" She tilted her head and scrunched her eyebrows.

He grinned. "Mom made one, and you ate half of it."

"I did not." She bumped his elbow with hers.

"Pretty sure you did. I ate the other half and Lucy didn't get any. She was ticked."

She chuckled. "We did, didn't we?"

"Want me to get you a piece? Or how about a whole pie?" He stood beside her.

"A piece will do, sir." She saluted him.

Sadie stared after him as he walked to the pie tent. Joel's swagger as he moved away left her with a tug of uncertainty. His uniform gave him an air of trustworthiness. Not to mention, he looked great. She wanted him in her life, not ... "Ugh."

Someone bumped into her from behind. She twisted to see who hit her. No one stood nearby. Could be one of the kids running around had knocked into her. She settled on the bench seat. On the picnic table, a piece of paper captured her attention. A black skull-and-crossbones, etched in marker, glared at her. The sketch resembled the one on her cottage.

Sadie's hands trembled. Her stomach clenched.

Joel settled the pie on the table and scooted close to her. She didn't move.

"What's wrong?" he asked.

"While I waited on you, somebody bumped me. I looked to see who it was, but didn't see anyone close to me. I found this on the table." She shoved the paper at him.

The black marks screamed off the page. "Same as on your cottage." With a napkin, he folded it over the offending paper and stuck it in his pocket. "I'll take it to the station. Things are wrapping up here. Let me walk you home." He took her by the arm and guided her through the crowd. "You didn't see anyone?"

"No. I looked behind me and didn't see anyone close by." Her legs shook.

"I'll talk to the other folks who were vandalized and see if anything similar happened to them." He folded her hand into his elbow to help steady her.

"Thank you." She searched his face. "Why did this happen?"

"We're nearing Halloween. Could be a prank." He patted her arm. "Whatever's going on, we'll figure it out."

"I hope so." She planned to make a home on the island, yet how could she if someone wanted her gone? Maybe Joel's theory explained the vandalism, but what if Bryce was trying to force her to go back to him?

# CHAPTER TWELVE

Monday night, wind beat against the tall, white, wooden door and the fragile glass windows of the Abbott Island Police Department. Hunched over the computer, Joel combed through old vandalism cases. The phone jangled. Still staring at the computer screen, he lifted the receiver.

"Grayson, here."

A husky voice whispered over the line. "That woman needs to leave the island. You know who I mean." The call clicked off, then silence. Caller ID offered no clue to the caller's identity.

Joel popped the phone into the cradle, leaned back in his chair, hands behind his head, and closed his eyes. Now what? Did the caller mean Sadie? For the most part, tranquility had filled his days since tourist season ended. He'd issued a few speeding tickets, rescued Mrs. Johnson's cat, and helped a couple kids with a school project. Other than Sadie's mystery, island crimes were down. He'd chat with his fellow officers. They hadn't mentioned any other incidents.

Joel climbed in the cruiser and drove around the island to check on his people. Thankful the wind died down to a breeze, he rolled his window down and perused the water. He traveled to the west side and parked in front of Sadie's house.

Nine o'clock and only the moon shone on her yard. He'd insisted she purchase an outdoor flood light with a motion sensor after that vandal painted the shaker siding. The beam should have flashed on when his car passed. Joel parked the cruiser in her gravel drive. With a flashlight, he approached the security light, and the sensor didn't trigger.

He waved the flashlight at the bulb and caught sight of broken glass. Who busted the new light? He stepped on the porch to rouse Sadie. The beam from the porch light flashed on. The curtain on the door moved, and she peered out. Her eyebrows scrunched as her lips formed a frown.

Joel smiled, and she opened the door. Sadie crossed her arms. "What's going on?"

"Sorry to bother you. I was out patrolling, and I noticed your security light didn't come on. I checked it. It's been smashed." He pointed to the corner of the house.

Sadie stepped out to the porch. "It was put in two days ago." She peered at the dark corner.

"I know. I installed it." He rubbed his chin. "You ought to leave the porch light on tonight. I'm sorry if I woke you."

"I wasn't asleep. I've spent the last hour reading one of Grandpa's mysteries." Sadie's eyes drooped as if she'd doze off.

Joel nodded. "He loved his mysteries, didn't he? He gave me a couple to read. They were pretty good."

A sound boomed behind the house. Sadie gasped. "What on earth? Do you smell something? Smoke?"

Joel vaulted over the porch steps, into the yard. He breathed in the pungent odor of burning wood and gasoline. His flashlight bobbed as he rushed around the corner of Sadie's house. Smoke billowed from the old shed. An eerie glow surrounded the rubble. He jerked his phone out of his pocket and dialed the fire chief.

"Sadie, turn on the hose." Joel dragged the water hose to the building and doused what flames he could. As he slowed the fire in the back, flames burst out in the front. He looked around to make sure Sadie was all right, but she had opened the valve and then disappeared.

Sirens blared and red lights flashed as the engine drove into Sadie's yard. The men and women jumped out, unrolled, and attached the hose to the hydrant to douse the fire. Light exploded through the burning building. The tin roof fell on singed boards.

Joel searched for Sadie. Her small form, hunkered on the front porch steps, made his heart trip up. He lowered himself to sit by her. "I'm so sorry."

"I don't know what happened. I've been careful." Her voice raised an octave. "I didn't put any cleaning supplies or paint in the shed, but there may have been a gas or kerosene can. I can't remember." She leaned her head into her hands. A soft sob escaped.

Before he stopped himself, he wrapped his arm around her shoulders. Her body shivered as she sank into him. He yearned to draw her into a full hug to comfort her, but in his official capacity he held back.

Had someone set the fire on purpose? If it proved to be arson, he'd track down the person responsible, no matter what he had to do.

~~~~~

When Sadie didn't toss and turn in bed, she paced. Someone lit a fire to her building on purpose. Why? Joel wanted to investigate the fire as arson. The chief needed to rake through the debris to find any answers. If they took too long to figure out the cause, the culprit might attack again.

Beside her bed, she dropped to her knees and prayed. "God, it's me, Sadie. I know I haven't talked to You much. I need help. I don't understand why bad stuff keeps happening. I want so much to have peace, but instead I get chaos. I want to have hope, but fear overwhelms me. I'm thankful Rosie is safe, and my bike and car weren't near the shed, but a person can only take so much. Please help Joel and the chief find answers, and cover me with Your protection. Amen."

She struggled to trust God even as she prayed for help.

~~~~~

At first light, with coffee in hand, Sadie traipsed to the vestiges of last night's fire. The acrid smell assaulted her nostrils. As she faced the pile of debris sheltered by a white tent, she saw destruction. Yet she longed to search and find one remnant of her grandpa's treasures. Some of his tools. A fishing pole, the shovel Gram had planted flowers with, anything to hold on to their memory.

After Joel finished the investigation, Mr. Cole might bulldoze the mess for her and help her look for anything worth keeping. He'd been trash picking and upcycling for as long as she remembered. Tourists grabbed his metal sculptures as fast as he produced them. Joel would know if he still ran his Upcycle Art business.

She ambled to the house, stopped on the front porch, and sipped her almond vanilla coffee. Joel had hugged her last night. Comfort wrapped around her when his arm drew her close. Warmth she'd not sensed in a long time flooded her heart. Not since Gram and Grandpa had she received care the way she had from him. She had rested against him and appreciated his touch, yet alarms had gone off in her head.

*Can you trust him?*

She pushed her thoughts aside, went to the kitchen, and located her project binder. Regardless of the burned shack behind her house, she'd finish the cottages, or she'd have no income.

The phone rang. She picked it up.

"This is Sadie."

"Hi Sadie, this is Becca, Lucy's friend. She said to call this number to make a reservation."

Sadie pulled a paper and pen from her binder. "It's so good to hear from you. Let me go over your options." She shoved her hair behind her ear. "I have the Old Ben, decorated in blue-gray and a log cabin quilt on the bed, or The Julia, a quaint English cottage with a floral nine-patch handmade quilt, pale blue walls, and a bookcase filled with novels and botanicals."

"I love the idea of the English cottage, but I think I'll take Old Ben. My husband will love it." Becca paused. "Maybe I'll come back with my girlfriends next summer for a girls' weekend and stay in The Julia."

Sadie finished the conversation, hung up the phone, jotted down the reservation, then lifted Rosie's paws and danced her across the kitchen.

"We have people coming." She'd work her fingernails off to finish the cottage. At least The Julia could wait a while.

A tap at the door stopped her mid-dance. She opened the door. "Hey, Joel."

"Sadie, I want you to meet the fire chief. I know last night you didn't get to talk to him. He has questions." Joel's eyes begged her to cooperate.

Her elation seeped out like a balloon with a pin hole. She stepped onto the porch and let the door close behind her. Rosie at her feet, she tromped behind Joel to the shed where the fire chief waited.

"Doug, Sadie. Sadie, Chief Larken." The chief reached his hand toward Sadie. She gave a perfunctory shake.

"It still smells smoky." She wrinkled her nose. She'd never explored the contents of the shed. Other than checking out the lawn mower and a few tools, she'd not darkened the doors. She had feared the rickety old shed might fall on her. If she had explored the contents sooner, she might have moved her grandpa's toolbox, but she'd waited too long.

The chief rubbed his chin. "Sadie, I'm considering arson. As we doused the flames, they burned yellow with black smoke. That's a possible indicator of the presence of an accelerant, plus the flames came from low to the ground, not in a wall or the ceiling. Did you have any flammables stored inside?"

"I think there was gasoline in a container at the front of the shed. I'm not sure." Sadie looked to Joel for confirmation.

Joel pointed at the building. "I know it was at the front. I mowed the yard at the end of summer and left the can by the mower. For easier access next year."

With a sigh, she nodded. "I was in there a few weeks ago to look for a hammer and screwdriver. That's when I saw the gas can."

Doug stepped closer to her. "Here's the thing." She shuddered at the chief's intense stare. "The fire started in the back. The flames we witnessed shot out of the north side of the building, then engulfed the rest. So it appears someone poured accelerant on the rear of the building. We're taking samples and checking our theory."

"How soon will you know, Chief?" Joel stood with his hands on his hips.

"It'll be a while. You know how it goes."

"Yeah, I do."

Chief Larken opened a notebook and poised to write. "I'm sorry, but I have to ask, where were you when the fire broke out?"

A headache formed at the back of Sadie's skull. "I was in the house reading when Joel stopped by to check on my light. Which is busted."

"So you didn't start the fire, maybe for insurance?"

"No. Of course not. Why would I? I don't even know what Grandpa kept in there." The pain crept into her neck and shoulders. Her eyes burned.

"I'm sorry, Sadie, I have to ask. It's part of my job." The chief gave a small smile. "Let me take a look at the light. There might be a clue, too."

"All right, it's around here." She led the men to the house.

Joel caught up with her. "We'll need a ladder."

"The ladder's in the garage. Please don't scratch my car." She pointed to the building where she parked her Mini-Cooper and stored the paint left over from the cottages.

Joel rolled his eyes at her. "Don't worry. I won't scratch your car."

He didn't understand. Coop allowed her the freedom to leave the past behind. She'd bought the car when she left for college. She and Grandpa had visited dealerships and purchased her together. If she continued to build a life for herself, she needed Coop.

Chief Larken climbed the ladder, and with gloved hands he ran his fingers over the broken glass. "Could be someone swung a ball bat or something and hit the lamp and destroyed the bulb."

On the ground, he poked around. "A footprint." He pointed in the flower bed. "Looks like a man's, size nine. What size do you wear, Joel?"

"A ten."

"Put your foot beside this one."

Joel stood next to the print. "Smaller than mine. I'll make a cast and take a photo. Since the light illuminated the whole yard, I'm guessing the same person who broke the light, set the fire."

A frown tugged the corner of Sadie's lips down. "So you think this was all on purpose?"

"I can't say until we finish the formal investigation." The chief shook his head. "In the meantime, go ahead and replace the light, Joel. Bring the broken one to the office as evidence."

"Yes, sir." Joel nodded.

The ache throbbed across Sadie's whole head. She begged for the peace Gram taught her from the Bible. *The peace that passes understanding. Is that too much to ask?*

# CHAPTER THIRTEEN

After two days of moping and wallowing in pity, Sadie drove Coop onto the ferry. She leaned along the rails and let the cool air and mist from the lake wash her stress away. Marblehead Lighthouse grew closer as waves slapped against the sides of the long boat. The tall structure had endured the elements and weather since 1821 and now stood as the oldest lighthouse in continuous operation on the Great Lakes. Sadie loved the old light, a steady symbol of hope. She'd climbed the seventy-seven steps to the top with Joel and Lucy when she and Joel were fifteen and Lucy was thirteen. With each step, she'd allowed herself a chance to dream of life on the island.

She refused to let a fire keep her from those dreams. Guests arrived in less than a week. The house hid the pile of ashes and debris from the view from the cottages. Determined to make this first reservation a success, Sadie perused the list she'd made for a few accessories for the Old Ben cottage. Maybe she'd find a painted canoe paddle for the wall, or a lake life wall hanging. She had visited the library and searched on their computers for kitschy shops on the mainland. Her search popped up a couple of thrift shops, a vintage store, and an arts and crafts mall. A day off-island promised fun.

After the ferry docked, she drove uptown, parked, and walked along the sidewalk to the Nifty Thrift Shop. She tugged on the handle of the solid oak door and the latch stuck. Sadie jerked harder on the knob and about fell on her bottom when her hand slipped.

A Southern voice called from inside, "Sorry about the door. The hinges need oil, makes it a bear to open. My hubby's comin' in tonight to fix it for me."

"No problem." Sadie searched the store for the person with the drawl.

"Hey there." A woman with dark, curly hair and brown eyes jumped from behind a clothes rack. "There I go again, scarin' a customer. You'll wish you hadn't stopped in." Her hands swiped the wrinkles on her t-shirt. "Is there something I can help you find, honey?"

She eyed the woman. No bigger than a minute, she sparkled with energy. Her smile shimmered against her mocha skin. "Yes, I'm looking for fun decorations to add to a cottage. I'm aiming for a lake life theme, greens and reds. A canoe paddle or fishing gear would be fun."

The lady tapped her finger on her mouth. "I know what you might like."

Sadie trailed behind her to a far corner of the store. "I have this mini canoe paddle made to hang keys on. See the little hooks." Painted pine green and whitewashed, about two feet long, three eye hooks stuck out.

"Perfect, the renter can keep track of the key." She added, "change the locks to deadbolts," to her mental list of repairs. If anyone broke into the cottages, she'd never get them ready for renters.

"I can take it to the counter for you, if you want to look around." This lady's thousand-watt smile gleamed. Sadie longed for life to offer something to brighten her days, so her smile would sparkle the same way.

As Sadie browsed the shelves, a row of carving tools captured her attention. She'd searched the house for Grandpa's set, but never found them. She lifted a palm tool and felt the weight, put it back, and wrapped her hand around a gouge. In his rocker on the porch, Grandpa had chiseled detailed animals and birds from black walnut and oak. She'd listened while he explained each tool's use. Her cherished moose that he had made for her stood on the mantel at home. She caressed the tool, then rolled the handle over. The letters BSR stared at her. *Benjamin Samuel Ross.* Grandpa had carved his initials on the gouge. As she flipped the other tools over, she found the same. Whoever set fire to the shed must have stolen the carving set. Why else would they be here? What else did they take?

Sadie rolled the tools in their case and tromped to the desk. She unfolded the leather roll on the counter. Her voice shook as she questioned the happy young sales lady. "Do you know who brought these in? When?"

The store owner stepped behind the check-out desk. "Let's see." Her curls bounced as she tapped her finger on her mouth again and placed her hand on the phone.

Sadie inhaled and crossed her arms. Did the tools belong to Grandpa? "Please, think."

"I am." For the first time the girl drew a frown. "Let me call Danny, my hubby. He'll know." She lifted her cell phone and walked away.

By the time the shop owner returned to the counter, Sadie paced the aisle ten times. "Danny said a young guy, around twenty, came in yesterday. Said he didn't know if they were worth anything, but if we sold them for him, he'd be happy."

Sadie sighed. "These were my grandfather's. His initials are carved on them. Do you have the name or number of the guy?"

"Here's the weird thing. He refused to give Danny his name. He said he'd stop in to check next week." She flashed her brown eyes at Sadie.

Flustered, Sadie shoved her hand through her hair. "They don't belong to him. They're my grandpa's." She bit her lip to keep from yelling.

The shop owner retreated a few steps. "Okay. I believe you."

"I'm sorry." Sadie bowed her head and rubbed her brow. *What now, God? What should I do?* "I need to make a phone call. Give me a minute."

"Sure thing."

The wind whipped Sadie's long brown hair as she stepped outside and snuggled into her scarf and coat. She settled on a wooden bench in front of the shop. The smell of chocolate drifted from a nearby candy store. Her hand shook as she dialed Joel's cell. *Please pick up.*

"Grayson." His voice echoed through the phone.

A sigh escaped her lips. "It's Sadie. Are you working?"

"I'm off today. What's up?"

The story of discovering the carving tools poured out. She paused to catch her breath. "What do I do?" A shiver from the biting wind crawled up her back.

"You're in Sandusky?"

She rubbed her forehead, as remnants of her earlier headache crept across her temples. "Yes."

"Give me the directions. I can be there in about half an hour."

Sadie stood and paced the sidewalk. "Thank you, Joel. I'll be waiting in the store."

~~~~~

At the dock, Joel secured his boat and hurried to meet the ride he had arranged. Thankful the ice and snow held off for a bit, he'd cruised across the lake to rescue Sadie. Or he should say help her. He was no hero. God blessed him with his post with the AIPD. He'd flounder in self-deprecation if not for his responsibility to keep the island folks safe. The song his mom strummed on the guitar, something about one day at a time, played through his head as a constant reminder to get up and get going every morning. Just the thought of his mom, and how he'd let her down, broke his heart.

An Uber dropped him at the Nifty Thrift Shop. With a hard tug, the door opened. His eyes adjusted from the brightness outside to the dim shop lighting. "Sadie?"

"Over here, Joel." Dark circles rimmed her eyes. Her expression begged for comfort. "They have Grandpa's tools. I want them back. What do I do?"

Joel scrubbed his hand over his face. "Let me talk to the owner." Out of his jurisdiction, he could ask for their cooperation, but he wouldn't force them to turn over the tools.

"Her husband just got here. He dealt with the guy." She shook her head. "Maybe I shouldn't have moved. Life's getting worse instead of better."

Joel stepped beside her and rested his hand on her shoulder. "No, Sadie. Things happen. Lucy and I are here for you, and Marigold. She's so happy you're here."

"Are you? Happy I'm here?" Her eyes shimmered.

He fixed his gaze on her face. "Yes. I've missed you ever since you left." He'd fallen for her the day they'd walked to the beach after work and played in the water. She hadn't minded his goofiness and he loved her laugh. On the beach, they'd poured their hearts out to one another for hours. He'd kissed her, and then she left five days later. So much had changed since then, so much she didn't know about him. She'd hate him as much as he hated himself, maybe more, if she learned the truth. He'd destroyed the life of a loved one. Now the scars strangled him. No matter how he tried to leave the past behind, the pain he'd suffered from his own stupidity haunted him.

"I've missed you, too." She blinked away the moisture in her eyes.

He wrapped her in a hug. When he released her, the warmth of the embrace evaporated too soon. "Let me talk to these people and see what can be done." Joel walked to the counter.

He surveyed the store. Clothes from the 60s and 70s hung from metal racks. Paintings, including those awful velvet ones, clung to the walls. Piles of books rested on a low table. "Hi. I'm Joel Grayson, law enforcement on Abbott Island. Can we talk about the tools Sadie found?"

The husband offered his hand. "I'm Danny, this is my wife, Joy."

Joel shook his hand. "Nice to meet you. What can you tell me about the guy who brought in the tools?" He pulled a notepad and pencil from his pocket.

Danny rubbed his hand over the back of his neck. "He didn't want to give me his name. I tried to tell him I didn't accept items without identification. He rushed out the door and yelled he'd stop in to check later. I put the stuff out. Figured if he never showed, I'd sell it and make some money. I didn't realize they'd be a problem."

"Can you describe him?"

"About six feet tall. Skinny, stringy brown hair that hung over the side of his face, and he seemed like he had a nervous tick. He didn't stand still much. Kept his hood pulled over his head." Danny glanced at his wife.

Joel jotted notes. "Thanks. I believe the items might be connected to an arson case. Is it okay with you if I take the tools and hold them as evidence? See if I can pull any prints. "

Danny nodded. "Sure, whatever you need."

Joel tucked the notebook in his pocket. "Did he bring anything else?"

Joy glanced at Danny. "Yes. He left a box of fishing lures and a couple of poles." Danny pointed to the other side of the store. "Let me get them."

"Thanks for your cooperation. If he comes back, try to get info on him if you can. If he gives you a hard time, don't push it. Any cameras around? They might have videoed the guy."

"No cameras. We've never had a need for one. Most people around here are honest." Danny rubbed the scruff of his neck. "Don't worry about returning the stuff. If it's stolen, I don't want it. If it's this lady's, we want her to have it back."

Joel pulled a card from his pocket. "Here's my info, I'd appreciate a call if you learn anything else."

Sadie stepped beside him. "I want to buy the key holder." She tugged her wallet out and paid Joy.

"All set." With gloves on, he and Sadie gathered the items and carried them to her car.

"Thank you. Maybe this will help find who set the fire." She slid into the driver's seat and buckled her seatbelt. "How'd you get here so fast?"

He leaned in the window. "My boat. I docked in the marina. Could you drop me off?"

"Sure. I have more shopping, want to join me?"

He wanted to spend every day with her. Of course he'd join her. "Sure." He climbed in and latched his belt.

She drove Cooper around the corner. "I hope you're into vintage."

Vintage, antiques, boutiques, wherever she wanted to go, he'd go. Was he into old stuff? Not so much, but if it involved Sadie, he'd shop until they dropped.

# CHAPTER FOURTEEN

After sunrise the next morning, arms overloaded with bags, Sadie fumbled with her keys and unlocked the Old Ben cottage. She dropped her purchases on the bed. Hands on hips, she eyed the walls. Where to put the mini-canoe paddle and wall hanging? Near the door, she pounded a nail and centered the paddle key holder.

Joel and Sadie had ended their shopping trip at the arts and crafts mall. He'd flexed his muscles and toted her bags like a packhorse. His fun and playful side shoved his masculine traits aside when he lifted a cinnamon candle and burst into a Christmas song. She'd giggled and hummed along with him. He'd surprised her with a Marblehead Lighthouse ornament to commemorate their climb to the top, when they were fifteen. Amazed by his patience and his sentiment about the lighthouse tour, her heart filled with emotion. Love and fear battled. She longed to trust her dear friend, but doubt slammed the door.

They'd strolled to a downtown cafe where the enticing aroma of pasta sauce coaxed them in for dinner. When they'd both reached for a breadstick, their hands brushed. Warmth had crept up her arm. Maybe his touch heated her up from the outside chill. Or ... she shoved the thought aside. Before she could stop him, Joel had paid the check. Was that a date? No, of course not. She visualized the meal as more of a friend feeding his distressed friend.

Sadie fluffed the pillows and arranged them in the comfy chair by the window. The cinnamon candle perched on the side table and the lake life wall hanging she'd found, for next to nothing, complimented her Gram's multi-colored quilt.

Arms crossed, Sadie surveyed the rest of the room, and her joy plummeted. A puddle glinted in front of the sink. "What on earth?" She jerked the sink's cabinet doors open. Water dripped from the pipe. A leak could ruin the hardwood floor.

She grabbed towels out of the bathroom cupboard and sopped the water. She wrung the towels out in the mop bucket. The steady drip left a pool of water under the sink. She stuffed the towels under the drain, then drew out her phone.

"Grayson, here." Joel's voice calmed her frustration.

"Um, hi. It's Sadie. I may need your help." She spilled her problem. "Any chance you could stop by?"

"I can stop after work."

Sadie stashed the empty shopping bags in the house and hung the lighthouse ornament on a hook on the mantel.

"Rosie, we've got a mess."

~~~~~

Sadie peered under the sink, as Joel loosened a PVC joint. Her gaze followed his muscular, masculine legs dressed in denim, stretched across the wood floor. Guilt pricked her conscience. She depended on him too much. The independence she sought crumbled a little every time she reached out to him. What was a girl to do?

He crawled out from under the sink. "I think the p-trap needs replacing. Looks like the washers are worn and the trap is backed up."

Sadie dropped on her knees beside him. "Can I get the parts at Lucy's?"

"No need. I've got some plumbing stuff at the house." He stood, then took Sadie's hand and lifted her to stand.

Her stomach fluttered at Joel's touch. "Oh, okay. I can pay you."

"No. They're left-over parts, and you aren't paying me to help you." He brushed off his jeans. "I'll be back in about twenty minutes."

Sadie sank onto the bed as he left. "What now?" A leaky sink and a gorgeous man didn't fit into her plans.

~~~~~

"I'm back." Joel trundled into the cottage with his arms full of plumbing contraptions. A toolbox dangled from his hand.

"Let me help." She reached to take the box from him. "Wow, you do have plumbing materials and another toolbox. Do you just keep extra stuff on hand?"

He unloaded beside the sink. "Yeah, I help a lot of people when no one else can. I've collected a bunch of extras no one can use. I brought two types to make sure one would fit your pipes." He squatted and held up a part. "I think this one will fit."

He crawled under the small cabinet. "Can you give me the tools as I need them?"

"Yes, no problem. I used to help Grandpa with stuff like this."

Joel's face warmed. At least she couldn't see him. When she called, he'd awaited the end of his shift, then hurried to her. Any time she needed him, he'd make sure he helped. At the corn maze her lips had invited a kiss, but she turned and ran like a deer. Her skittish response left him discouraged. No matter, he'd care for her anyway. He couldn't stop himself.

"I need a wrench to loosen this joint." He reached out.

"Here you go." The tool slid into his outstretched hand.

"I'll give you the old p-trap and washers, then pass me the new one."

"Sounds good." Sadie took the old pieces and dumped them in the bucket. "Here's the new parts." She placed the washers and parts in his hand.

Soon Joel grunted and shoved his way out of the cabinet. "All done." He rose from the floor. "Let's try this." He ran water and no drips. "Looks good."

Sadie threw her arms around him with a quick hug, then backed away. "Thank you so much. I thought I faced a disaster."

"You're welcome. Any time I can help you, I will." He held her gaze. Her beautiful green eyes sparkled. The hug left him itching to hold her. Instead, he lifted his toolbox and unused pieces from the floor. "I better go. I'm trying to get the leaves under control at home."

"Thanks again, Joel. I'd like to make you dinner sometime. You know, to pay you back."

"That would be great. See you later." He'd love to eat dinner with her. Anything to spend time with her.

~~~~~

The next morning, Rosie loped behind the bicycle as Sadie sailed down the road. The cold air whipped her scarf. She looked forward to another weather day in the fifties, as she tugged her hat over her ears.

She parked the bike, then climbed the stairs to the General Store's porch. "I smell breakfast cooking at the Corner Restaurant, Rosie." Sadie breathed in. She'd visit the restaurant soon and indulge in their omelets.

She shoved the General Store's door open. "Hey, Lucy. Do you still allow dogs?"

"You bet I do." Lucy hugged her. "I'm so glad you're here."

Sadie's heart swelled. Her island friends loved her. She agreed with Joel, she'd found good people here, and she needed to stay.

"Thanks." She took in the inventory of the store. Lots of touristy shirts and items hung from the walls. She should snap up a snazzy souvenir to add to the cottage.

"Are you shopping or visiting?" Lucy straightened the sepia-toned treasure maps piled on the counter.

Sadie patted Rosie's head. "I was hoping to visit. Are you busy?"

"Not too busy for you." She flipped her door sign to Closed. "This time of year, we're slow. I'm getting ready for the folks who come for the 5K. Let's sit in the office in my comfy chairs." Lucy dimmed the lights in the front, and Sadie trailed her to the office. She pointed to an overstuffed flowered chair, a survivor of the 60s. "Have a seat."

"I can't believe you still have this old chair." Sadie sank into the flowers.

"Mom made me get it out of the house. I couldn't part with it. Your gram gave it to me, you know."

"I remember. Your mom wasn't happy about it. Somehow you won. You always did." A laugh escaped Sadie's lips. Pure bliss bubbled from a shared guffaw with her friend.

"So, how's it going being back? Joel told me you've had a couple of incidents." Lucy popped a pod into the coffee maker. "Cream?"

"Yes, to cream and to trouble. First the graffiti, then a fire. I should have stayed away."

Lucy gave her the stink eye, a trademark of hers since childhood. If she got aggravated, her glare told the world. Sadie loved her dear friend for her honesty and loyalty. She'd defended her many times and never asked for anything in return. Like a true friend, Lucy had forgiven her for the unanswered letters and email.

Sadie accepted coffee from her friend. The smell of hazelnut wafted from the cup.

"Nonsense. You belong here. Joel will figure out what's going on. He's good at his job and the other guys will help him." She filled a cup with coffee and sipped. "You can't give up. You've got a way to make money, a beautiful place to live, and friends who love you. Besides, I believe God sent you here."

Sadie about choked on her coffee. "God sent me here? My father's disregard and my ex-boyfriend's anger sent me here." She'd spilled too much. She had intended to keep the past in the past. Not to drag it out as a crutch. She didn't want pity for her poor choices. Yes, she believed in God, but did He bring her home? Gram had quoted Bible verses about how much God loved His people, yet she doubted the One who created the universe paid attention to her life.

Lucy tilted her head. "What do you mean, your ex's anger?"

"Nothing. I didn't mean anything. I gotta run to the grocery for milk." Sadie grabbed Rosie's leash and led her out the door.

~~~~~

Thunder boomed overhead as Sadie peddaled home from the grocery store. She jogged to the porch and dragged her bicycle onto the wooden floorboards. The smell of wet smoke lingered as the rain pounded the ground. Maybe the storm would wash away the smell once and for all, and then she'd find someone to clear the mess away. Joel had collected the evidence from the pile of rubble. At least she'd get her grandpa's tools back, after the police finished with them.

Once inside, she stashed the milk in the fridge. Thankful for the little island grocery, she tossed Rosie a treat. "Jane made dog treats again. Enjoy."

What possessed her to reveal Bryce's anger to Lucy? Not a wise move. If Lucy blabbed, she'd tell Joel first. The lightning flash over the lake and the thunderstorm reflected her mood.

The news predicted the storm to last all night. Waves crashed on the shore, and the din shook Sadie's windows. At least the road split the sandy beach from the yard and cottages and gave her distance from the lake's angry waves. Her grandpa had mapped out a great place to build. He understood the dynamics of the lake and the land. Blessed beyond measure, she'd never leave. Whether God led her to the island or not, she thanked Him for her new home. Safe, dry, and warm. She refused to complain.

After dinner, she settled on the red leather couch, dressed in her flannel jammies, and wrapped her hands around the warmth of a peacock blue mug. She breathed in the aroma of hot chocolate, Gram's recipe. With the waves and rain penetrating the quiet, Sadie released her mug to the coffee table, then bowed her head.

"God, I'm confused. Did You send me here? If so, why are these things happening to make me doubt? I love the island, and I plan to stay. Maybe a sign or something would convince me. I want to know I'm where You want me." She swiped away a tear. "What about Joel? Can I trust him? I want to, but the fear Bryce pounded into me makes me doubt."

*Trust Me.*

A voice echoed in Sadie's head. "God? Am I hearing things?"

*Trust Me.*

The voice sounded in her heart.

"I want to trust You, God."

Where had she spied Grandpa's Bible? From the built-in shelf under the stairs, she uncovered the precious book. On the couch, she opened to a place he'd bookmarked. He'd circled Psalm 28:7. *The Lord is my strength and my shield; my heart trusts in him, and he helps me. My heart leaps for joy, and with my song I praise him.* Grandpa and Gram had trusted God. When they left the cottages to Sadie, maybe they'd asked God to lead her home.

"Okay, God. I'm going to try this trust thing, at least for now." She lifted the mug to her lips and took a long sip of chocolate.

# CHAPTER FIFTEEN

*Who is pounding on the door?* Sadie traipsed downstairs in answer to the knocking and drew the front door open. Sunlight outlined Joel and highlighted his toned arms. The long-sleeved, blue t-shirt hugged his muscular chest. Whoa. Why did she notice his arms as soon as she saw him? Those arms hugged and comforted her the night of the fire. He'd enveloped her against his chest and stroked her hair. Her cheeks warmed from the memory.

She blinked away her yearning to calm her embarrassment. "Hey, Joel, come in."

He ambled into the living room and tucked into one end of the couch. Sadie settled on the opposite side.

"News, I hope." She bit her lip and rubbed her hands together.

"We got prints off the tools and fishing gear. I eliminated the shop owners and yours. One print is still in process. It doesn't appear to be in the system. I'm still hoping we come across it." He hugged a pillow in his lap, same as when they were kids. He'd squeeze the stuffing and flip it from end-to-end while he worked through his worries. "Sadie, I'm trying to figure all this out. Be careful, okay?"

"How much trouble am I in?" She stood and paced across the room.

He pushed up from the couch and stood in front of her. "I'm not trying to scare you. I want you to stay alert to your surroundings. By the way, did you know you have a flat on your bike? I saw it when I came in." He nodded at the door.

"No. It was fine yesterday when I rolled it on the porch." She took a step to the door. "You coming?"

Outside, Joel knelt beside her bicycle. "Man, I hate to say this. Looks like somebody slashed a hole in it."

She glared at the cut. "Are you kidding? This is getting ridiculous." She gritted her teeth.

"Is there anyone in your life who'd do this stuff on purpose? A person in your past who might want to hurt you?" His gaze locked with Sadie's.

"Have you been talking to Lucy?" She broke eye contact and stomped across the yard. Torn between spilling her story or pulling up her boots and moving on, she crossed her arms over her chest and stood at the edge of the yard. The waves had calmed after the storm, but her emotions swirled over the ground like the debris on her little beach.

Joel trailed her. "I haven't talked to my sister. Should I?"

"No. I haven't told her anything." Still drawn into herself, she gazed into Joel's eyes and witnessed tenderness and concern. His compassionate demeanor tempted her to tell him everything.

He touched her cheek and cradled her face. His warmth sent chills through her. She shoved the desire to be held away from her heart.

"You know, Sadie, you aren't the only one with secrets." He let go and walked away.

~~~~~

*Stupid.* Sadie knocked her forehead with her fist. Joel wanted to listen, and she let him go. To admit she'd tangled with an abuser scorched her cheeks with embarrassment. She'd fled to her grandparents' haven, yet fear bubbled inside her from the recent incidents. If Bryce chased her, he'd pursue her until he wore her into a pile of emotional rubble. Yet he slaved through long days at the office, sometimes twelve hours a day. He would not take a minute off the job for anything, not even chasing Sadie. So who did his dirty work?

On the parcel of sandy beach she owned, Sadie wadded up garbage and tossed debris in a bag. She scoured through pebbles and driftwood for any treasure the waves washed ashore. Red glass, smaller than a dime, frosted and smoothed by the ebb and flow of the water, caught her eye. In the years she and Gram had combed the beach, they'd never found red. Gram had told her if she ever discovered a beach ruby, she'd better hold it tight. She fingered the red glass, as rare as the peace she chased. The waves had smoothed the sharp edges. She hoped life on the island would heal her heart and soften her fears.

"Rosie, come to the house." The red-haired retriever galloped across the yard. As Sadie approached the house, she glimpsed a shadow pass across the porch. What now? Rosie stayed calm, not barking. That was a good sign.

Marigold's purple and orange maxi dress swished with the rhythm of the creaking rocker.

"Hey, lady." Sadie waved, then tossed her bag of debris by the house.

The aroma of homemade cinnamon rolls drifted to her nose. "Did you make my favorite?"

Marigold stood, then offered Sadie a cake pan. The bottom of the pan warmed her hands. "Here you go, friend. Thought you might need a boost."

"They smell amazing." Sadie hugged the pan. "Come in the house. I'll make tea."

Inside the house, Marigold slipped into a kitchen chair. "Joel stopped by my place last night."

Sadie heated water, arranged teacups and saucers on the vintage red and blue rose tablecloth, then poured the water into a pot to steep some tea. "Of course he did."

Marigold rubbed the edge of the fabric between her fingers. "Go easy on him. He's got stuff he needs to work through."

"Joel? The guy who's lived a perfect life with an amazing family on this incredible island. What on earth does he have to work through?" She used air quotes for the last two words.

"It's his story to tell." Marigold flattened her lips. "I'm saying you need to be considerate."

Sadie placed her hands on her hips. "I am kind to him and that won't change."

"Of course you are. You know he's worried about you."

Sadie poured from Grandma Julia's Brown Betty teapot. She trembled, and Marigold grasped the handle and took over the task.

"Thank you."

"What's up with the shakes?"

"It's nothing. I just get tired sometimes." She blew off any discussion of her frayed nerves, scooped a roll for each of them onto two saucers, then scooted her chair to the table.

"How about we enjoy our treat?" Marigold sliced off a piece of the gooey delight with her fork and stuffed her mouth.

Sadie did the same, then closed her eyes and relished the cinnamon and sugar. "Heaven."

"Indeed."

"My tummy thanks you." Another reason to stay on the island, Marigold's friendship filled her with joy.

Marigold licked her fork. "I love rolling the dough and slathering on the butter, cinnamon, and sugar. It's a rewarding task when I make them for a friend."

"I'm happy I'm on the receiving end."

Marigold had shined, a bright spot in Sadie's life. She had mothered her when her own mom didn't.

While they enjoyed Marigold's homemade treat, her friend's conversation about upcoming events, the crafts she'd created for the local fairs, and a few memories of past summers comforted Sadie.

Marigold set her fork on the empty plate. "Are you doing okay? Holding up?"

"I'm fine. Like I said, just tired. I've been getting the cottage ready for my guests."

"Lucy told me. It's a great idea to do a trial run."

Marigold deposited her cup in the sink. "I'm heading to the house. I've got Christmas gifts to make."

"Already?" Sadie had dreamed of Christmas on the island. Mom and Dad had allowed her to visit Gram and Grandpa for a couple of holidays. Most of the time they kept her home to make an appearance at their fancy parties. This Christmas, she'd embrace the peace and love of the people who mattered.

"Yep. Gotta get a head start." Marigold hugged her. "I'm glad you enjoyed the rolls. I know you've had a time, Joel told me about the tools and fishing items you found. The couple who run the Nifty Thrift Shop are great people. If they know anything, they'll tell the police. In the meantime, be careful."

"Did Joel tell you someone slashed my bike tire? He's worried about me." Even so, she refused to hibernate and hide in her house.

"He did. I want you to pay attention and watch your back." Marigold searched Sadie's face. "Any idea who might be after you?"

"Not for sure." At least not anyone she wanted to discuss.

~~~~~

Sadie paced the porch and kept an eye on the road. The past week flew by and her guests were due any minute. They'd called and confirmed their reservation the day before yesterday. This morning, she'd arranged a cheese plate, a basket of apples, bananas, and pears, and sparkling water on the cottage's table. She hoped for an excellent review. If not, a long road of improvement stretched ahead of her.

She prayed nothing else went wrong, no fire, theft, or graffiti. *God, help me put my best foot forward and not trip over it.* She caught herself praying more often. Between church and reading her grandpa's Bible, the brick wall she'd built around the trust she was able to give crumbled a tad every day. Her faith doubled as God's providence played out. She allowed a sense of assurance to inch into her life.

The crunch of tires drew her attention to the driveway. A man and woman climbed from a red Wrangler.

"Good morning." Sadie jogged down the porch steps. "You must be Becca and Reece. I'm Sadie. It's so nice to meet you. Welcome to the island." Her words streamed like a rushing brook.

"We're happy to be here." The woman with a pixie cut and petite frame smiled.

"Can I help you with your bags?"

The man, handsome in a rugged way, lifted two suitcases from the rear of the Jeep. "No, I'm good."

She retrieved a key from her pocket. "I have your information, and you paid ahead. Let me show you to your cottage." Was she too exuberant? She paused and breathed in the crisp air.

As they neared their home away from home, Sadie turned to the woman. "Did you have issues with the ferry?"

"Not at all. We stood on deck and enjoyed the lighthouse and view. It was chilly, but refreshing."

Sadie nodded. "Here we are." She unlocked the door and handed over the key. "If you have questions, please let me know. Here's my card with my cell number. Good luck with the race tomorrow. The weather's supposed to be pleasant."

In the house, Sadie plopped on the couch. Rosie rested her head on her lap. "Well, girl, we've got people." She patted her buddy's head and stared out the window. "Hope all goes well."

~~~~~

From the woods, Bryce peered at Sadie, giddy as she welcomed her guests. A long weekend off work allowed him time to check out his plan to drive her back to him. The person he had hired had failed so far. The little twerp needed to step up the game.

His eyes on her, he yearned to go after her and drag her home where she belonged. She'd crossed him, now she'd pay. He'd hoped to marry her. Make his tie to the family business permanent. Certain he'd made himself indispensable, he just needed to secure his prize. If he scared her and pushed her to return to her daddy, he'd call checkmate.

Thanks to a guy who lived in the woods on the north side of the island, he'd arranged a place to sleep. Not the Hilton, but a clean bed and food. Why did Sadie want to live on this stupid island in the middle of nowhere? The air stank with wood smoke. He'd have to toss his clothes. They reeked of the woodsy odor.

Women made no sense to him. The ladies his dad had run through their two-bedroom shack taught him females were useless unless they offered something in return. Dad had tamed his women with threats. If his menacing didn't work, he knocked them around. Of the parade of dad's ladies, Bryce had liked Lola, who cooked and did the laundry, and Jade, who cleaned the house and tried to mother him with toys and trips to the park. Neither had lasted long.

When he ogled Sadie, dollar signs flashed like neon. Big money dripped from her old man, but her sickening sweet attitude annoyed him. How had her old man produced a wimp? He'd heard her mom bordered on manic. What if he'd push her so far, she'd follow suit? No, he wanted her to worship him, bow down, and look pretty. No problem, he'd prod until she ran to him. He rubbed his hands together in anticipation.

What if he threatened the skinny jerk he'd hired to plant something questionable on Sadie's property? Her new boyfriend might arrest her.

The thought of Sadie dragged to jail by her cop friend brought a belly laugh.

He'd swoop in and rescue her and convince her to get her head on straight and return to the mainland to live with him. Nope, marry him. He wanted every benefit: money, prestige, and a trophy wife.

Yeah, he wanted her. Once she moved home and groveled to her dad to take her back at the company, Bryce would map out his takeover. He'd snow the old man and hold his lucrative future in his hands.

The skinny idiot he'd hired refused to fire a gun and scare the wits out of Sadie. Maybe he'd pull the trigger himself.

# CHAPTER SIXTEEN

In the town square, Sadie chuckled at a scarecrow who sat in the driver's seat of a small Case tractor. Her hand brushed the bumpy yellow and green gourds piled on the fenders. She ambled to an antique fire truck adorned with purple and white mums and a pile of pumpkins. Autumn's scent drifted from dried leaves as a crisp breeze blew. She snapped a couple of pictures with her phone, then sauntered to the street.

Had Gram and Grandpa strolled along Main Street in the fall? Did they hold hands and enjoy the rhythm of the waves as they hit the shore? Sadie had never stayed with them through the school year. A few times, she visited for Christmas. If she'd had her druthers, she would've lived with her grandparents year-round. Maybe she and Joel ...

*No, I can't go back.*

A runner zipped past.

"You're doing great. Keep at it." Sadie shouted encouragement and applauded the runners, as they loped through downtown. The canopy of red and yellow leaves cast a golden glow over the street. Her stomach growled at the smell of hot dogs and hamburgers from a nearby grill.

"Hey, Sadie." Joel and his dog, Griff, strolled along the sidewalk.

"Hi, Joel."

His muscles filled out the snug uniform shirt and slacks and made her heart thump. Her doubts melted more every time he flashed his dazzling smile. She'd vowed not to let a charming, handsome man slip into her heart again. She had traveled the disappointment road before and never intended to go there again.

He sidled up to her. "Running in the race today?" Griff sat at attention beside him.

"Me? No. I jog for fun not for competition." Long runs gave her a chance to release stress. Weird sounds in the woods had spooked her a few times, but she refused to quit. She figured the deer and rabbits ran with her.

"How do your guests like the island?"

Two runners sprinted along the street.

"There they go." Sadie waved at them and gave them a thumbs up. "I think they're enjoying themselves. I took them apple muffins and wished them luck this morning. They couldn't wait to tour Abbott Island by foot."

He faced her. "Good. I hope they let their friends know about your place."

"Me, too." His gaze held hers. Her stomach fluttered and the old sparks flew. She longed to hold his hand the way they had in high school. A potent attraction to adult Joel coursed through her and yanked at her heart. Yet a sense of fear smothered her desire.

He touched her arm. She startled. "Hey, you checked out for a minute. I'm heading over to keep vehicles off the running route. I'll catch you later."

"Sure." Good thing he couldn't read her mind.

~~~~~

Several racers sprinted to the end, while a few stragglers limped to the finish line. Joel strolled to the corner and watched the organizers pass out awards. He applauded Becca and Reece, who took second and third in their categories. Good. If they enjoyed a pleasant, positive experience, they'd send more people to Sadie's rentals.

As he smiled and nodded to the winners, Sadie's fire and the stolen tools nagged him. What had he missed? He'd take another, more thorough look at the evidence. The fire chief had called the case arson. Now they'd dig in and pinpoint the perpetrator. He'd search through the debris again. If the team overlooked a clue, he'd find it.

After the race ended and the streets cleared, he checked in at the police station and signed off for the day. Joel changed into jeans and a sweatshirt, then drove the golf cart to Sadie's. Griff rode beside him. He'd stow away the cart soon, before the weather changed to bitter cold and he had to drive his truck. For today, he took pleasure in the freedom.

He'd brought a metal detector, with plans to search the burned rubble pile. The tool might ding on a clue he'd missed. The island's police department lacked top of the line digital equipment, but he'd use the items he had. He'd prepped Griff, letting the German shepherd sniff the leather case and the carving tools. If he poked around, maybe he'd dig up a clue. Sadie needed him to solve this mystery. He yearned for her to see him as a responsible and trustworthy man.

So as not to startle her, Joel tapped on her door. No answer. She might have stopped at the store to visit Lucy.

"Come on, boy."

Griff trailed him to the back of the property. When he turned the corner, a person dressed in jeans and a dark hoodie jogged toward him. The runner dodged him and raced around the corner. Joel and Griff dashed after him, but whoever it was had already disappeared into the wooded area that bordered Sadie's property. Joel stood with his hands on his hips.

"Whoever that was, they didn't want to stop." The musty odor of the fire lingered. "Let's go, buddy. See if we can find some answers." He patted the dog's side.

The metal detector beeped several times. Joel scavenged several coins, penny nails, and a rusty hammer. One last sweep revealed a lighter, which could be the fire starter. Doubtful though, since this piece of evidence sat at the edge of the ashes, not buried beneath. He examined the small silver canister in his gloved hand. The letter B, embossed on the side, intrigued him. The lighter appeared fancy, expensive, and not charred. Did he hold a potential clue to who harassed Sadie, or something the runner dropped? It could have fallen from the sprinter's pocket.

"Hey. What are you doing, Joel?" Sadie's voice broke into his thoughts. Her gentle voice had soothed him on those days when they worked at the store and a customer complained. The same musical voice had lingered in his dreams for years, and now she stood in front of him. He soaked up the sight of her long brown hair in a braid and those adorable dimples that showcased the slightest smile.

Griff stood at attention beside his owner.

"I wanted to pick through the ashes before you have this bulldozed." She hurried her steps. "Are you still on duty?"

"No. Since the weather's nice, I wanted to give a look." He fingered the lighter.

"Find anything?" She petted Griff.

He lifted the lighter. "I found this. When I got here, I spooked someone. They'd been in your backyard. Whoever it was darted off before I ID-ed him."

"A lot of people are on the island today who don't live here. You think a tourist wandered through?" She glanced at the road.

"Possible, but why run?" Joel ran his hand through his hair. "This lighter is embossed. Could be a gift or trademarked. I'll look into it."

She stared at the lighter. She paled, clutched her stomach, and bent over. Her hand covered her mouth. He heard her bare whisper.

"Bryce."

"What did you say? Are you okay?" He touched her on the shoulder. "Let's go in the house."

Sadie stood still as if concrete held her feet.

Joel pulled her to him and cradled her in his arms. "Let me help you into the house."

She raised her head and gave him a slight nod.

With his arm around her waist, they stepped around the debris and moved to the grass. With a gentle nudge, he escorted her across the yard. She lifted one foot at a time on the steps and into the rear door of her house. He guided her to the couch and wrapped a quilt around her.

"Tell me what's going on?"

~~~~~~

Gram's friendship quilt offered comfort, but not enough to shove away the fear bubbling in Sadie's stomach. Tears rolled from her eyes as she stared straight ahead. Her shoulders shook.

"I can't."

"You can't what?" Joel brought a wooden kitchen chair close to her. He covered her hand with his. "I'm not here on official business, I'm here as a friend. Talk to me."

81

A sharp pain attacked her stomach. She threw her hand over her mouth and escaped to the bathroom.

Her body expelled her lunch. Unconcerned if Joel heard her, she let her stomach empty.

After a few minutes, she stepped out with a wet washcloth pushed against her mouth. She searched his eyes for any accusation and saw none. The cloth dropped to the floor as she ran to him.

"I'm so ... scared."

He wrapped her in his arms. She prayed he'd hold on and never let go.

Sadie settled on the couch. Joel draped the quilt over her, then squatted in front of her. "You said the name Bryce. Does he scare you? Is he someone you should worry about?"

He moved one hand to her cheek and let his thumb brush her face. "I'm here for you. How can I help?" He bowed his head in front of her and moved his lips as if he prayed.

Hadn't God led her here? Yet now the evil followed her. Had God allowed Bryce to come to the island and stalk her? Scare her? Joel was her friend. Her heart told her to trust him, but her fear screamed not to trust anyone.

"Sadie?"

She'd longed for the comfort of his touch. His eyes bored into hers as if he tried to read her mind.

"We've all got secrets, a past," he said. "There are times you have to ask for help."

"Joel, you won't understand. My life's a mess. I escaped here to get away. To leave my past, and now I'm afraid it's chasing me." She pulled away from his touch. "He's followed me."

"Bryce followed you? Who's Bryce?" Joel sat beside her.

Sadie tightened the quilt around her shoulders. She wanted to crawl into the quilt, like a caterpillar, and pray she'd come out as a butterfly, able to fly away and exist in simplicity.

"Bryce is my ex-boyfriend and Dad's right-hand man. He's evil. Full of himself, arrogant. Doesn't care who he hurts." Her voice wobbled.

Joel leaned in to meet her gaze. "Why's he after you? Obviously, you broke up. Right?"

"Yes. Last time I saw him I hit him in the head with a lamp."

"Wow. I'm guessing he deserved it." He scrubbed his hand over his chin. "If he's here, Griff and I will track him down. And I'll find out if he's behind the fire." He stood and paced in front of her. "I don't suppose you have a piece of his clothing. Griff could sniff and follow a trail."

She bit her lip, then twisted her mouth. "I think I might. Let me check upstairs."

~~~~~

Footsteps rattled in the loft. A thump, then a scrape across the floor sounded from above. Sadie must have unearthed something. Discomfort tensed Joel's spine. She had hung on to a piece of her past with the jerk. Sadness and disgust filled him with anger toward anyone who would hurt her.

Footfalls on the stairs directed his attention to the woman he vowed to protect. He admired Sadie as she descended the steps with a red and gray sweatshirt draped over her arm. Despite the trouble she faced, her strength and determination remained.

"I found this in the bottom of a box. I meant to toss it, but I've been busy with the cottages." She passed the shirt to Joel.

He clutched the garment. "Good thing you still have it. Griff and I will cruise the island and see what we can find." He grabbed the lighter they'd put in a plastic bag and zipped it closed. "You recognized this, didn't you?"

Her stature appeared smaller as she wrapped her arms around herself. "I gave it to him for his birthday last year. He threw a fit because I didn't get his full monogram embossed. He smoked cigars with the boys and wanted to show off his expensive lighter. I had ruined his expectations, because I was too poor to have all the initials printed." A shuddering sigh escaped her lips.

Joel approached her as if she cowered like a skittish fawn. He reached his hand to her shoulder and prayed she accepted his affection. As she moved closer, he wrapped both arms around her. Her body slumped as she leaned into him. He rubbed her back and let her sob. He'd find the jerk who'd hurt this kind, beautiful woman and get him off the island. His island.

# CHAPTER SEVENTEEN

From the porch, Joel listened for Sadie's lock to click. Satisfied she'd bolted all the doors and windows and drawn the curtains, he stepped into the yard, Griff at his heels. No matter what or how he had to accomplish it, he'd map a strategy to catch her menace.

Joel trotted to the cart. "We'd better get moving, Griff. Up." The dog leaped into the seat.

The golf cart bumped along the road to the north end of the island. The shadowed woods invited a lurker to hide. Joel sensed Sadie's threat holed up somewhere nearby. He'd choose easy access to her place, but far enough away to not be suspect. The acid in his stomach burned at the thought of Sadie in the crosshairs of a maniac.

He ticked off the information he'd gathered. The fire chief didn't find the lighter when his crew checked the remains of the building. The sheen of the silver appeared new, not scorched by a fire. Wouldn't the heat have blown it up or melted it? A guy with an athletic build and dark clothing had jogged from Sadie's yard. Bryce may have sped from Sadie's lot, but did he ignite the fire or drop the lighter to taunt her?

Joel eased the cart into a gravel lot. "Griff, work your magic. Sniff this lighter and shirt, then we'll hike into the woods." He offered the fabric to Griff's sensitive nose.

Boot prints marred the muddy trail.

"How about here?"

Griff dragged him into the forest. He paused and raised his head, his liquid brown eyes trained on his master.

Joel held the shirt to him again. Nose down, Griff zeroed in on a definite path in the underbrush. He followed with soft, sure steps.

The dog's ears perked at the sound of branches breaking. In the dusky light, he spotted a tall, dark figure. The shadowed man rushed through the trees as the wind rustled brush and limbs. Griff barked and chased the runner. Joel sprinted behind the dog.

Their prey disappeared into the thicket, where Griff lost his scent.

"We lost him." Joel led the dog onto the dirt trail.

A log cabin rested in a nearby clearing. Moss covered one side, and the grass had grown into a jungle. Wood smoke swirled down from the chimney.

Griff dragged him to the front step and yelped. A man jerked the slat board door open.

"What do you want?" He growled louder than Griff.

85

"Sir, I'm Officer Grayson. This isn't an official visit." Joel tried to reassure the man. "Can we talk a minute? I'm looking for someone who might be visiting the island. I thought he might be staying around here."

"I've not seen anyone trespassing here, but you." The man pushed his greasy hair behind his ear. "How am I supposed to know you're a real police officer? Take your dog and get off my property!" He shook his fist.

With a nod, Joel and Griff backed away. The dog resisted. Joel tugged his collar, then checked over his shoulder as they backtracked to the woods.

~~~~~

Bent at the waist, Bryce whispered to the forest between pants. "Stupid cop. He and his mangy mutt couldn't catch me." He released a low, wicked laugh. "Good thing the guy in the cabin needed money. Chump change and he zipped his lips." From behind a spruce tree, Bryce glared at the cop and his dog as they exited the brush. "No way Mr. Policeman will steal my Sadie. Next time, I'll shoot." The light of the moon glinted off the weapon tucked into his belted jeans. "He'll never know what hit him."

Twenty minutes later, he walked across the pier and jumped into a boat and sped away. "I'll be back. Don't you worry, my Sadie." The engine roared across the waves.

~~~~~

Sadie shuddered as she climbed the steps to the limestone police station. Other than a speeding ticket, she had never had any direct dealings with the police. However, Joel had asked her to come in and talk, so here she stood.

The police station door opened before she turned the knob. Joel stood there, holding the door open for her to come in.

"I saw you coming." He waved her to a seat in front of his desk.

She scrunched her face and pursed her lips as she eased into the wooden, straight-back chair. "Why couldn't we talk at the house? This place makes me nervous." She wrung her hands.

Joel sat down and propped his elbows on his hardwood desk. "I understand, but I need to make certain I know who I'm dealing with and what he's capable of. I prefer to interview you here where I know you're safe and no one will hear us." He pulled a pad and pen from a drawer. "I searched the woods for a couple of hours the other night. We chased the scent until we came to a cabin. I hoped we had a lead, but the man in the cabin said he hadn't seen anyone." He made eye contact with her. "Remember Emmet? He stays to himself most of the time, so I didn't expect much conversation from him. I did, however, hear a boat take off nearby. I'm guessing Bryce, or whoever it was, left the island when he figured out I was searching for him."

Sadie tightened her hands into fists. "I hope he left. I never want to see him again." She let a breath whoosh out. "I didn't know Emmet still lived in the woods. I remember him coming into town once in a while. He stopped in the General Store. He looked sad all the time." She smiled at the memory. "We'd sneak an extra treat in his bag."

"I remember. You and Lucy had a soft spot for him." He clicked the pen. "What can you tell me about Bryce? I'm still asking as your friend, even though the info will be used for my investigation. Any personal notes I'm jotting down are for me, not the entire force."

She gnawed her lip. "I met him at my dad's business when I went to work for him, after college. Bryce had worked for Dad for about four years." "So he's older?"

"Yeah, he's seven years older than me." She squirmed in the hard wooden chair. "When we started dating, he poured on the romance." Sadie flashed air quotes. "You're so beautiful. You work so hard." She shook her head. "He took me out to dinner in expensive restaurants and bought me gifts. I tried to refuse the items and turn down the invites. He insisted. I knew Dad liked him, so I think part of me wanted to please him."

Joel jotted on his note pad. "Big spender, huh?"

"I guess, but with a catch. When he started buying me clothes and jewelry and telling me how to dress and act, alarm bells went off. My friend Anne sensed my uneasiness. She questioned me about him, and I let it slide for way too long." Sadie took a breath. "He told Dad I ignored his calls and avoided him. True to a point. I wanted to break up with him, but truth is, I was scared."

Joel frowned. "What were you afraid of?"

"On our dates, if I didn't react or converse the way he thought I should, he'd pinch or poke me. One time in the car, he screamed at me. Told me my manners lacked finesse, and I embarrassed him. I opened the car door to get out, and he grabbed my arm and bruised me. He'd squeeze my arm or leg when he was mad. I wore long sleeves and pants, even in the summer."

Joel rested his pen on the desk. "Why didn't you tell your dad?"

Sadie let a sorrowful sigh escape her lips. "I did, but he didn't care. He saw me as his workhorse. Any extra paperwork he didn't want to deal with was sent to me, and I was expected to stay until I finished. After I worked hours on end, he'd call me lazy because I didn't get a last-minute file finished. So no, telling Dad didn't help." She rubbed her temples, exhausted by the memory.

"Anne, my friend from Columbus, convinced me to tell her about Bryce. I'd suffered the abuse for over a year. She said enough. A week later I resigned from my job, removed all my savings from the bank, broke my lease, and went to tell him I was done. He tried to force himself on me, and I knocked him out with a lamp. Anne let me live in her apartment for three months."

Joel shook his head. "I'm so sorry for the heartache you've gone through."

Sadie tilted her head. "No need for you to be sorry. You didn't do anything." She wiped tears off her cheeks. "So now you know my secrets."

He stood and walked around the desk. "Everybody has secrets." He reached for her hand and helped her stand, then wrapped her in a hug. She rested her head on his chest. His woodsy scent calmed her.

She scanned his face. "I can't imagine you have any."

He tugged her close and whispered in her ear, "You have no idea."

~~~~~

Quiet immersed the downtown. No tourists, no runners, only the locals coming and going. Sadie pushed open the door to the General Store. Racks of t-shirts and sweatshirts lined the aisles. Twenty-five percent off raincoats called shoppers to buy now. A stand of postcards and stickers needed to be replenished. Island winters left holes to fill before spring.

"Lucy?"

Her friend rose from behind the cash register. "How's it going?"

Sadie jumped. "I didn't expect you to pop up like a Jack-in-the-box."

Lucy sauntered around the counter. "So sorry. I was looking for the price gun. My help thinks it's funny to hide it from me."

Sadie giggled. "We used to shove it as far under the counter as we could. Then cover it with a shirt."

"We did, didn't we? I'm surprised we didn't get fired." Lucy laughed.

"Me too."

Sadie opened her phone and called up her browser. "I've got to show you something. I got my first review of the cottages. Your friends posted five stars. Look at this."

*We stayed in this quaint cottage while we visited Abbott Island in November. The place was so cute and clean, with plenty of towels and accoutrements. The hostess is a sweet lady who provided us with muffins and hospitality. We'll be staying there again.*

"I'm so excited." Sadie grinned.

"Wow, fantastic." Lucy grabbed her hands and twirled her friend in the aisle.

"I need to finish the other cottage. The mess with Grandpa's tools sidetracked me the other day. I had to catch the ferry before I finished buying everything I needed."

"Come to Mom and Dad's with me for Thanksgiving. We can stay all night and hit the sales on Friday." Lucy tilted her head and smiled like a child who wanted ice cream.

"I don't want to interfere with your family time." Sadie's mind spun. If she ate Thanksgiving dinner with Lucy, she'd be with Joel. He'd listened to her pitiful story. He knew her secrets. When he looked at her, would she and the disaster of a life she'd lived appall him? What if he let something slip? If his folks picked up on her insecurity, they might question her.

Sadie's stomach rolled.

Joel's mom, Amy, the sweetest lady on the planet, could read her feelings no matter how hard she tried to hide them. Amy might sense her fear, or worse, her attraction to Joel.

Lucy grasped Sadie's arm, and she looked her in the eye. "Joel will eat with us, afterwards he'll go home. He's on duty Friday."

"I guess I'm pretty transparent." She nibbled her lower lip. "I'll think about it." She hugged her, then walked across the street to the island's grocery store.

A zip of joy ran through her at the idea of dinner with Joel's family. Then a bolt of fear struck the happiness away. If she let her guard down, would whoever wanted to frighten her follow her to Joel's parents' house?

# CHAPTER EIGHTEEN

Goosebumps rose on Sadie's arms. "Brrr ... It's cold today, Rosie." She lifted a dented saucepan onto the stove's burner, the one Gram kept for hot chocolate. With a wooden spoon she blended milk, cocoa, sugar, and a pinch of salt into the pot. Eyes closed, she inhaled the sweet chocolate fragrance of the creamy mixture.

A heavy knock sounded from the front door.

She dialed the burner's knob to warm, hurried to the living room, and pulled the door open. "Hi, Joel."

Rosie stuck her nose out the door and sniffed his leg. Joel's red-rimmed eyes told her he'd patrolled last night.

"You look exhausted."

"Gee, thanks. Can I come in?" Joel caught his foot on the doorjamb and tumbled into the room. Sadie grabbed his upper arm. The ripple of his muscles warmed her face as she helped right him. His rumpled flannel shirt hung from his broad shoulders and mud caked the shoes he slipped off. Griff lumbered in and sniffed Rosie. The two dogs ran in a circle, then curled in two balls beside the table. She closed the door as tension stretched across the room. What had he discovered last night? In his depleted state, something pressed him to stop at her house.

Without pause, Joel plopped on the couch as Sadie stood in front of him. He balled his hands and twisted his neck as if to relieve stress.

"Do you want hot chocolate? I made it with Gram's recipe." The sweet, hot drink might lift his spirits.

"Yeah, sounds good. Do you have anything to make a sandwich?" Joel's stomach growled. "I haven't eaten since lunch yesterday." The corner of his mouth raised into a small smile.

By the time Sadie finished making a ham and cheese sandwich and heated a cup of hot chocolate for him, he'd dozed off. Peace enveloped his face. Should she wake him? She needed to hear what information he had found, but she'd award him an hour of sleep. After she stashed the sandwich in the refrigerator and turned the hot chocolate back to warm, she poured herself a mug and left him to rest.

She bundled in her coat and rocked on the porch. The chocolate warmed her as waves crashed on the shore. Most days the power of water fascinated her, but today the burden of not knowing what he had discovered roared through her mind louder than the waves.

After an hour of worry, she woke him.

"Joel." Sadie shook his knee. "Hey, I have your food ready."

He rubbed his eyes. "Sorry. No rest last night." He pushed himself from the slump. "I didn't mean to doze off. How long did I sleep?"

"About an hour." She sat beside him and handed him the plated ham and cheese sandwich. "It's on the wheat bread you like."

"This looks great." He raised the sandwich to his mouth and took a bite. "Mmm. Thank you." His head against the couch cushion, he closed his eyes and chewed.

Sadie admired his strong jaw, his wavy, dark blond hair, and his lips. Those kissable lips. The kiss they had shared so long ago wrapped her in a sweet memory.

Joel placed the rest of the sandwich on his plate, then sipped the chocolate. "Amazing. The best I've tasted."

The pleasant daydream floated away. "Thanks."

Hands on his knees, he faced her. "We need to talk."

She twined and untwined her fingers. Whatever he'd found must be bad.

Morning light shone through the window. The rays played on the wall and created a colorful display. A rainbow sealed the deal for Noah, when God promised no more devastating floods. Grandpa had shared God's promises to protect and guide. He'd taught her about the Holy Spirit who lived in her heart when, as a twelve-year-old, she had accepted Jesus. Now the Spirit's comfort escaped her. When anxiety threatened, shivers of fear woke her at night. *God overcomes fear.* If only she believed.

"I told you, I took Griff to check on Emmet. I wanted to see if he'd seen anyone he didn't know hanging out in the woods." Joel took another bite. "He said he hadn't seen a soul. What I didn't tell you is I think he lied." He sipped the drink. "So, Griff and I meandered through the woods behind Emmet's house." He repeated what he'd told her before, that he'd seen someone running and then heard a motor on the water.

"Somebody left the island in a small boat. By the time I got to the water's edge, he was well on his way to Lakeside." He rubbed his chin. "Thing is, Griff sniffed Bryce's shirt and tracked him. No doubt he was here. Griff hasn't missed a lead yet." He took another bite of the ham and cheese, chewed and swallowed. "Last evening, we searched the trails and beach, and I found a business card in the sand. Griff and I spent the night in the woods in case he came back. I doubt he dropped the card on purpose, but it looks like he was here."

Sadie leaned her head on the couch. Joel's callused hand embraced hers, then he ran his thumb over her skin. Comfort inched along her arm. She wanted to trust him. Her heart said yes, but her head screamed no. He'd spent the night in the woods to help her. Her heart and head needed to stop combating each other.

Sadie searched his face. The bags under his eyes didn't hide his handsomeness. This man she'd known as a boy wrapped himself around her heart. He'd sacrificed his sleep for her safety.

She squeezed his hand. "I think Bryce planted the lighter and the card. He wanted to send me a message to assure me he's still in control. He wants to scare me." Sadie bent her neck and stared at the floor. "He expects me to return to Columbus and my old job, and I won't." Her eyes met his. "I'm afraid he'll go too far. He can be violent."

Joel grasped her shoulders and turned her to look at him. "You said he pinched and poked you, did he hit you?"

Tears washed her cheeks. "Yeah, he punched me a couple of times. Then the next day I'd get roses from him. He charmed everyone at work. He left them with the impression of this amazing boyfriend. They had no idea. And my dad loved him."

He reached for her face and wiped away the tears. "Don't cry. Griff and I will find him and not let him hurt you anymore. I lo ... I'll figure this out." He dropped his hands into his lap.

~~~~~

"Idiot woman thinks she got away from me. No way." Bryce propped his feet on his handmade oak coffee table. "I can't believe Sadie thinks she can ditch me." He flipped on the television. "She's mine and she's going to find out how far I'll go to get her."

Sox, his Siamese cat, slunk across the couch. "I'm telling you, Sox, she's mine." The cat stretched and strolled away. Music from a crime show reverberated from the television.

Bryce grabbed his phone. He hit the buttons to call her, but got a recording claiming the number had been changed, again. How dare she? He tossed the cell on the coffee table. She wanted to ruin his charade at work. He'd snowed everyone, including her dad. The old man had no idea of his plan, but he'd run the company soon enough.

The pitiful cop followed Sadie around like a puppy. Bryce needed to ramp up his scheme to control her again. After all, the president of a corporation needed a pretty woman on his arm. He'd possess her again.

Thanks to the money-hungry little wimp who lived on the island, his plan continued to play out with the graffiti and the fire. His pulse accelerated at the notion of the next ploy. The terror he incited would push her to run to Daddy. He rubbed his hands together in anticipation.

~~~~~

Rosie chased the stick and trotted to Sadie.

"Good girl." She patted her on the head. "No more playing. Let's get to work."

Sadie dragged the paint buckets and rollers to the Julia cottage. The door creaked open. She dropped her supplies on the floor. In the daylight, the little place looked promising. The floor sparkled as light gleamed through the clean windows.

"Hey, girl." Lucy stood in the doorway. "Ready for my help?"

Sadie grinned. "Yes. How'd you know?"

"I rode by on my bike and saw you carrying the paint bucket."

"This your day off?" She spread the drop cloth across the hardwood floor.

Lucy tugged an edge and straightened it. "Yeah, I get one once in a while." Her laughter reached the rafters.

Rollers in hand, they splashed the new color across the walls.

"I love the light blue. It gives an airy feel to the room, and it already smells fresher. You can coordinate touches of red and green with it. I can see a floral bedspread and bright throw pillows scattered across." Lucy pointed to where the bed rested.

Sadie raised her eyebrows. "I have one of Gram's flower garden quilts, and how about birds?" She rolled another layer. "If I remember right, birders visit the island."

"They do. Every year we host a banding event and the naturalist who works part-time on the island helps people mark owls and some other birds they're observing. It's a pretty big deal."

Sadie switched brushes and trimmed around the windows. "That's cool. I thought I might gather inspiration from our shopping trip, too."

"So you're coming to Thanksgiving?" Lucy smiled her "I'm getting my way" grin.

Sadie poured paint into the roller pan. "Yeah, I decided I'd survive if I come to your dinner and spend the night. As long as Joel doesn't hang out with us."

"I can't promise, but I'm pretty sure he has to work the next day."

"Only pretty sure?" If Joel hung out, Sadie might fall deeper into the pit of admiration and desire. How could she protect her heart from her handsome prince in a police uniform? Maybe she wouldn't.

~~~~~

In the afternoon, Joel assessed the old man's cabin. Tattered curtains hung along the sides of the window, and nothing moved inside. Emmet might have walked to the creek and stuck his fishing pole in the water, even though the temperature dropped to forty degrees. He had witnessed him fishing at all hours. Maybe if he caught his supper, he'd be in a good mood and spill about the guy who darted through the woods, the one he suspected planted the lighter. Joel hunkered into the seat of his squad car with his binoculars. Whatever it took, he'd catch the jerk who taunted Sadie.

Movement caught his eye. A scroungy dog scurried across the muddy path, the one he'd seen running around the north end of the island. The mutt needed to be corralled in case of rabies.

As he lifted his phone to dial Randy, to catch him and take him to the Sandusky Shelter, a howl screamed through the woods. He threw open the door to the squad car, hopped out, and dashed through the brush. The scream let out again, one that was hard to tell if it was a man or animal. Joel followed the sound, and guarded his step, in case a wild animal lunged from the brush. He unholstered his gun in case he needed to put the creature out of its misery. Not his favorite thing to do.

Grunts echoed through the woods, then yelps. Joel closed in on the sounds. Under a tree, the source of the noise squirmed and cried. As he crept closer, blood spurted out of the man's leg.

"Emmet, what happened?"

# CHAPTER NINETEEN

The clean scent of a fresh coat of paint filled the cottage. "What a difference the crisp color makes." Sadie admired the walls of the Julia. "I like the light blue walls and the screen will be perfect behind the bed. What do you think?"

Lucy folded the drop cloth. "I agree. It looks great and gives an inviting vibe." She shoved the plastic wrapper from the cloth into the trash bag. "What else needs to be done?"

The couch moaned as Sadie stood. "I'm thinking about checking the thrift stores for a small couch or an over-sized chair. The bookcase I found in the attic will fit on this wall. I want the renters to feel at home." Offering her guests an experience they'd love should establish return customers.

Finger tapping her lips, Lucy rotated a three-sixty around the room. "Are you offering rentals to the men and women who come to fish?"

"I don't want to. The thought of a smelly fish station makes me gag. I want the cottages to have a vacation feel, relaxing, and cozy." The curtains fluttered and reminded Sadie to push the windows closed. "My dream is to lure artists and writers to retreat here and work on their art. Plus there are the folks who want to relax and enjoy the nature on the island. They'll want a respite from their busy lives." She closed the panes against the sills.

"I remember the sketchbook you carried everywhere." Lucy helped her shove the bed into place. "Do you have art you'd decorate with?"

"No. I don't think anyone wants to see my college art. I haven't made anything since then. Haven't had time, but I found my portfolio in Grandpa's loft. I gave it to him to keep for me when I graduated." She rinsed the brushes and rollers in the tiny kitchenette's sink. "I enjoyed fiber art. We did weaving and quilting. Reminded me of Gram. I've got a few pieces I might hang in my house."

"I'd love to see them."

Arms burdened with supplies, they trooped to the house.

Inside, Sadie removed a jug of tea from the refrigerator. "Want a glass?"

"Yep. I'd love one." Perched on the couch, Lucy tugged one of Gram's quilts from the back and ran her hand over the intricate stitches. "She did beautiful work. When Mom got hurt in the crash, your gram gave her one with pinwheels at the center of every block."

"The friendship star, Gram's favorite. She made several of those and gave them away. She said she wanted the recipients to feel her hugs whenever they wrapped themselves in her quilts." Sadie offered Lucy a glass of tea, then cuddled into a corner of the couch. "How long ago was your mom in the wreck? No one has told me what happened."

Silence echoed from the other end of the couch, as the clock ticked off a full sixty seconds.

Lucy cleared her throat. "I was nineteen, Joel was twenty-one. He had come home from Bowling Green University for the summer. I was up to my eyeballs with tourists at the store, while I took online accounting and business classes."

"What happened?" The sweet tea slid down Sadie's throat, refreshing her thirst.

Lucy placed her glass on the table, half full. "Joel can answer better than me. You may want to ask him. Or not." She stood. "I gotta go check on the store before I head home."

"Okay." Before Sadie rose from the couch, Lucy hurried out the door, a string of questions unfurled in her wake.

~~~~~

Sadie dumped the remainder of Lucy's tea in the sink. Out the window, the waves swirled toward the shore, and a storm stretched on the horizon. If the rain fell hard enough, the last of the gorgeous golden and red leaves would sail to the ground. An uneasiness shrouded her like a moonless November night.

Life on Abbott Island held the promise of new beginnings, but Sadie struggled to shake her fear. If Bryce planted the lighter in the fire's debris, then he'd been on the island. Chills seized her spine. At least the restraining order she'd placed against him might hold up in court. She'd chat with Joel about the legitimacy, when she saw him again.

"Rosie, what do you say we climb to the loft and dig through my portfolio?" The dog rubbed her furry head against her leg as if to say, "anything for you."

A large, brown, lightweight cardboard container rested against the wall in the loft. Sadie dragged the bundle onto the twin bed she'd slept in summer after summer. The contents spilled out. She lifted a small watercolor painting of Marblehead Lighthouse. The most photographed of Ohio's lighthouses, Sadie loved the way the painting captured the prominent beauty. She tugged on a piece of fabric. Out came the miniature quilt she'd pieced and hand-quilted. The nine-piece squares created a colorful background of blues and greens. On top, she'd appliquéd a red and white sailboat with a full mast. Among several sketches, she spied one she'd drawn from a photograph of Joel, Lucy, and herself. She'd captured their youth in charcoal.

In the sketch, she'd portrayed their last summer together on the island. Lucy looked straight ahead while Joel and she looked at each other. Back then, she'd perched him on a pedestal as her hero, the one to rescue her from her dad. She had dreamed he'd sweep her off her feet and marry her. The notion proved ridiculous and no more than puppy love or desperation to get away from her father. Yet, she'd escaped Dad's tightened tentacles, thanks to Gram and Grandpa and her own determination.

In the bottom of the container, Sadie discovered a piece woven in red and blue yarn and a watercolor art quilt of Lake Erie and the island. When she unfolded the fabric, a piece of paper fluttered to the bed and landed on Sadie's pillow. She unfolded the letter and read.

*Dear Sadie,*

*I guess you opened your portfolio. It's about time.*
*Young lady, you are a talented artist. I wish your Gram had seen all the beauty you created. You remind me so much of my sweet Julia.*
*Despite what your dad thinks, you have the ability to do whatever you want.*
*Always remember, I love you and even though I'm most likely gone by the time you see this, I'll always be in your corner.*
*Your talent is a gift from God, please don't waste it.*

*Love you,*
*Grandpa Ben*

Sadie held the letter to her heart. "Oh Gramps, you have no idea what this means to me."

When they'd sat on the porch, him carving and her sketching, he'd repeated time and again she needed to find her passion, to follow her heart and create the beautiful things she'd drawn. For a few years in college, she'd embraced the arts between the economy and accounting classes. What if she offered art classes to her renters?

*Thanks, Grandpa.*

"Rosie, I think I'll hang the watercolor quilt downstairs. Maybe the painting of Marblehead, too." She tucked the portfolio under the bed, then placed the letter in her journal. "Come on, Rosie. We have things to do."

~~~~~

Two days later, rain beat on the roof while Sadie sorted through the drawers of an antique oak secretary. Grandpa had cleared out most of the personal items, but she found the occasional pile of papers or books scattered throughout the house. Drawer by drawer, she unearthed paperwork from her Gram's cottage rentals. She tossed any old bills and receipts as she emptied the chest. From the top drawer, she drew a leather ledger and a notebook. She carried the items to the kitchen table, fixed herself a cup of tea, and then perused the contents. A dusty odor rose from the notebook, a diary of sorts. Gram had penned a detailed list of seasonal repairs and updates with check marks, noting each job's completion. The rest of the pages listed her comments on the guests.

Sadie set aside the notebook and drew the ledger in front of her. She ran her hand over the smooth edge where the leather had rubbed off. She unwound the thin strap wrapped around the middle and cracked open the book. On the first page guests had written their names, dates of their visit, and the occasions they celebrated. The first couple honeymooned on the island over twenty years ago. According to the dates, they'd stayed for a week. Curious whether Gram had written anything about the couple, she opened the diary. She ran her finger over the entry where she'd noted their stay. Her first renters had enjoyed canoeing, a campfire in the evening, and gone to bed early every night. Sadie chuckled at the last entry.

She flipped the ledger pages to the end. The date reflected the summer she turned twenty-one and was penned by Grandpa. One name jumped out. *Joel Grayson.* Why on earth had he stayed in one of the cottages after Gram had died? Hadn't Grandpa closed them? Sadie almost knocked the big book off the table as she scrambled to open the notebook and see if Grandpa had written a journal entry.

*I feel so bad for Joel. I hope a few days spent by himself will bring healing. I pray for him each night.*

~~~~~

A loud crack split the air when the ax sliced through the timber. Log after log, Joel drew the ax, then crashed it into the wood to drop it to the ground. With every swing, the angst that plagued his soul spirited away, a bit at a time. The desire to confess to Sadie gnawed at him. He hated secrets. The ones he kept buried, hidden from a person he cared about, proved the worst.

Marigold sashayed into the muddy yard. "What did the lumber do to you?"

Joel dropped the ax and ran the sleeve of his red and green plaid flannel shirt across his forehead. "Hey, Mari."

His friend plopped into a metal lawn chair. "Take a load off and talk to me."

He breathed a deep sigh. "I could use a break."

He scooted into the seat next to her and wiped his face with a bandana, again.

"Worked up a sweat, did you?"

"Guess I did. Getting ready for winter. You know how cold it gets, and we lose electricity so often." He stretched his neck.

Marigold looked around the yard. "You've got enough for two or three homes."

Joel pursed his lips, then turned toward her. "Some of this is for you, and Sadie will need logs and kindling. She's got a fireplace and no way to cut wood." Another good reason to spend time with her.

"Ah, yes, Sadie. She does pretty good for herself. I heard she had a successful first guest experience."

"She did. She's also trying to figure out what happened to the shed."

Marigold swung her leg. Her long skirt fluttered in the wind. "So you're helping, in a professional capacity?"

A mourning dove landed on the ground and picked at pine needles. "I'm working on tracking the facts and who might have started the fire. There was another one burnt across the island. They might be connected."

"What's the real reason you brutalized those pieces of wood?"

He studied his boots. "Preparing for winter."

"You need to tell her. She's not going to think any less of you. Sadie's a good person who's been hurt. How can she trust you if you don't tell her the truth? You can't keep secrets. Besides, you need to deal with your guilt and move on." She patted his arm.

His gaze drifted to two seagulls playing in the yard. "I know."

*The question is, how do you tell the woman you love that you put your mother in a wheelchair?*

# CHAPTER TWENTY

Maples and oaks released the last of their color to the ground. Sadie swished the broom and tumbled the dried leaves off the porch. "I'd better finish cleaning up out here before winter blows in, Rosie."

She rounded the house in search of a rake. An acrid, smoky smell from the shed's ashes assaulted her nose. The remnants of a rake and shovel hid under the debris. Sadie hit her palm on her forehead. "What was I thinking? I don't have tools anymore."

With Rosie secured in the house, she settled in the Mini-Cooper and drove to the General Store. What else did the fire destroy? Before spring arrived, she'd inventory the outdoor tools and invest in a trowel and hoe to care for Gram's flower beds.

Sadie swung the store's door open. "Hello."

Lucy dropped a dust rag on a shelf behind the counter, then greeted her friend. "Hi. How's it going?"

"Pretty good." She scanned the store. "I'm in need of a rake. I lost Grandpa's in the fire."

"I believe I have one left in the back. Let's check." Lucy led the way to the rear of the store where she kept hardware items.

Nails, hammers, screwdrivers, and pliers lined the walls, and metal pegs gripped shovels and a rake.

"I'll take the green one." Sadie grabbed the wooden handle and tugged the tool from the wall.

Lucy's laughter filled the room. "Good thing, since it's the last one."

At the register, she cashed out the rake, a sweatshirt, and a pair of warm socks Sadie picked up along the way to the front. "Has my brother been around?"

Sadie shook her head. "I haven't seen him for a few days."

The bell above the door tinkled.

"Speaking of ... "Lucy nodded at the entryway.

Sadie's heart fluttered as butterflies flitted in her belly. "Hi, Joel." She rested her hand on her stomach to calm herself. The surge of attraction to this good-looking man betrayed her resolve to stay single.

The corners of Joel's mouth lifted. "Um ... I saw your car and stopped to say hi. I haven't seen you in a few days."

"You missed her, didn't you?" An ornery grin crossed Lucy's face.

He ignored his sister. "Looks like you've got work to do." He nodded at the rake.

Lucy smacked the counter with her hand. "Good call, Captain

Obvious."

Sadie rolled her eyes at her friend. "I went to clear the leaves in the yard and realized I'd lost the outdoor tools in the shed fire." She lifted her bag from the counter and moved to the door. "I'd better get going or I'll never get done. Later, Lucy. Bye, Joel."

"See you." Lucy waved her fingers.

When Sadie lifted the trunk to shove the rake in, the hair on her neck prickled. Across the street by the grocery store, a young man perched on the stoop and stared at her. His menacing grin shot sparks through her.

A touch on her arm made her jump.

"Joel, you scared me."

"Seems to me you were already spooked." He held her arm.

She shook him off. "Do you know the guy across the street?"

Joel peered around the car. "I don't see anyone."

He'd disappeared. "Whoever he was, he stared at me while I loaded my stuff in the car, then gave me a leering grin and freaked me out." She shut the trunk and turned. "He looked about six-foot tall, skinny, longish hair, dressed in jeans and a hoodie."

"I'd guess you saw Emmet's grandson. He stays on the island sometimes. I'm not sure why he's hanging out on the main street. He could have walked to the grocery store for his grandpa. As far as I know, he's harmless. He's been in trouble a couple of times on the mainland, fighting and shoplifting. I'll keep an eye on him."

"Thanks."

"No problem, and by the way, I found Emmet in the woods the other night. He yowled the way a bear with a thorn in his foot cried. I followed the noise and found him under a tree. He'd fallen and a sharp limb ripped his leg open." Joel patted his thigh. "I helped him to his house and cleaned and bandaged him."

"I hope he's okay."

"He is. More important, he told me he'd rented his old shack to a city slicker."

Sadie wrapped her arms around herself. "Bryce?"

"There's a good chance. He said the guy left a paper bag with cash for payment on the bed and hightailed it off the island." Joel rested his hand on Sadie's shoulder. "I'm guessing it was the same guy I heard leave in the boat."

"I pray he stays away, but I'm afraid he won't." She shuffled closer to Joel, and he pulled her to him. She rested her head on his chest. Comfort seeped into her as her protector tightened his hold. She longed to let her heart love him.

"We'll get him, Sadie. We're getting closer." His breath whispered across her ear.

She stepped away. "I know you will."

He opened her car door, and she climbed in. "I want to get my yard work finished before we have another storm."

"Want help?"

Sadie bit her lip. Working side-by-side with him might break her resolve to keep her feelings to herself.

~~~~~

Joel stuffed the last of the leaves into the heavy-duty trash bag. "Finished." He stacked the sack on the pile for the town to gather. "Grandma used to say, many hands make light work."

"Gram said that too." Sadie propped the rake against the porch wall. "Thank you so much. It would've taken me hours to get this finished by myself. I'm not used to a man who says he'll do something and then expects nothing in return."

He moved closer to her and held her hand. "You're easy to help, and I enjoy being around you. I hope you know I'm not like other men."

Her green eyes sparkled in the sun. "I enjoy being with you, too."

He inched closer, then lifted a finger to brush a speck of leaf from her face. The softness of her skin under his callused hands encouraged him to caress her cheek. She closed her eyes at his touch. He longed to kiss her, but he drew back. No use sharing tangled emotions until he unburdened his conscience and told her the truth. As Joel dropped his hand, Rosie jumped on Sadie and pushed her away. The moment dissipated.

"You silly dog." Sadie knelt and nuzzled her, then grinned at Joel.

He scrubbed his hand over his face. "I guess I'd better go."

"Do you want to stay for a bowl of vegetable soup? It's been simmering since early morning."

Did he see hope in her? "Yeah, sounds great."

~~~~~

A spicy tomato smell filled the kitchen as steam rose from ceramic bowls. Sadie sliced cheddar cheese and added the yellow wedges to a plate of saltine crackers. "Milk or tea to drink?"

"Milk sounds good. Do you have any peanut butter?" He placed spoons and napkins beside the bowls.

Sadie poured the drinks, then opened the kitchen cabinet. "Of course I have peanut butter. Do you want jelly and bread?" A smile crossed her lips as he set the table. Joy bubbled in her because of this man in her kitchen, one she cared for and trusted. *Don't let me down, Joel.*

"No. I spread the peanut butter on my crackers." He took the jar from her and placed it on the table. Then he grabbed a knife from the drawer.

At the table, he reached for her hand and bowed his head. "God, thank You for bringing Sadie to the island. I ask protection over her, and thanks for this delicious smelling food. Amen."

Sadie looked at his strong but gentle hand. He let go and raised his gaze to her. Warmth heated her cheeks. "Thank you." She could swim in those blue eyes all day. The risk she took if she fell for another man, one whose kindness wrapped around her deepest being, pierced her heart. She'd known Joel for years, yet he held back when he could have kissed her. The words "baby steps" echoed through her mind.

He scooped his spoon into the steaming soup and tasted. "Delicious. I was starving by the time we finished."

She crumbled crackers into her bowl. "Me too." She paused, spoon halfway to her mouth. "I don't want to bring up bad news, but have you found out anything else about the fire and graffiti?"

Joel left his soup to cool. "I wanted to wait until we finished eating, but I guess we can talk now." He stiffened his back as he raised to his full seated height. "We know the lighter belonged to Bryce. Jason, one of our forensic guys, found a match to the partial fingerprint. I think he left his print on purpose to intimidate you, and he drove the boat I saw leave. I had Levi make calls to check where Bryce has been spending his time. The day the shed burned, he has an alibi, and the day the graffiti marred your shed, he was at work. I'm thinking he's paying somebody to do his dirty work."

"I never imagined I'd be in this mess. Thank you for trying to figure this out. I mean, I know it's your job, but I appreciate your help." The spoon shook as she lifted the soup to her mouth.

"I'm hoping we'll have enough to put him behind bars for at least a year or two. We'll have to see. No doubt he'll hire a fancy lawyer to plead his case." With the knife, Joel spread peanut butter across the saltine.

He held the cracker out to Sadie. "Want one?"

"Thanks." It crunched as she bit into the saltiness. She sipped her tea and swallowed. "I hope you get him, too. I know he's behind this. He wants to control me. Or at least make me think I should crawl back to him, but I won't. He scares me." She dabbed her mouth with a napkin. "Did I tell you how charming he was when we first met? He complimented me all the time. After we started dating, he changed. If one of my friends called while we were together, he'd take my phone and swipe ignore. At work, he isolated me from everyone."

"I'm sorry you had to go through such abuse." Joel took her hand and held it.

"The lies hurt. He told them so often, I think he believed them. He used them to promote himself at work, too. All I wanted were honest answers and someone to trust. It wasn't Bryce."

He released her hand and moved away.

~~~~~

The police station's two desktop computers hummed. "Hey, Joel. I found more info on Emmet's grandson, Derrick. Did you know he was arrested for arson when he was eighteen?" Joel's co-worker, Levi, stood over the printer.

Joel clutched the file and read the incriminating words. "No. I hadn't heard. Thanks for checking."

The front door swung open, and a chill walked into the office with Chief Jansen, head of the police department.

Joel waved the report. "Hey, Chief. Levi found more about Derrick. He has arson in his repertoire."

The chief plopped in a chair by Joel. He leaned away and tapped his fingers together. "You want to bring him in and question him?"

"Yes, I do, but maybe I'd be better off to go find him." He studied the chief's face for his reaction. "He was sitting in front of the grocery the other day, eyes on Sadie. She felt uncomfortable, like he zeroed in on her. Considering the other stuff that's happened, I think there's an accomplice with this Bryce guy. It might be Derrick." The chair squeaked as Joel spun to toss a water bottle in the recycle bin. "My last encounter with Emmet was less than pleasant, but I think I'll take a ride out there today."

The chief perused Derrick's information. "Sounds good, just be careful. Emmet doesn't appreciate trespassers, legal or not."

# CHAPTER TWENTY-ONE

The logs on the old cabin had weathered to a sad shade of gray. The hinges had rusted and the porch step wobbled. Joel knocked on the door. Emmet's grandson should spend his time helping his grandpa fix the place.

The door creaked open.

"Hey, Emmet. Got a minute?"

"What do you want?" Emmet's frown exaggerated his wrinkles and creases.

Joel grimaced. The old man must have eaten lemons for breakfast. Regardless, he coaxed a smile on his face. "I was hoping to talk. It won't take long."

Emmet blocked the entry. "I listened to you jawing the other night, after my accident. What else you want to know?"

Joel inched closer. "I have a few questions."

With a shrug, Emmet swung the door open.

Joel stepped into a dim room, with the curtains drawn. He spied a couch and chair, an old television, and not much else.

Emmet pointed to the couch. "Sit yourself down."

Joel suppressed a sneeze as a musty odor attacked his nose. He blinked as his gaze met the old man's. "Is your grandson here?" Roosted on the edge of the couch, he pulled out a pad and pen.

"He's been around. Why you asking?" Emmet's chair sank under his weight.

Another odor drifted through the room, the strong smell of cabbage. "I wanted to talk to him." The cuckoo clock on the wall ticked. A little bird popped out. "Cuckoo."

Emmet rose from his chair and cupped his hands to his mouth. "Derrick. Get yourself out here."

A fellow six-foot-plus, skinny and unshaven, waltzed into the room. "What's up?" Early twenties, hair hanging around his face, he shuffled to the couch and parked himself.

Joel stuck out his hand, but the man fist bumped him, instead. "Hi, I'm Joel Grayson, AIPD. Can we chat for a minute?"

"I guess." He burrowed into the couch and stretched his arm across the back.

He scooted toward the young man. "Derrick, do you spend much time on the island?"

He twisted his lips as if thinking. "Enough. I'm here when I'm not working."

109

"What kind of work do you do?"

"Whatever I can find. I do repairs for people and yard work. I take about any job anyone will give me." He jerked a stretchy band from his pocket, ran his fingers through his hair, then twisted the hunk into a man bun.

"Has anyone from out of town contacted you to do any work?" He cocked his head to one side to get a better view of Derrick's face and read his expression.

The man's eyes darted to the side. "Yeah, I've had a few jobs from people I don't know." He shifted on the couch. "Hey, they pay good, so why not, right?" He raised his head and grinned at Joel.

"Have you met anyone named Bryce?"

"Nope." He stood and ran his hand over his wrinkled shirt. "Man, I gotta go. I'm heading to Sandusky to meet my lady, so I want to catch the ferry."

Joel stood. "Thanks for your time. Emmet, glad to see your leg is on the mend." He placed his cap on his head. "Derrick, have a safe trip."

In the squad car, he pinched the bridge of his nose. A headache crept behind his eyes. He extracted his notes and read over Derrick's reactions to the questioning. His nonchalant attitude defied his eyes darting and his constant movement. *Something's off.*

~~~~~

The island junk collector had hauled off the worn couch from the Julia cottage. Sadie swept the floor and fussed over where to arrange comfy chairs, once she found some. A car crunched over the gravel in her driveway.

"Someone's here, Rosie." Her dog ran in front of her as she stepped out of the rental cottage.

A young redhead opened the rear door of her car. Sadie didn't expect any visitors or renters. The girl looked familiar, but she didn't recognize her. "Hello."

The young woman jumped and grabbed the neck of her coat. "You scared me. I didn't think anybody was here."

"I'm sorry." Sadie grabbed Rosie's collar. "Rosie, go to the porch." Once the pooch settled, she met the girl in the driveway. "Can I help you?"

The redhead tugged a long white box, wrapped with a huge pink bow, out of the backseat. "I have a delivery for Sadie Stewart."

"I'm Sadie." A sick feeling stirred in her stomach. Did Bryce send these? The box sagged in her arms. "Thanks."

"Welcome." The delivery girl hopped in her car and sped out of the drive.

"Rosie, come on. We're going in." She dropped the box on the table. Tempted to throw it in the trash, her curiosity won. She slid the bow off the slender container then lifted the lid. A dozen pink Rosita Vendela antique

110

roses rested in green tissue paper. Only one person sent her favorite roses. Her stomach churned. As sweet as the blooms smelled, she wanted to throw them in the lake.

A small white envelope peeked from under a bud. Her hand shook as she lifted the card from the bundle.

*Dear Sadie,*

*I'm sure you miss me by now. Come back to me, please. I promise I've changed. I want to show you I can be the man you want me to be. I need you.*

*Love, Bryce.*

She tossed the card on the floor as if it was a snake ready to attack. A nearby chair caught her as she sank. Rage coursed through her. *How dare he think I'd run back because he sent flowers. This has to stop.*

She lifted her phone to call Joel.

~~~~~

At Sadie's kitchen table, Joel scrutinized the box of flowers. Anger etched her beautiful face, while her eyes mirrored fear. More than anything, he longed to hold her and tell her everything would be okay. Instead, he pressed his notebook to the table and prepared to interview her. "Can you describe the person who delivered them?"

"She was a young woman with long, red hair, and she seemed in a hurry." Sadie rubbed her fingernails. "She acted jumpy, too."

He studied the box of roses. "Looks like you opened them." Gloves on, he lifted the box and looked at the underside. A florist's sticker from the mainland adhered to the lid.

She crossed her arms in front of her. "Yeah, I pulled off the bow, opened the box, and took the card out."

He took a photo of the sticker and the flowers. "These came from the Flower Factory. We don't have a florist on the island. When flowers are delivered, they come on the ferry. Susan or one of her employees drives a delivery van with big daisies and tulips painted on it."

"This girl drove a small car. A Honda Civic, I think, gray with a scrape across the side. The back bumper looked dented." Sadie uncrossed her arms. "You can take them with you. I don't want them. If he thinks I'm going back, he's crazy."

Joel nodded. "Good."

He turned to her and placed his hands on her shoulders. "It's not illegal to send flowers, but it's suspicious for him to have his own delivery person. We'll figure this out."

Her eyes sparkled with unshed tears. Her mouth softened with a slight grin. He wanted to kiss her, yet he hesitated. *Patience.*

*I hear You, God.*

~~~~~

In his office, behind a locked door, Bryce settled behind his massive glass and steel desk. He lifted his phone and tapped out a number.

After three rings, a voice whispered, "Yeah. What now?"

"You have to scare her off the island," he barked into the phone. "The lighter I planted freaked her out. Now the fancy cop's nosing around."

"Whadda you want me to do?" A grunt echoed through the phone.

Bryce's fist slammed on his desk. The only photo he displayed, a picture of him and his cat, fell over. "Figure out something to send her running to me. The flowers didn't work. I wasted a hundred dollars on a stupid bouquet."

He paced beside his desk. "I want her. She's my ticket to the top of this thankless company." He yanked the receiver from his ear and slammed it in the phone's cradle. One more way to cheat the boss, use the work phone for personal errands.

A tap at the door drew his attention. He unlocked the latch. "Come in." The new accountant waltzed in. "Close the door, Josie." Before she placed the file on the desk, Bryce tugged her to him, and planted his lips on hers.

~~~~~

Sadie curved her bike around the sharp bend. The tails of her hand-knit wool sweater flapped in the breeze. Lake water churned like a washing machine and slammed waves against the shore. As Rosie galloped beside the bicycle, the chill of November sent shivers down her spine. Yet the cool, crisp air gave her a burst of energy. She peddled up a small rise, then pulled into her driveway. After she hopped off, she dragged the bike onto the porch. Thank goodness she'd spared it from the fire.

Sadie pushed Rosie aside and glared at a package propped by the front door. "What's this?" She nudged the box with her boot. Silver duct tape rounded the container.

Her name scrawled across the top in bold black marker spelled SADI. Weird.

She shoved the package away. "Come on, Rosie." Inside, she punched in Joel's number. She got a recording, instructing her to leave a message. "Are you working today?" She snuggled on the couch. "When you get this, please call me."

Rosie laid her head on Sadie's lap.

"I'm so tired. This whole mess has sucked my energy." She patted the dog's head.

Sadie's mouth stretched into a mid-afternoon yawn. She fought sleep, but her eyes blinked closed.

*A man with a rose in his teeth chased her. Her legs pumped the bike pedals with all the energy she mustered. Pain shot through her muscles. The man's laughter echoed as the rose dropped to the ground. The petals melted into a puddle of blood as she popped over a hill, then sailed toward the lake. She squeezed the brakes. Nothing happened. The bike careened into the water as the man's cackle faded.*

A musical melody jolted her from her dream. She patted the table to find her cell. "Hello."

A scratchy voice crawled through the phone. "Did you get the box? Open it yet?" A raucous laugh echoed, and the call cut off.

She stared at the blank screen. The melody blared, again. Sadie jerked and dropped the cell on the floor. From her perch on the couch, she read Joel's name. With a sweep of her arm, she grabbed the phone and answered. "Joel?"

"Hey, what's up? You okay?"

"No. Can you come over?"

~~~~~

On Sadie's porch, Joel knocked. No answer. He looked around and saw a box with Sadie's name misspelled. Without touching the duct taped cardboard, he creaked the door open. "Sadie, you here?"

She cowered on the couch. Her red-rimmed eyes glimmered.

He sat on the couch and pulled her to him. "Hey, what's going on?"

"There's a box on the front porch. I found it when I got home from biking." She gulped in air. "I didn't open it. I wanted to talk to you first. Then I got a call from…" She sobbed.

He tightened his embrace. "A call from?"

"From someone who asked if I'd opened the package. He had a deep, scratchy voice and a horrible laugh."

"I'm going to step out on the porch." Warmth left his body when he released her.

He put on gloves before picking up the box and taking it out to his cruiser, to use the trunk as a working surface. The box measured six by eight inches.

"Whoever it is can't spell," he reported to Sadie, who watched from her front step. He put the box in the back seat of his cruiser. "I'm taking it to the office."

"Can I come?"

"Best you don't. I need time to figure this out."

She crossed her arms. Joel admired her tenacity and her cuteness. He dared not verbalize his thoughts.

"Thanks for the info on what the caller said. I'm sending Lucy to stay with you."

"Not necessary. I'll be fine." Her voice quivered, and she blew her nose.

"Look, you get Lucy or Marigold. Which one?"

A whisper escaped her bowed lips. "Lucy."

# CHAPTER TWENTY-TWO

The oversize clock in the living room ticked off every second. Low lights glowed around the room, as Rosie's snore wrapped Sadie in comfort.

She set her coffee cup on the table, then tucked her legs beneath her. "Lucy, what do you think he found, and when's he going to tell us?"

In the overstuffed chair, Lucy swung her leg. "I'm sure we'll find out tomorrow. I'll spend the night and hang with you 'til then." She stood. "I'm going to fix you soup or something." Her friend trekked to the kitchen.

"Not hungry."

Rosie woke and whined and stepped to her owner. Sadie cradled the dog's head in her lap and ruffled her fur. "What are we going to do?" The dog tilted her head as if to say, "No idea, but it will be okay."

Lucy called from the kitchen. "You're going to eat."

Minutes later, steam wafted from the jumbo bowl she parked on the table. "Tomato soup for you. I'm grilling cheese sandwiches. Dig in."

"Fine. I'll eat." The liquid soon warmed her throat. "Thanks, Luce. Sorry I've been difficult."

Her friend slid into the chair beside her. "No problem, but you've got to let Joel do his job."

"I get it. I dread the answers, though." She sipped a spoonful of soup. "I'm angry at myself and Bryce. How could I let myself get tangled up with such a jerk?"

~~~~~

The plastic-covered chairs at the police station chilled Sadie when she sat down. She tucked her hands under her legs to generate warmth. Joel stood behind the desk, facing her and Lucy, who had brought her over. The open box rested on the corner of the desk between him and the ladies. He nodded toward it.

"No explosives or anything of the sort." He stuttered. "Um, there was a note and photos."

Sadie leaned toward him. "Well, what did it say?"

He lifted his face and locked eyes with her. "It's a threat. Whoever it is said they wanted you to go back to Columbus or your dog, Rosie, might not survive."

Sadie stood and slapped her hands on the desk. "What do you mean?"

"I mean, he threatened to hurt Rosie. I'm not showing you the photos." He fumbled for the best word. "They're...graphic. They'd upset you. I want you to keep an eye on Rosie and not let her out by herself." He stood and moved around his desk. "Do you feed her outside?"

"Never. She always eats in the kitchen." A panicked look covered her face. "She's home by herself." Sadie tore out the door.

Lucy caught up with her outside. "I drove. I'll take you home."

"Wait," Joel called, following them outside. "I'll take her home." He motioned to the squad car. "Get in."

She hunkered down in the front seat. Her voice shook. "Can you hurry?"

~~~~~

Before the car fully stopped in her driveway, she jumped out and sprinted to the house, jumped over the porch steps, and shoved the front door open. "Rosie. Where are you?"

A flurry of fur lunged from behind the couch. Sadie plopped to the floor and hugged her. "I love you, girl. Nothing's going to happen to you." She peered over the dog's head as Joel followed her inside. "What am I going to do?" Her eyes pleaded with him.

"I'm off duty in an hour. How about I come back and we'll talk." He turned the rim of his hat in his hands.

"Okay, I'll make dinner. Gives me something to do." She stood. "Rosie will stay by me the whole time."

"Lock the door behind me."

She gave him a thumbs up.

~~~~~

Hours later, Joel broke off a piece of the multi-grain treat. "Homemade bread and stew. You've been busy."

Sadie's giggle tinkled. A joyful sound after the day they'd had.

"It's frozen bread you thaw and bake," she admitted. "I'm no magician, just a smart shopper."

After they'd eaten, then ridded the table of the plates and silverware and washed the dishes, he trailed her to the living room. Warm light from the blazing fire in the fireplace enveloped the room.

"Sit with me and tell me what to do." Sadie patted the cushion.

Joel lowered himself to rest beside his beautiful friend. The flickering light from the fire danced across her face. More than anything, he wanted to take the pain out of those green eyes. He wanted to wrap his arms around her long enough to fill her with confidence. Why had the guy who terrorized her evaded him? His gut told him Bryce threatened her peace and maybe her life. Who did the dirty work?

"I can't tell you what to do." His hand reached for hers. "I can suggest safety precautions, but I can't force you to do them."

Rosie nosed between them, shoving Joel's hand away from Sadie.

"I think she knows something's wrong," she said.

"She might. She's a smart one." He patted the dog's head. "One thing I can offer is for you to call me, no matter what time, if you need help."

"Do you offer those services to all the people on the island?" She peered at him. Her green eyes glistened.

"Only the ones I spent hours with in the summers of my youth." He placed a soft kiss on her cheek.

~~~~~

With her cell phone on speaker, Sadie rested her head on the couch, while she ran her hand over her companion's furry back. "Are you sure your parents want me to bring Rosie?" she asked Lucy.

"Yes. Joel explained to them you need to keep her with you. He didn't tell them why. Didn't want to upset them." Lucy's voice echoed through the phone. "Besides, Mom will love having a friend while we're shopping. She had a retriever when she was a girl, we heard stories about Rosco all the time. No worries, Dad will keep Rosie safe."

"Okay. I'll pack her food and bed. Let's take my car so I don't have to load her stuff in yours." She twirled her hair. A week had passed since the package arrived on the porch. Nothing had happened. She'd noticed no signs of tampering or malice. Yet, each time she attempted to relax, her senses kicked into overdrive. Every snap of a branch, creak of the old house, or shadow in the yard made her jump.

~~~~~

A ramp led to the porch of the green craftsman bungalow. A white railing wrapped the front porch where two white wicker chairs invited company. Joel opened the door to his parents' home.

"Come in ladies." He knelt to pet Rosie. "Hey, girl. Good to see you."

Lucy nudged him with her foot. "Joel, can you help unload the car?"

"You got it." He lugged in Rosie's bed and Sadie's suitcase. "I'll get yours too, Lucy."

Lucy hugged her mom and dad. "You all remember Sadie." She grinned at her friend.

"Of course we do. You are as lovely as ever, dear," Amy gushed. "I'm so happy to see you and Rosie. I miss having a dog."

Wes took their coats. "Make yourselves at home. Dinner will be ready in about an hour. My lady and I have cooked a feast." He patted Amy on the shoulder.

"He exaggerates. We've prepared a traditional dinner. I hope you enjoy the turkey." Her laughter eased any tension in the room, as Joel relaxed. He had feared his secret might spill out, even though Mom's discretion protected him from further self-punishment. After her accident, her life changed, but her attitude didn't. She still awoke every day thanking God for His blessings. He needed to learn from her. His mom suffered through months of therapy to find out she'd never walk again, yet she still praised God.

Dad had altered his lifestyle after Mom's surgery, from a workaholic to a contented husband. After Mom's accident, he vowed to be available to his family. As a result, he'd since retired and now refurbished furniture in his workshop. Mom developed her artistic skills and tole painted some of the pieces. Together, they created interesting, usable art, perfect for the artsy community.

Lucy rubbed her hands together. "They set up Scrabble in the living room, if you want to play while we wait for dinner."

"We gotta watch out for her. Lucy likes to cheat." Joel took Sadie's hand and led her to the front room.

Lucy threw a pillow at her brother. "I do not."

After an hour of competition, Dad called into the living room, "Dinner's ready. Come and get it."

"This smells amazing." Sadie found her place at the table and scooted into a high-back oak chair. "Thank you so much for inviting me."

Amy rolled to the end of the rectangular table. "We're happy to have you." She reached out to take Sadie and Lucy's hands. Joel found Sadie's other hand and caressed it in his. Wes bowed his head and blessed the food and their time together.

"Now, let's eat."

"Mom, I love the dressing." Lucy spooned another serving on her plate.

"You say that every year." Amy chuckled. "I hope the potatoes aren't too lumpy." She winked at Wes.

"Hey, I did my best."

Sadie giggled at the couple's banter. "I like lumps in my potatoes."

~~~~~

The love she witnessed around the holiday table tugged at Sadie's heart. She dreamed of a family who cared about each other. One who had each other's backs and encouraged each other. Gram and Grandpa planted that desire. She shook her head. What happened to her mom? She didn't get the kindness gene. Not a smidgen. What caused her selfish, bitter attitude? She'd never know.

"Sadie?" Joel touched her arm.

"Yes?" She startled, then looked around the table.

He leaned toward her. "You okay?"

"I'm fine. I guess I got caught up in memories of my grandparents." She touched her napkin to her lips. "I spent a few holidays with them when I was young. I loved Gram's pie. She made great pecan pie."

Lucy stood and cleared her place setting. "You're in luck. Mom makes amazing pie, too. Apple, pumpkin, and pecan."

"Wow. I'm not sure I can try them all." Sadie rose to help her.

"Have a seat, Sadie. You're our guest. Joel will help Lucy." Amy reached toward her. "No worries, when you come a second time, you can help. This time you're our guest." She patted her arm. "Now tell me about your rentals and what you're doing with them."

Sadie admired this sweet woman who reflected a beauty most women never attained. She lived her life in a wheelchair, yet she beamed with joy and peace. Perhaps God read Amy's heart and poured peace over her. She prayed God would bless her with a similar level of calm.

She faced Amy. "I've enjoyed bringing the cottages to life. Lucy's been a huge help. I can't wait to shop tomorrow. There are so many fun things to look for. The first cottage--"

Sadie's phone chirped. "Excuse me." The caller ID revealed an unwelcome number. Her finger slid across the ignore button. *Sorry, Dad.* The man never gave up. He must have asked one of his tech friends to track down her number.

# CHAPTER TWENTY-THREE

The next day, Sadie parked in front of the specialty shops in Sandusky. "I hope we walk a lot today. I'm still stuffed from the turkey and dressing." She and Lucy climbed out of the car. "Your mom's pecan pie reminded me so much of Gram's."

Lucy stopped in front of Paddywhacks Gift Shop. "When Mom married Dad, your gram taught her how to cook. She had moved to the island with Dad from Illinois and never learned to cook at home."

White lights sparkled in the windows, under an overcast sky. Candy canes stood at attention on each side of the shop's door, and the smell of fresh pine lingered in the air. "No wonder I enjoyed your family's dinner so much."

Sadie bubbled with joy as *Joy to the World* played over the store's speaker. This year, she'd have friends to give gifts to and a home big enough for an eight-foot tree. Gram and Grandpa had mailed her an ornament each year since she was born. For her eighth Christmas, they added a house-shaped Advent calendar to her package. Every year on Christmas day, she'd open a tiny door and find baby Jesus in a manger with the story of His birth. She'd cradle the babe in her hands and remember her grandparents' love. The ornaments and the calendar, worn from years of use, had traveled with her to the island. This year she'd display the house on the mantel in honor of Gram and Grandpa.

Inside the entrance of the store, Lucy perused the hand-knit hats and gloves embellished with ribbons and beads. "These are pretty."

Sadie stopped beside her. "Those are cute. Do you mind if I check out the housewares?"

Lucy modeled a glove on her hand. "You go ahead."

The store owner had stacked an array of pillows, with scarlet, yellow, and teal birds, on one end of a display. A jar filled with lake glass rested on a rugged table. Sadie flipped over the price tags. The shopkeeper offered the pillows for half price. *Perfect.* She piled four into her cart and gazed at the jar, as a do-it-yourself idea popped in her head. A small round oak table caught her attention, but the sticker screamed "out of your range." On the way to the counter, she tucked a pair of the baby blue mittens in with her purchases. She'd save them for Lucy's Christmas gift.

At the Flying Crane Thrift Shop, Lucy sifted through a bowl of beads and buttons, and Sadie browsed through paintings. A motion to Sadie's left caught her attention.

"Lucy," Sadie muttered.

Her friend looked around the room. "Did you say my name?"

"Yes." She lifted her finger to her lips. "Do you see the girl beside the quilts?"

Lucy's eyebrows made a V-shape. "Sure do."

Sadie leaned into her friend. "She's the girl who delivered the roses. Do you know her?"

"She looks familiar. She might have lived on the island when she was a kid." Lucy lifted her cell and snapped a picture.

Sadie pushed the phone down. "What are you doing?"

She waved as if to swat a fly away. "Taking a photo for Joel. She didn't see me."

Sadie winced at the idea of getting caught. "We need to finish shopping." She tugged on her arm. "Let's go."

After three more shops, she and Lucy stuffed their purchases in the back seat of the car.

"Other than the chair I want for the corner of the cottage, I'm set." Sadie started the Mini-Cooper.

Lucy buckled her seatbelt. "I found a couple of gifts and a cute box I can use to organize the stuff under the store's counter." She leaned her head on the seat. "Shopping wears me out. I'm hungry, too. I bet Mom will have coffee and dessert ready for us at the house."

"Sounds good." A twinge of heat warmed her cheeks. "Will Joel still be there?"

"I'm not sure. I know he worked today." Lucy's smile brightened the interior of the car as she looked at Sadie. "Why do you want to know?"

Because Joel's presence wrapped her with comfort and security. "Curious, is all."

Seeing the red-haired girl and the threat to her beautiful pet pushed her anxiety beyond her grasp. She shivered with fear for Rosie's safety.

~~~~~

The fragrance of fresh coffee drifted from a carafe on the enamel workstation of a white Hoosier cabinet. Pans of leftover pie, lined up beside the coffee, tempted Sadie as she sat between Amy and Lucy at the dining room table.

"Girls, this has been the best Thanksgiving." Amy squeezed her hand. "I wish Joel had stayed."

Lucy smirked. "Sadie wishes so, too."

An elbow landed on Lucy's arm, along with a threatening glance from Sadie.

She faced her hostess. "Amy, thank you so much for everything. This has been a much-needed break."

Wes stepped in the kitchen from the backdoor. "What are you girls up to? Any pie left for me?" He scrubbed his hands and dried them on a towel.

"Sure, honey. Lucy, get your dad coffee and pie."

"I can get it myself," said Wes.

"Lucy, go help your dad and bring us pie and coffee, too."

She nodded at her mom, then hiked to the kitchen.

Amy leaned toward Sadie. "I wanted to talk to you, alone. My boy Joel needs to let go of baggage. He'd be mad if he knew I told you. Please be patient with him ... he's a good guy."

Sadie breathed and steadied herself. "He's a great guy, but to tell you the truth, I have obstacles myself."

Amy tightened her hold on her hand. "I know, sweetie. I'm praying for you."

A weight lifted from her shoulders, even as she longed for faith like Amy's. Her own beliefs wavered, yet the words of this wise and wonderful woman poured peace into Sadie's heart.

Lucy placed a tray of pie and coffee on the table. "Help yourselves."

Sadie nabbed a slice of pumpkin, then dolloped whipped cream on her coffee. "Thanks, Lucy."

Wes settled beside Amy with a cup of black, steaming coffee and hot apple pie. "Lucy tells me you're looking for a chair for the cottage. We finished a Danish low-style chair made of teak wood a few weeks ago, complete with light blue and red checked upholstery on the seat and back. It's a beaut." He sipped from his cup. "Want to take a look?"

She hesitated. A chair with a fancy pedigree must be out of her price range. "I'd love to."

They finished their pie as they chatted about the treasures Sadie and Lucy found in town.

Wes rose from the table and collected the plates and forks. "Let me put these in the dishwasher, then we'll take a look at the chair."

Sadie trailed Wes to the workshop. The walls of the workspace held tools and small buckets of nails. A few pieces of furniture waited for repair and refinishing.

Wes nodded to a chair in the center of the room. Sadie hurried to it and ran her hand over a smooth wooden arm. "This is what I had in mind. I can't--"

Wes raised his hand as if to stop the conversation. "It's a welcome home gift from Amy and me. We want you to be successful, so if a piece of furniture helps, we want you to have it."

She felt the fabric. "I don't know what to say. Thank you."

"Don't say a word." Wes side-hugged her. "I'll have Joel deliver this to your door. He's got time before the lake freezes to drive the boat over."

If only her own dad had embraced her longing to revive Gram's business. "I appreciate this so much."

~~~~~~

Monday evening, Sadie watched the sky shift from orange to pink. Thankful her picture window faced the sunset, she perched in Gram's rocker and relaxed. She'd arranged and re-arranged the cottages today. Old Ben popped with color after she added the red and yellow pillows and the plaid wool blankets she'd found. She'd propped a folding screen behind the bed in the Julia, as a headboard. The screen's painted pine trees against the off-white background drew out the nature theme. Her thrift shop find, a watercolor of a bluebird in a flowering tree, hung above the spot she saved for the new chair. Once Joel delivered it, she'd be about ready for spring guests. She anticipated a few brave souls would venture to the island in the winter, but in the meantime, she'd work on her website and make plans to update the outside.

Rosie sprawled at Sadie's feet as she surveyed the horizon. Amy's comments about Joel's baggage niggled at her. *He's a cop, so his record must be clean.* What if he'd caused trouble in college? *No,* she shook her head. *No way.*

A knock at the door startled her peace. "Hang on."

Joel and Lucy stood on the other side of the door.

"Hey." Lucy waltzed in.

Sadie held on to the door. "Hi. What are you two doing?"

He pointed at his truck. "I picked up the chair today." He smiled as if he'd won the lottery.

"Thank you. I'm so excited to add it to the cottage."

"Where do you want it?" He peered at the rentals.

"Bring it in here for now. It's cold out there." She waved him into the house.

Joel lifted the chair from the truck's bed and carried it through the door. "Not near as cold as the boat." He placed the piece next to the kitchen table.

She twisted her mouth. "I'm sorry your dad volunteered you. I didn't know what to say."

"Did you bring in the table?" Lucy peered behind her brother. "I told Dad you needed a small table. He had one perfect for the chair." She grabbed it from the truck. "Like it?"

Sadie's hands flew to her face. "I think I'm going to cry."

"Don't cry. We love you and want you to succeed." Lucy patted her back.

"Your parents are so kind." She touched the smooth surface of the end table. "You guys want to sit?"

Lucy stood by the door. "I have to go. You two have a great evening." She wiggled her fingers in a wave before she darted out.

*Well-played, Lucy.* "How about it, Joel? Want a drink or a snack?"

"Not now, thanks. I can take this chair to the cottage for you. No point in you having to move it." His hand rested on the piece.

"Thank you, I appreciate it." She lifted the table and followed him out the door.

In the cottage, he placed the chair under the bluebird painting. "Looks great in here. You did it in so little time. I thought it would take all winter."

"Thanks, Joel." Warmth waved over her at his kind encouragement.

As he wandered across the room, she lowered herself into the new-to-her chair. "This is so comfortable. My renters will love it."

Joel stood with his hands in his pockets. "Dad loves helping."

Just like his son. Joel poured himself into his job and assisted people in his time off.

"You're a lot like him. And by the way, I have something I could use your help with."

He sat his backside on the bed. "Yeah, what have you got?"

"I need to make certain the cottage's entries have ramps." She paced to the door. "After visiting with your mom, I realized I'd neglected to consider easy access." She opened the cottage door and nodded to the entry. "It's not much of a step, but a small ramp would give total accessibility. Gram had already made the doorways the appropriate width and added oversized showers. If she installed ramps, they must have rotted and Grandpa took them out."

"I took the wood out for him. You're right, the rot ate right through. I can build new ones." He bounced one foot on the step. "We can put the ramps over the steps, then everyone can use them."

Sadie noticed a shadow pass over Joel's face. Maybe the job took too much time. Yet, he promised to build them.

"I saw lumber in the shed." She smacked her hand to her forehead. "Never mind. It burned in the fire."

"Yeah, I thought the same thing. No worries, I have some in the shop at home." He followed her outdoors. "By the way, Lucy showed me the photo of the red-haired girl. She looked familiar. Her family rented here for a few years, then moved to the mainland. Most folks can't handle the winters. She may have moved back."

Sadie opened her mouth, then stopped and pointed. "I left the door open." She jogged across the yard and into the house. "Rosie." No fur ball appeared as Sadie and Joel searched the main floor. "She got out, and it's all my fault."

Joel combed the upstairs. He huffed as he descended the steps. "Not there." He reached for Sadie and wound his fingers with hers. "We'll find her."

"It's dark. She could be anywhere." She let go and rubbed her temples.

Joel locked the front door to the house, then called Lucy, told her about Rosie, and asked her to bring a couple of camping lanterns to Sadie's.

By the time Joel and Sadie had searched the yard, Lucy joined them. Bundled in coats and scarves, Joel drove the truck as Sadie called out the window for her beloved pet.

Two hours later, he drove into Sadie's driveway and shut off the

# Penny Frost McGinnis

engine.

A faint whine met Sadie's ears. "Rosie?" She leaped out of the vehicle and bumped Lucy out of the way. Behind the first cottage, Rosie limped to her. At the sight of her dog, Sadie ran and landed on the ground in front of her. She touched the dog's side where wet, sticky gunk seeped through her fur. The light of Joel's lantern revealed blood as it dripped to the ground.

126

# CHAPTER TWENTY-FOUR

The dark made the lake's waves appear ominous. As Joel guided the boat across the rough, cold water, he watched Sadie snuggle Rosie. If only he could comfort her and let her know everything would be all right. But he couldn't. Not yet. Not until he found the person behind the threats.

With the boat docked, Joel lifted Rosie to his dad, then helped Sadie climb to the wooden planks of the dock. Wes loaded Rosie into the back seat of his SUV, as Sadie hustled behind him. She climbed in and tucked the thick blanket around Rosie, then wrapped her arms around her precious dog's neck.

Joel buckled his seat belt. "Thanks, Dad."

"No problem. What happened?" Wes navigated a couple blocks, then parked in front of the veterinarian's office.

Joel rubbed his forehead. "We're not sure. She got out of the house and when we found her, she was hurt."

He opened the back door for Sadie, then lifted Rosie out of the seat.

Wes stood on the sidewalk. "I'll wait here for you. I want to call your mom and tell her you made it."

Sadie shoved the vet's door open, and Joel pushed past her into the waiting room. The bags under Sadie's eyes and her sad expression broke his heart. She loved Rosie like a mom loved her child. If Bryce did this, he'd find out and stop this nonsense.

A woman with auburn hair, wearing a white lab coat, rose from the welcome desk. "Joel?"

"Hey, Claire." He nodded to his friend. "I'm sorry to call so late. Thanks for seeing us."

"No problem. I'm finishing paperwork."

Rosie whimpered as Joel redistributed her weight. "Sadie, this is Claire, the best veterinarian in northern Ohio."

Sadie offered a weak smile. "Nice to meet you."

Claire smiled. "Let's look at Rosie." She led them to a small sterile room.

He lifted the dog to the exam table, where she rested against his arm. Sadie held Rosie's head and rubbed her ears. The dog's soulful brown eyes gazed at her master.

Claire ran her hands over Rosie's side and examined the wound. "I'm giving her a local anesthetic so I can get a closer look." She poked her with a needle, gave it a few minutes to numb, then pushed aside a patch of fur. "It's pretty jagged. Could be another animal tore into her, or she got caught in a fence."

Joel rubbed his hand over his one-day scruff. "Are you sure? Anything else you can tell us?"

"It's not a clean cut. Looks to be about a six-inch tear."

With a cloth, she wiped away blood and cleaned with an antiseptic. "Is she up-to-date on her shots? Rabies in particular."

Rosie moaned, and Sadie petted her head. "Yes. She's had all her shots and meds."

"Good." Claire pulled out a razor. "I'm going to shave this area, so I can put in stitches." She ran her hand over Rosie's abdomen. "I don't feel any other obvious injuries. I'd say whoever did this looks worse than she does."

"Who would do this?" Sadie's pleading eyes met Joel's. "She's such a good dog." She shook her head. "I know Bryce can be mean, but this ... flat out evil?"

Claire glanced from him to Sadie. "You think someone did this on purpose?"

Not wanting to disturb Rosie, he kept his arm under her. "We're not sure. There are reasons to be suspicious."

The vet stitched the wound and tied off the thread. "I want to keep her overnight, to watch her and be certain she's okay. You can pick her up tomorrow. I know you had to take the boat tonight, but I'd recommend you bring your car to pick her up. She'll be drowsy and sore."

Sadie pressed her face to Rosie's forehead. "I don't want to leave her."

"She'll be safe here." He laid his hand on her arm, as fury roiled in his stomach. Bryce's heart must be stone. How could he arrange for an innocent animal to be harmed?

"We have an excellent alarm system." Claire pointed to a box of numbered buttons on the wall. "I'll set the code tonight and be back here early tomorrow morning."

"Okay, I guess." Rosie nuzzled Sadie's neck.

"No problem. I hope if someone's responsible, you catch who did this." Claire patted Joel on the arm. "Can I have a word with you?"

"Sure thing. Sadie, I'll be right there." He watched her walk to the lobby, arms wrapped around herself, head down. He had to stop this ridiculous game before someone else got hurt.

~~~~~

On the ride back, Sadie listened to the choppy water smack the side of the boat. The dark, cold, and unpredictable winter pressed against her, much like her mood. Her best buddy lay in a vet's office because she made a poor decision and dated a man who cared more about himself than anyone else.

When they reached the island, Sadie climbed out of the boat onto the pier. "Joel, I appreciate your help."

He moored the boat and covered over the top while Sadie waited on the dock.

After he tied the last knot, he lumbered over to her and wrapped his hands around hers. "Sadie, let's talk."

Her stomach flipped. What now? "Want to come to the house?" Did he know who stole Rosie? Goosebumps swelled on her arms.

"Yeah. Let's go." He led her to his truck.

At the house, Joel unlocked the door and led Sadie inside. "I think we should check the house to see if anything else was bothered or taken, besides Rosie. We hurried her to the vet and didn't make a thorough check."

"Okay."

"Put on gloves before you touch anything."

Sadie slipped them on, then walked around the downstairs. "Nothing seems out of place."

"Let's check the loft." Joel climbed the stairs with Sadie on his heels.

She moved across the loft. "My dresser drawers are open."

"I saw that when I was up here looking for Rosie, but I didn't know if you'd left them open."

Sadie lifted a stack of t-shirts. "Gram's ring box." She pushed the clothes aside and searched every part of the drawer. "Her engagement ring is missing."

Sadie sank to the bed. Someone had rummaged through her dresser and found the only valuable she owned. Her stomach rolled at the thought of someone violating her privacy and taking a precious heirloom.

"I'll call it in and we'll see if we can track it down. Good chance whoever took it will try to sell it." He pulled a notebook out of his pocket. "Can you describe it for me?"

After she'd given a detailed description, and Joel assured her he'd try to find it, head down and shoulders hunched, she descended the stairs to the kitchen. She filled the kettle with water, place it on the stove, and turned on the heat.

"Want me to get the cups?"

"Sure. The cabinet on the left."

Joel pulled two flowery cups from the shelf. "Were these your gram's?"

"They were. Her sister sent them to her from England. Aren't they beautiful?" The sadness in her eyes betrayed the attempted joy in her voice.

"Yeah, they're pretty. A little dainty for me, do you mind if I get a mug?"

His comment brought a smile to her face. "Sure, they're in the back."

After the water heated, they settled side-by-side at Sadie's table, with steamy decaf tea. Her head throbbed and her back ached, but she was determined to listen to Joel and find answers.

Joel's breath whispered across her cheek. "We may have a clue. Claire found fabric in Rosie's mouth. There's a possibility we can use it to figure out who took her, assuming someone did, but it might not be enough."

A sandy film irritated Sadie's eyes. She leaned away, shoved her hair out of her face, and blinked. "Why didn't you tell me this on the ride home?"

"I needed to think. To figure out how I'm going to keep you safe." He wrapped both hands around hers.

The warmth from his touch traversed her arms and penetrated her heart. With Rosie injured and life unsettled, her head said to pull away. "You aren't responsible for me."

He nodded. "Yes, I am. I'm part of the police department. You are one of our citizens." He released a hand. "Besides, there's more at stake. I care about you. I don't know what I'd do if something happened to you." His head dropped, and the next words were mumbled. "I've already caused enough grief in my life."

"What are you talking about? All I hear about you is how amazing you are and all you do for everyone on the island. Even Emmet told Lucy you went above and beyond."

"It's late. You need your sleep." Joel walked around the table and lifted Sadie from her chair. He tucked a strand of hair behind her ear and kissed her cheek. "I'll see you tomorrow."

~~~~~

The next morning, Lucy and Sadie trundled onto the ferry in the Cooper with Rosie snoring in the back seat. The threat of a storm brewed to the north as wind whipped across the water and clouds hovered overhead. Canada often shared her chilly weather with the island.

Lucy flicked through her phone, looking at the pictures she had taken. "I remember where I've seen her."

"Who?" Sadie shut the engine off and peeked at Rosie. Poor baby, she'd taken the trauma for her owner. Why didn't they come after her instead?

"The redhead we saw at the thrift store." Lucy pointed at her phone. "She applied for a job at my store in the spring, but I didn't have any openings. She was nice until I told her I couldn't hire her. Then she yelled at me, said I didn't understand her situation. I took her pic in case she caused me any trouble."

"Did Joel tell you Claire found fabric in Rosie's mouth?" Sadie reached behind her and rested her hand on Rosie, as waves crashed against the side of the ferry. "They've got to figure this out. I'm done with Bryce's games." She stared at the choppy water. "I've considered confronting him." A knot tightened in her stomach.

Lucy shook her head. "There's no way Joel will let you."

Sadie hit the steering wheel. "How's he going to stop me?"

~~~~~

Joel moved photos and notes around on the investigation board he'd set up in his bedroom, a duplicate of the one he'd made at the station. He worked on Sadie's case while on duty, but he wanted the freedom to think without interruption. Bryce's photo hung in the middle. He tacked Derrick's photo on the side, along with the red-haired girl and Emmet. He arranged

Post-its in chronological order. What was he missing?

First the graffiti, then the fire, and the lighter. Roses and a box of pictures with a specific threat. Rosie injured.

Bryce traveled to the island to plant the lighter. Instead of a florist, a random woman delivered the flowers. He ran his hand through his hair. They all appeared strong enough to wrestle with Rosie, except the girl. No more than five foot two, she might weigh ninety pounds.

A tap on the door disrupted his thoughts.

"Hey, big brother." Lucy peered around the door jamb. "Want to eat? I fried hamburgers and whipped up a salad."

"Sure. I'll be there in a minute." With one last perusal of the board, he dropped his marker on his desk and hiked down the steps.

Joel scooped the juicy burger from the pan. The meat dripped with cheese as he wrapped the beef in a bun. He joined his sister at the table. "This looks great, Luce. Sorry I haven't been cooking as much."

A thousand-watt grin crossed Lucy's face. "You've been busy, saving a damsel in distress."

"Very funny." He dumped a good dose of French dressing on the lettuce and vegetables. "I'm doing my job. Remember, I'm an officer of the law." He jabbed a carrot and cucumber with his fork.

Whenever he stood near Sadie or caught a glimpse of her, his heart sped up. He'd loved her since forever, then she'd left, and he had made a mess of his life. After Mom's accident, he'd prayed to God for mercy, to release him from the hurt. God forgave him, but he'd never been able to forgive himself.

Lucy's voice cut through the silence. "I know you've got feelings for her. Why not tell her?" She drew a knife through her lettuce.

Joel placed his fork on the table and faced his sibling. "Yes, I care for Sadie. You know as well as I do, now isn't the time to pour my guts out. She's dealing with her own garbage. I don't want to add myself to the pile." He stuffed his sandwich into his mouth.

"When we brought Rosie home, Sadie talked about going to her dad's business and confronting Bryce."

He raised his eyebrows as his mouth opened. "You're just now telling me this?"

"Sorry. I haven't had a chance to talk to you."

Joel stuffed the rest of the burger in his mouth, grabbed his coat, and bolted.

~~~~~

"Hello, you've reached Sadie's Cottage Rentals. Sadie, speaking."

Three different tourists called to reserve cottages for the holidays, and they had each booked flights with the local airport.

"Good thing you're flying over. You never know about ice in December." She applauded the airport for staying open all year round.

"Where did you hear about our rentals?"

The first two callers had learned about her rentals from the folks who stayed during the 5K, but the third one didn't say.

Sadie entered information into her computer, then hustled upstairs to dig through Gram's Christmas decorations. She would splash the cottages with holiday color and décor. Slower than normal, Rosie trailed close behind.

"Look, girl, Gram has a ton of holiday decorations." Dust motes flew as Sadie opened a carton filled with boxes of vintage Christmas bulbs. She lifted the lid of a dated cardboard box with a cellophane window. Blue and pink fluted baubles sparkled.

"I remember these." She held one to the light. The few times she'd visited in December, she and Gram had decorated the tree. She longed for the peace of those times, a quiet life of love, and laughter. *God, can I have the joy my grandparents possessed?*

As Sadie rummaged through the trimmings, she prayed for the peace she'd never known.

*Give Joel the wisdom to stop Bryce and please allow me to live a tranquil life.*

A light reflected from the corner of the attic. Sadie followed the glint, as Rosie shadowed her. The last of the evening sun spilled in and glistened off a piece of metal. She lifted the silver object from the floor. Gram's Christmas star. She'd adorned the door with it every year. Her gram's voice whispered, as if she stood beside her.

*It belonged to my mother. I brought this beauty from England. It reminds me there is always hope, especially this time of year.*

"Come on, Rosie." She bundled a few of the decorations and scurried down the steps.

Someone beat on her door. *What on earth?*

She opened it. "Joel? What's with all the racket?"

He shoved in past her and held his hands palms up. "Do you think I can't do my job?"

"What are you talking about? Of course, I know you can do your job." She backed away and shuddered at his aggressive behavior.

"Lucy said you wanted to confront Bryce. You can't." He scrubbed his hand through his hair.

"Oh. I did say I might go see him, but I'm not. I know better." She plopped onto the couch. "I was desperate." She peered at him.

He dropped beside her. "Good. More than anything, I want you safe." He wrapped her face with both hands. His lips touched her forehead. "Please, be careful." He pulled from her and left.

# CHAPTER TWENTY-FIVE

Wind whistled through the windows' old seals, as snowflakes blew across Sadie's porch. Fluffy flakes floated to the ground and piled into drifts. The night sky had dumped at least five inches of white across the yard. The furnace hummed and poured heat out of the registers. In the kitchen, she planted herself on the largest vent, wiggled her sock-covered toes, and warmed her feet.

As a child at home, she'd jump on the metal slatted vent in her bedroom first thing in the morning. The warmth radiated, toasted her toes, and blew her granny-length nightgown around her like a balloon. She'd giggled and danced until her mom had called her to breakfast. Around the table, the fun ended. Dad had checked her homework and berated her for any mistakes, and Mom had fussed over Sadie's school uniform.

Sadie shook off the memory and called Rosie. "Come here, girl. Get your paws warm." She and her pet pranced about until she fell on the floor laughing.

"Rosie, thank goodness you're healed." She nuzzled her buddy. "You're the best gift Grandpa gave me."

Rosie raised her head and a deep rumble rose from her chest.

"What, girl?"

A scraping sound rubbed across the porch and brought Sadie to her feet. She moved the curtain away and peered out the door's window. Joel shoved snow away from the entry and pushed a shovel full into the yard. Bundled in a parka, red wool hat, and black gloves, his broad shoulders and muscular arms worked the snow away from the house.

Sadie's heart warmed more than her toes had on the register, yet she hesitated to greet him. His abrupt exit yesterday still stung. After a few minutes, she shrugged, rubbed her hand over her sweater to flatten any wrinkles, unfastened the door's lock, and tugged it open.

The sound of the shovel swooshed against the sidewalk.

Sadie slid into her boots and coat and stepped onto the porch. "Joel."

He lifted the shovel and dumped a load of snow away from the sidewalk, then turned to her. "Good morning." His red nose and cheeks added charm to his bright smile.

"Good morning, yourself." She closed the door and met him on the sidewalk. "Quite a snow, huh?"

He leaned on the shovel. "First good one of the season. We expected an inch, but God had another idea."

She gazed across the yard at the cottages. "He did. Isn't it beautiful? I love the snow."

"Do you have a snow shovel?" He fingered his hat.

"I don't think so."

He tapped the shovel on the walkway. "I figured. You can have this one when I'm finished."

"Do you come with it?" Sadie's eyebrows raised and she covered her mouth with her hand. Did she say that out loud? "I mean, thank you, and you're doing a fine job shoveling." Heat rose to her cheeks and warmed her chilled face.

A smile spread across his face. "I come with a price."

"Oh yeah?" She rubbed her hands to warm them.

He set the shovel against the porch rail and climbed the steps to meet her. "Hot chocolate and come sledding with me."

Sadie sank into his twinkling blue eyes. "You're on. Which comes first?"

"Sledding, of course. Bundle up and meet me out here in twenty minutes. You're going to love this."

~~~~~

Division Street gleamed with drifts of white, untouched perfection. "Check this out." Joel parked the truck along the side of the road. "There's enough slope, we can sail all the way to Main Street."

Bundled in a wool coat, fur-lined boots, pink fuzzy hat, mittens, and scarf, Sadie glowed in the brilliance of the sun sparkling on the white. "It's amazing. Part of me hates to mar the perfection."

"Don't worry, we won't be the only ones." While he grabbed saucer sleds from the truck's bed, Sadie helped Rosie out of the truck. The dog loved snow almost as much as Sadie.

They tromped to the top of the rise, and he positioned the green saucer on the snow. "Want to be first?"

Sadie twisted her lips and looked from the saucer to Joel. "Can we go together?"

"Sure." He plopped the blue disc beside the green one. "Take a seat, m'lady."

"Yes, sir."

They lowered onto the cold seats and pushed off. Rosie raced beside them.

Sadie raised her arms and spun across the smooth path. Snow sprayed from under Joel's sled and sprinkled her face. "Whoa... whee..." At the bottom, she crashed into him.

He wrapped his arms around her, and they tumbled into a drift. When they landed inches apart and face to face, their breath mingled. The smell of her lavender shampoo tickled his nose. Her soft lips within kissing distance tugged him toward her. She didn't move away, but he couldn't make a promise, yet. His heart ached to draw her closer, yet his conscience said no, not until he'd come clean and told her what had happened.

With an awkward push from the ground, he lifted Sadie to stand. The question in her eyes tugged at his heart. He shook off the snow and grabbed the saucers.

"Want to go again?"

~~~~~

Snow blanketed Sadie's coat after a roll in the drift. He'd almost kissed her. She'd dreamed of his hugs and affection too often and resolved to deflect them. Yet when his lips, a bare whisper away, turned from her, her heart cried, "Come back."

She plodded behind him to the top of the hill, thankful more people joined them. Lucy waved from the corner as a young boy and his big brother sailed the path.

"Hey, Lucy." Sadie hiked to her friend. "You going to sled?"

She rubbed her mittened hands together. "If my brother brought a sled for me."

Joel laid an old wooden Flexible Flyer with metal runners at Lucy's feet. "There you go."

"This is the one we played with. I love the way it glides, and I can lay flat and see the sights zoom by. If I don't close my eyes." Lucy's laugh echoed across the road. "We've done this every year since I was three, and Mom and Dad brought us. It's a tradition when the first good snow falls, the town shuts down and folks grab a sled and have fun. Tonight, the shop owners will build a campfire at the square, and we'll roast marshmallows and drink hot chocolate." She took a breath. "It's a blast."

The clouds overhead peppered fresh snowflakes on the ground.

"Sounds fun," Sadie said. "I wonder if my mom did this when she was young."

"Good chance she did. Dad said his parents brought him. They'd have been close to the same age. Right?"

"I guess so. She never shared her life on the island with me, except she hated living here." She brushed flakes off her face.

Joel bumped his sister's arm. "You going to show us how it's done?"

"You bet I am." Lucy adjusted the sled to face downhill and lowered herself to lay flat. She held on to the guide bar, and Joel shoved her sled.

She sailed downhill, as white powder flew in her wake.

He shook his head. "My sister's a big kid."

Sadie lifted her saucer. "Much like her big brother." She grinned, then sat on the disc and flew off to meet Lucy.

At the bottom, Lucy waited to walk with her. Eyelashes covered in snow, Sadie brushed away tiny icicles. "I'm having so much fun."

Lucy linked her arm with Sadie's. "I shouldn't tell you Joel rushed out of the house this morning to invite you to sled."

The disc slipped from Sadie's hand. She bent to pick it up, and a

135

snowball landed on her backside. "Hey, who hit me?" She chuckled and brushed the snow off, then looked around to find the culprit.

Another snowball flew in the air. Lucy nailed Joel in the head.

"Lucy, you know the head rule. No hitting above the neck." He tossed one and hit her in the arm.

Sadie ran behind a tree and rolled a ball the size of a softball and winged it at Joel. Her target moved, and the snowball slammed into Marigold, who was walking past.

Sadie waved and stepped from her hiding place. "I didn't mean to hit you."

Marigold threw a baseball pitch and nailed her in the chest. She fell on the ground and laughed until her sides hurt.

Dressed in a snowsuit and purple crocheted cap, Marigold lumbered to Sadie and offered a gloved hand to lift her from the ground. "No problem. I've been playing this game for years."

Sadie pushed her hair into her hat. "Do you remember if Mom ever did this?"

She pressed her fingers against her temple. "I came to the island when I was eighteen. Two years before your mom met your dad. She would have been sixteen." She tugged on her snowsuit. "Your grandparents helped make hot chocolate to celebrate the first big snow. I'd see your mom with friends, then later she'd help your gram."

Sadie tossed a snowball from hand to hand. "It's good to know she had some fun."

"When your dad started coming around, she changed. We'd sort of become friends when she told me she wanted to leave the island. I encouraged her to wait, but your mom was strong-willed. She'd found someone who'd take her away." Marigold placed a mittened hand over her heart. "I said too much, didn't I? I'm sorry, but you need to know your mom never was a cheerful person. I double dated with your parents a few times. Once she left, we didn't keep in touch, except through your grandparents."

The sound of people laughing and playing floated in the background as Sadie digested Marigold's words. Mom had led a miserable life, even after she had married Dad. Sadie refused to follow her mom's path. Her mom had taught her the graces of society, so she'd make a good outward impression, while her soul longed for peace and inward beauty.

Sadie lifted the saucer from the ground and trudged to the top of the street. She sat on the hard plastic, raised her hands to the sky and asked Lucy for a push. The chilly air stung her face. She spun in circles and crashed into a drift. Head back and eyes to the sky, snowflakes kissed her cheeks. Even as voices called to one another, Sadie heard the quiet in her heart, and the settled satisfaction of life on the island.

# CHAPTER TWENTY-SIX

Pink and indigo streaked the winter sky, while the tantalizing scent of hot chocolate filled the town square. Sadie, Joel, and Lucy eased onto the General Store's steps and balanced plates and mugs.

After a few bites, juice from the sloppy jo sandwich dripped down Sadie's chin. "This tastes yummy."

Joel lifted his napkin and wiped the red streak from her face. "Tastes good and looks good on you."

"Thanks a bunch." She bumped his shoulder with hers. "Or should I say, thank you for making me presentable?"

He lifted his drink as if making a toast. "Any time."

Sadie rested her plate and cup on the porch steps. "It's been good to forget about stuff for a few hours. Thanks for inviting me today. I had fun."

Lucy leaned into her friend. "We all need to enjoy life every once in a while. It's fun to act like a kid now and then."

Joel and Sadie nodded. He rose from his seat. "Let me get rid of the plates and cups, then I'll drive you home, Sadie. Lucy, you want a ride?"

She stood. "I'm going to work for an hour or two, then I'll walk home. Thanks, though."

He opened the truck's door for Sadie. She loaded Rosie, then hoisted herself into the passenger seat and latched her belt.

He climbed behind the steering wheel, then reached over and wrapped his rough hand over her soft, small one. "I'm glad you enjoyed the day. Like Lucy said, I think we needed a fun day."

Her fingers twined with his. This man's touch spilled security over her and a jolt of something more. Trust, perhaps? Or did the tingle traveling along her arm and straight to her heart mean more? At the release of his hand, the warmth evaporated and left her chilled. She longed for the comfort and tenderness of his touch, yet he withdrew again. He'd almost kissed her at the bottom of the hill, then stopped. Had the problems with Bryce shoved a wedge between them? As he drove, a distance spanned the truck much larger than the few feet separating them.

~~~~~

Streams of sunlight danced across Sadie's face. She yawned and checked the time. Eight o'clock. She rolled to the edge of the mattress and hung her feet over. Her muscles ached and eyelids fought to stay open. Too much to do to stay in bed. She shuffled to the bathroom.

After breakfast, she retrieved the star she'd found and applied silver cleaner she'd discovered under the kitchen sink. The star glowed with a glimmering sheen.

On her porch, she positioned the star on the door and added twigs of holly for a festive air. To the left, she propped a wooden sled, older than Grandpa, adorned with a wreath of greenery from the woods. The sweet scent of pine permeated the air. She hummed a favorite Christmas tune. An island squad car drove up and parked on the road.

"Hey, Sadie." Joel stepped out. "Getting ready for guests?"

He approached in full uniform, and his jacket didn't hide his solid build. Confidence and assurance oozed from his stride. She and her mom agreed on one thing: a man in uniform pleased the eye.

"Hi. How'd you hear about the guests?"

He trooped up the steps and planted himself in front of her. "Lucy spilled it at breakfast this morning." His gaze moved to the decor. "I remember the star. Your gram hung it every year."

"I found it and a bunch of other Christmas decorations in the attic. I'm going to splash holiday charm on the cottages, too." She adjusted the pine boughs on the sled.

"If you want, I can come by later this afternoon and help you carry the stuff downstairs." He inched toward her until they stood toe to toe.

She closed her eyes and breathed in the woodsy fragrance of his spicy aftershave. When she opened her eyes, he stood so close the whisper of his breath touched her face. "I'd love for you to help me."

His hand caressed her cheek. The rough calluses caused her skin to tingle. He touched his lips on hers. A brief, gentle kiss left a desire for more. He backed away. "I'll see you later." He got back into his car.

Sadie stood with her fingers on her lips as Joel drove away. She sank to the step. So different from last night. What changed? The chill of the air swirled as she stared at the cottages.

Footsteps crunched through the snow in her yard. Sadie rose from the step, ready to bolt into the house.

Marigold tromped through the snow. "Hey. What's got you out in this cold, today?"

Sadie exhaled. "Hi. I'm getting ready for Christmas." She pointed to her gram's star. "Want to come inside?"

"I'd love to. Got any tea?" She followed Sadie into the house, slid out of her boots, and ambled into the kitchen. "I didn't ask yesterday, how's Rosie?" At the sound of her name, the dog trotted in to join them. "There's my girl." Marigold rubbed the dog's fur. "She's looking good."

"She's great. All healed." Sadie laid out teacups and a plate of cookies. "I baked oatmeal chocolate chip cookies this week. Enjoy." The kettle whistled, and she filled the teapot to let the leaves steep. Fresh tea made the house smell happy. "What have you been doing, besides nailing me with a snowball? I hadn't seen you in a week, until yesterday."

Marigold snatched a cookie. "I took a trip."

Sadie poured the tea. Steam lingered above each cup and filled the kitchen with an orange spice fragrance. "A vacation? In December?"

Her guest stirred a spoon of honey into the drink.

"Where did you go? If you don't mind my asking."

"I don't mind, but you might." With a tap, she shook the excess honey from the spoon, then rested the utensil on the tea cozy.

Sadie tilted her head. "What do you mean?" The peacefulness she'd encountered with Joel's sweet kiss dissipated.

Marigold stood and paced behind her chair. "I confess. I went to visit your father." She raised her hand toward her. "I'm tired of you getting hurt, so I talked to him. I told him to stop this nonsense and control Bryce. Who, by the way, is a nasty person."

"I'm not sure I follow. You went to see my dad, a man you don't know?"

She rubbed her forehead. "I told you I met him when he dated your mom, early on. You forget how old I am." A chuckle left her lips.

Sadie nodded. "You said you double dated with them. I didn't realize you knew him well enough to go see him. I doubt he realizes Bryce is threatening me. What did he say?"

Marigold chomped on her cookie, then swallowed. "He told me to mind my own business. Then he asked what's going on. He confused me for a minute, then I plowed through and told him. By the end of the conversation, he said he'd consider what I'd said." She brushed cookie crumbs into a napkin. "Your dad's a tough nut. I'm not surprised he's a brilliant businessman."

"He's brilliant all right. Not much more." She wrapped her hands around the delicate china cup. "Will he say anything to Bryce?"

"I don't know. Sorry if I overstepped the boundary, but I care about you, kiddo, and I want this craziness to stop." Marigold stood. "I got to go. Stuff to do."

Sadie hugged her friend. "Thanks for trying."

"By the way, he said he misses you." She walked out the door.

Doubt pushed away any inkling of hope her dad missed her. He'd never welcome her back, even though Bryce pushed for her return.

~~~~~

Later in the afternoon, Sadie and Joel surveyed the contents of the attic, as dust moats floated in what little light shined through the window. Sadie motioned to a stack of cardboard boxes. "Can you grab those?"

Joel lifted the large boxes and carried them from the attic to the living room. "These aren't too heavy."

With a few smaller ones stacked in her arms, she trailed him. "Good. I wouldn't want you to hurt yourself on my account." She laughed, then dropped the smaller ones on the coffee table. "Let's sort through them here."

Boxes littered the floor as dust settled. She unfolded the flaps on one of the bigger containers, and lifted one of Gram's ceramic Christmas trees, wrapped in tissue paper. As the paper unfurled, she ran her hand over the sparkly surface. White dashed with glitter, the tree held tiny lights. A cord with a bulb fell from the inside.

"Wonder if it still works?"

He carried the tree to the socket and plugged in the cord. The lights glowed. "Looks good to me."

"Here's another one." Sadie held an identical one. "I want to put one in each cottage. They're kind of retro, don't you think?"

He placed the one he held on the table. "Yeah, I guess so."

"Can you scoot the copy paper boxes over? I snagged them from Lucy to sort out what I want in the cottages. The handles and lids make for easy moving."

"Sure." He pushed a couple to her.

She lifted the lids and tossed them in the corner. "I've meant to ask, have you found Gram's ring yet?"

"Not yet. I've contacted several businesses in the area that might deal in jewelry. A few pawn shops and some vintage stores, but haven't had a lead. Don't worry, I haven't given up."

"Thank you. I appreciate your efforts." She lifted her arms above her head and stretched. "Guess we'd better keep working."

After she emptied two large boxes, she bent over one of the small ones on the table. "Let's see what's in here. There's writing on the top that's worn away. Does it say Marcus?"

She removed yellowed tape and raised the lid. Inside the box, a note lay on top of tissue-wrapped ornaments.

*Dear little brother,*

*I miss you every day, and I'm so sorry. I tried to pull you from the lake, but the tide carried you away too fast. I know this letter won't help, but I miss you so much. Mom and Dad say it's not my fault, but it was. If I'd watched you better, you'd still be here. I was eleven, and you were three. Now I'm twelve, and you've been gone a year.*
*As soon as I can, I'm leaving the island. I can't live here and feel the ache of losing you every day. I love you, Marcus. I'm putting this in here because Mom never opens this box, and it's got your memories in it.*

*Your sister,*
*Jenny*

Sadie blinked and read the note out loud. "Mom had a younger brother. Why didn't I know this?" Her hand shook as she held the revelation. Mom had blamed herself for her brother's death. Why keep the boy a secret? Mom's sadness and distance made sense now, but wouldn't she want to do better by her daughter? Perhaps in her own way she did. Made sure Sadie lacked nothing. She'd built an invisible and safe fortress around her.

Joel sank to the couch beside her. "You okay?"

"I guess. I had no idea. Did you?"

He wrapped an arm around her shoulders. "No. I'd not heard of a little boy. Your grandparents never mentioned him."

She gazed around the room. "I've never seen any photos of him, either. Kind of strange."

He rubbed her arm. "Maybe they didn't want to remind your mom of whatever happened."

"Could be." She leaned on the cushion and Joel pulled his arm away. Her mom's twelve-year-old handwriting scrawled across the page. She had suffered deep hurt, thinking she'd let her baby brother die.

"I can't wrap my head around this. I wonder if Marigold knows? She and Gram were such good friends. Maybe Gram confided in her."

"Possible. You want me to ask her?"

"No. I'll talk to her and perhaps Dad, too." She folded the paper and tucked it back into the box. Her fingers touched on a piece of slick paper. With care, Sadie pealed back tissue paper and discovered a black and white photo. A girl about ten with a baby on her lap, sitting with Santa. "This must be Marcus and Mom. She's smiling ear to ear. I've never seen her so happy. She must have loved this little guy." Her heart ached for her mom. For the first time in forever, she wanted to hug the woman who gave birth to her. After one last look, she wrapped the photo and letter, tucked them away, and closed the lid. She shook away the desire to curl into a ball and cry. Work she needed to do wouldn't get done if she shrank into the confusion of her mom's life.

"Will you take this and put it on the kitchen table? I'll sort through the rest later. Maybe with Marigold." She faked a smile.

"Of course."

Sadie attacked the next carton as if it might bite her.

"Let's carry the items for the cottages out, so I can decorate them. Gram kept tree ornaments in the big box by the stairs. I'll use those in here. If you grab these four paper boxes, we'll go outside."

He peeked around the load. "You carrying anything?"

She grabbed a hammer and nails to hang the wreaths she'd found. "Of course, I am." She fluttered her eyelashes and waved the hammer at him.

# CHAPTER TWENTY-SEVEN

Inside the Old Ben cottage, Joel lifted the lid from the cardboard box and passed Sadie one of the ceramic trees. "My mom made one of those trees when I was a kid. She displays it every year."

Sadie arranged a silver sleigh with a flameless candle beside the tree. "I love the glitter and the tiny lights. Thank goodness a mouse didn't chew the wires." She plugged in the ceramic creation. "Look, isn't this the cutest?"

"Sure is." His eyes focused on her as he edged to her side. He stood so close he needed to step away, or he'd be an inch from her face. His feet didn't budge. Her eyes widened and her lips parted. His pulse quickened as he ached to sprinkle her face with kisses. He cleared his throat and wrapped his hands around hers, as his heartbeat sped.

"Sadie, I promised myself I wouldn't fall for you again, but it's too late." Before he could stop himself, he bent his head to hers and caressed her lips with his. His hands released hers and he reached to cradle her face. He deepened the kiss and sensed a pleasant hint of vanilla. She wrapped her arms around his neck and stepped into his embrace.

Joel tasted her lips one last time, then he rested his forehead on hers as his hands hugged her back. "I've wanted to kiss you since you came home." He stepped away and looked at the ground.

Sadie touched his face and lifted his chin until his gaze met hers. "I've wanted you to kiss me again since the brief kiss on my porch." She flattened her hand on the front of his sweater. "Give me time, please."

He planted a tender kiss on her forehead. "I know you've got a lot going on. I won't push, but I don't want to lose you again."

~~~~~

The pine wreath sported an enormous red bow, which complimented the white door. The pine roping they had strung across the top of the entry smelled heavenly. Sadie admired their handiwork. "What do you think?"

Joel held the boxes for the other cottage. "Looks great, a warm welcome for your guests."

With Old Ben finished, he ambled behind her to the Julia cottage.

From the step, she poked the key in, and pressure nudged the door open before she turned the key.

"Joel, it's unlocked. I know I locked it." With her free hand, she shoved the door all the way open. "No."

She dropped the hammer and nails. Someone had slashed the log cabin quilt she'd washed and dried from her gram's stash. *Ruined.* A pastel drawing of seagulls lay on the floor with a cracked frame. The jar of lake

143

glass she'd collected lay shattered.

"This is too much." She sank to the bed and clung to Gram's beautiful handiwork, now sliced to ribbons. Anger and sorrow shoved aside the joy that had buoyed her from Joel's kiss. What vile person did this? *Oh Gram, I'm so sorry they ruined your quilt.* Artwork meant for comfort, shredded into an abhorrent pile of hatred.

With his shirt sleeve wrapped around his hand, Joel lifted a piece of paper. He held it out for her to read. *"GIVE UP YET?"* in bold black letters.

"Bryce. He's done it again. Someone is doing his dirty work. Someone has fallen into his trap." Sadie covered her face with her hands.

"You can't decorate in here until we search for evidence." He placed the paper on the dresser. "I'm sorry."

"I can't believe this. Can't he leave me alone?" She stood. "I'm going to the house."

"I'll call Levi to help me go through the cottage." He wrapped her in a hug. "We'll figure this out."

~~~~~

After another sleepless night, Sadie sipped coffee with almond creamer. The boxes of decorations piled in the corner taunted her. She had to delay decorating the Julia, but what about her house? She pushed from the couch and opened a box she'd not touched yet.

Piece by piece, she unwrapped the tissue paper and revealed a nativity set. Grandpa had carved all the pieces, including the stable. On the mantel, she arranged Mary, Joseph, and baby Jesus. She positioned the shepherds and sheep to the left, then added the wise men and camel to the far right. Gram adored her husband's carvings. She'd shown Sadie the creche after Grandpa completed the final piece, an angel meant to hover over the scene. Sadie tapped a nail in the wall above the mantel and hung the winged cherub.

As she studied the scene, peace washed over her. *God, I know You've got the situation in hand and You've kept me safe from Bryce. Thank You. Please help Joel figure this mess out.*

She carried the empty container to the bottom of the stairsteps and sat. Rosie nuzzled her leg and laid her head in Sadie's lap. "We need a tree. An eight-foot spruce with huge limbs, or a Charlie Brown tree we can love. Let's see what we can find."

In the Mini-Cooper, Sadie and Rosie drove to a farm at the edge of the island. Evergreens lined a fence, wrapped and priced to sell, and a sign announced, "Cut Your Own Tree." With no one to help her saw a tree down, she hoped she'd find the perfect pre-cut tree.

"Welcome to Reynold's Farm, ma'am." A kid, about fifteen, popped out of nowhere, smiled, and tipped his hat.

Charmed by his enthusiasm, she smiled. "Hello. I'm here for a tree. Do you have any recommendations?"

"You can't go wrong with a fir. We've got some ready to go. How big you looking for?" The young man hiked to a fence line where pre-cut trees stood.

Sadie and Rosie tromped through the snow behind him. "About eight foot."

He drew one out of the bunch. "Here's one a little over seven feet. I think we can fit it on top of your car."

She ran her hand over the branches. The evergreen scent penetrated the air. "It smells wonderful. I'll take it."

He nodded at a small outbuilding. "Head on in the shop to pay, and if you don't mind, I'll tie it to your car."

"Thank you." She entered the little store packed with ornaments and all things Christmas. "Wow."

A plump woman in a red and white dress stood behind the counter. "Hello, dear, and welcome." Her cheeks pinked with her pleasant smile.

"You've got so many decorations." Sadie gawked at the tinsel and bows. "This place looks so festive." She spied several wreaths with holly leaves and berries. "Is this where I pay for my tree?" She opened her wallet. "I'd like to buy a wreath and a tree stand, too."

As if by magic, the lady reached under the counter and retrieved a tree holder. "Many people need one, so I keep them handy." She removed a wreath from the wall and placed it on the counter. Then she lifted a plate of cut-out cookies decorated with swirls of colorful butter icing and sprinkles. "How about a treat?"

"Those are beautiful, thank you." Sadie bit into a corner of the star cookie. "Oh my, delicious."

The woman's smile twinkled as she gave a slight curtsy. "Thank you."

She placed the rest of the cookie on a napkin and opened her wallet. "How much do I owe you?"

"Let's see, you owe $25."

"That's all?" *How do these people stay in business?*

"Sweetie, we've heard about your troubles since you came to the island. I gave you a bit of a discount." The woman pursed her lips. "Perhaps I shouldn't have said anything."

"Who told you about my business?" Sadie gripped the counter.

The lady sauntered around to face her. "It's a small island, dear. News travels."

Sadie tossed her money on the counter, grabbed the tree stand, and hustled to the car.

The lady's voice followed her. "You forgot the wreath."

Outside, the boy called to her. "All set, ma'am."

She waved her hand. "Thanks." She loaded Rosie into the car and slammed the door.

The entire island had discovered her business. How embarrassing. *And*

*I forgot my cookie.*

~~~~~

At the house, Sadie untied the tree and dragged the fir through the snow and onto her porch. "Ugh. Rosie, this tree is heavy and messy." She balanced it against the wall and brushed off the flakes.

"Hello, Sadie." Marigold's voice drifted in the wind.

Sadie swung around and waved. "Hey, Mari."

Dressed in a teal wool coat embroidered with flowers, Marigold kicked snow off her boots and stepped onto the porch. "Need help with your Christmas tree?"

"Yes, please. I struggled to get it this far."

They each took an end and carried the tree into the house. Warmth snuggled Sadie as she settled the tree into the corner. "I think I'll display it in front of the window so the lights shine outside."

Marigold nodded. "I believe your gram put it there, too."

"Makes sense."

The two of them wrestled the fir into the stand and fluffed out the branches. "I love the fragrance. Kind of a spicy orange." Sadie brushed a branch.

Marigold rubbed the needles. "It's a delicious scent."

Sadie perused the tree and checked the evenness of the branches. "Looks good. All this tree stuff has made me hungry. Want a sandwich and tea?"

Her friend settled at the table. "If it's no trouble."

Sadie layered ham and cheese on wheat bread, topped with tomato slices and mayonnaise. She poured two glasses of sweet tea and carried them to the table. "Here you go. Thanks for your help."

"Thank you. I'm glad I got here in time to help." She bit into the sandwich. "So good."

Sadie fingered the edge of her plate. "Can I ask you something?"

"Sure."

"How do people all over the island know my business? The lady at the tree farm said she'd heard all about my problems." She wadded her napkin.

Her friend placed her hand over hers. "Honey, the people on this island talk. They always have and always will. Typical of life in a small community. I'm sure she meant no harm. Sounds more like concern. Was she Mrs. Reynolds?"

Sadie withdrew her hand and pressed her fingers along her temple. "Yes. I think so. I went to the Reynolds' farm."

"Try not to worry about it. If nothing else, folks care about you."

She lifted her sandwich from the plate. "I hope one of them can help Joel put a stop to all of this."

"Me too." As Marigold reached for her tea, her hand bumped the box Joel had placed on the table yesterday. "Ornaments?"

A frown wrinkled Sadie's brow. "No, it's a box of memories and a mystery. I hope you can help me understand."

"Me?"

"I hope so. Let's finish eating, then we can take a look."

After lunch, Sadie carried the mystery box to the living room. Marigold perched on the couch cushion beside her. When she opened the lid, her heart sped. The worn, yellowed letter reminded her of the secrets her family hid. She lifted the paper and the photo from the container. "Read this."

Marigold read the twelve-year-old's writing. Her face softened, and her eyes misted.

"What do you think? Did you know Mom had a brother?" Sadie showed the photo to her. "This is Marcus."

Marigold stared at the picture of Jenny and her little brother. "Your Gram told me, years ago. I thought you knew." She passed the photo to Sadie.

"No one told me." Sadie paced across the room. "Can you fill me in?"

"I guess it won't hurt anyone, now." Marigold patted the couch cushion. "Come sit."

# CHAPTER TWENTY-EIGHT

Marigold handed the letter and photo to Sadie, then settled into the couch. "When I met your mom, she seemed distant from most everyone. She had a few friends she hung with, but not many. After she left with your dad, your gram cried for days. Said it was all her fault because she could never get over losing Marcus."

She twisted her body to face Marigold. "Who couldn't get over losing him? Mom or Gram?"

Marigold hugged a pillow. "Both. Your gram blamed herself for your mom's grief, and your mom blamed herself for Marcus's death. They both kept it bottled inside."

Sadie studied the photo. "How did you find out?"

"One day I helped your gram can vegetables. Since the room temp hit ninety degrees, we sat on the porch and snapped green beans. She had a faraway look, so I said, 'Penny for your thoughts.' She spilled the story."

Marigold took a breath. "Your gram took Jenny and Marcus to the beach. The kids played at the edge of the water while your gram sunned on a chair a few yards away. She said she chatted with her friend and kept an eye on the children from her seat. Marcus had wandered into the water and a wave washed over him and carried him out. Jenny screamed, but they were too late. She and your gram tried to get to him. The water took him instead. The lifeguard tried to reach him, and he couldn't find him. A few days later, divers found his body. Your gram and Jenny blamed themselves."

Unshed tears burned Sadie's eyes. "I can see why Mom was a mess. How did Gram live with her guilt?"

"She said she locked it away for a long time. The guilt ate at her and drove a wedge between her and your mom. As an adult, your mom understood the accident wasn't her fault, but she blamed your gram. Jenny said Gram didn't tend to them close enough and shouldn't have put the responsibility on her. Your grandpa got caught in the middle. He grieved the death of his son, even as he tried to comfort his wife and daughter. He felt helpless."

Her gram kept the fact she had an uncle from Sadie. Perhaps she would have understood her mom better if she'd known. "All those years and no one told me."

Marigold patted Sadie's hand. "Your grandparents wanted to protect you. Your mom left here as soon as possible, and when she had you, your grandparents vowed to provide a happy oasis for you. It took a lot for your mom to trust your grandparents, but they begged for a chance to love you. I think your dad convinced her to let you visit. You were five years old the first summer you came."

The older woman scooted to the edge of the cushion. "I've told you all your gram shared." Her crow's feet framed the sadness in her eyes.

Sadie faced her friend. "I remember the first summer. Mom dropped me off and left. She didn't talk to Gram other than to say be careful. Mom was a mess, always distant. We never shared a bond like I did with Gram and Grandpa. I figured she sent me to the island because she wanted me out of her way. Maybe she wanted to give Gram another chance. I guess I'll never know."

They rose from the couch, and Marigold wrapped her in a mama-bear hug. "I hope you understand, your Gram grieved until she died, but she also had peace. In her heart, she understood God forgave her. I'm not sure your mom ever did."

~~~~~

After Marigold left, Sadie emptied the contents of Marcus's box. She fingered a pair of sky blue, hand-crocheted booties. His little feet had worn those. Sadie lifted a hand-carved rattle and a baby's first Christmas ornament from the box, then she flipped through his baby book. A stuffed sheep and a tiny white shirt with a green bowtie rested on the bottom of the cardboard. Three years old and these were the remnants of his brief life. She carried the booties to the Christmas tree, tied them together, and laced them through the branches.

"We didn't meet him, Rosie, but we can honor him."

For a moment, she dropped her own baggage and embraced her gram and mom's grief. Joel and the police force worked to solve Sadie's problems. Mom and Gram's could only be resolved through faith.

At least Gram made peace before she died. Mom's restless spirit continued to torture her over her loss. No wonder Mom and Dad had kept a tight rein on her. Dad realized Mom couldn't handle losing a child. She pictured her mom with a scarf on her bald head, staring out the hospital window. She'd approached her and hoped to make peace. Mom shook her head and told her to leave. The woman Sadie tried to love died two days later. Her heart ached for her parents and their hurt. She prayed God would close the gap between her and her dad.

~~~~~

"Why haven't I heard from Joel in two days?" Sadie perched on the edge of her couch. Hands curled around a cushion. "I need to get the cottage ready by Friday."

Lucy swung her foot as she leaned on the other end of the red leather behemoth. "The real question is, why do you still own this enormous piece of furniture?"

"Lucy, stop. You remember how tall Grandpa was. Gram wanted him to be comfortable." She settled into the couch. "I'll think about furniture next year." Arms crossed, she glared at her friend.

Lucy snatched a cookie from the coffee table. "Joel will contact you soon. He's not been home much. I bet he's working on your crime scene."

"He hasn't been here. Levi strung yellow tape around the cottage, took samples, photos, and dusted for prints. I'm not sure they'll find any fingerprints but mine. I need the okay to clean the cottage and prepare it for my guests." Sadie munched on a snickerdoodle. The taste of cinnamon and sugar lingered on her tongue.

Lucy stood and walked to the Christmas tree. "Your tree is about half-decorated. Want me to help you finish?"

She brushed cookie crumbs from her jeans, then joined Lucy. "I guess so. We might as well do something constructive."

Lucy fingered the booties. "What's this?"

Sadie's heart thudded. "Those belonged to my uncle."

She whirled around to face her. "What?"

Sorrow swelled in Sadie. "My mom had a three-year-old brother who died. I found out about him a few days ago."

Lucy wrapped her hand around her friend's. "Wow, what a shocker."

"It was, but I've made peace with it." Sadie let go of Lucy, sorted through the ornament box, and hung a Father Christmas bauble on a branch. "I learned about Marcus from Marigold. She filled me in on the story. She thought Gram told me. I guess my family kept secrets."

"Most families do." Lucy tucked a snowflake on the tree. "I'm sorry they didn't tell you. You okay?"

"Yeah. I'd be better if I heard from your brother."

~~~~~

Gram's quilt invited Sadie to curl into a ball and sleep. She stretched, then crawled under the cozy covers. The scent of fresh sheets wrapped her in comfort. When her head hit the fluffy feather pillow, her phone chimed. "It's after ten." She didn't recognize the number. What if one of her guests called to cancel? She hoped not.

"Hello."

A low voice crawled through the phone. "How's my girl? Ready to come home?"

She clicked the end button. No need to talk to a drunken Bryce.

One night after they'd started dating, he'd imbibed too much. He had shoved himself into her apartment and proceeded to pull at her dress. With all the strength she had mustered, she'd shoved him out the door and twisted the lock, then phoned his buddy to pick him up. Why had she been so stupid to fall for him and his fake charm? How did he get her number this time?

She dialed Lucy. "Hey, is Joel around? I need to talk to him, but I don't want to bother him." She twisted the ends of her hair.

151

"Hello to you, too."

"Sorry." She sat on the edge of her bed and pushed her feet in her slippers.

"He's on duty tonight. You might catch him at the station."

"Thanks, Lucy."

Sadie rubbed her eyes and climbed out of her comfortable cocoon. She put on jeans and a sweatshirt, traded her slippers for a pair of boots, then grabbed her coat, and Rosie. With her keys, she tromped to the car.

~~~~~

As the station door clicked open, the old stone building echoed the sound.

"Hello?" Joel stood from behind the desk. "Sadie, what are you doing here this late?"

Her eyes, rimmed in red, stared at him. "Lucy said I might find you here."

He eased toward her. "What's going on?" With a gentle touch, he took her hand and guided her to a chair and brushed a strand of her hair behind her ear.

Tears fell on her cheeks. "I'm so tired of all this. Have you found anything out yet?" A sob followed.

He wrapped her in his arms. This beautiful woman's pain pierced his heart.

She pulled away. Her pale skin and down-turned mouth told him he'd waited too long to give her any news.

"Bryce called again, drunk. I hung up on him." She didn't move, not even to talk with her hands.

He touched her arm. "When did he call?"

"Tonight. I had just climbed into bed when the phone rang." She wiped her nose on a wadded tissue. "I can't take this much longer, Joel."

How much he revealed might affect the case. With caution, he shared a bit of hope. "I expect to find out tomorrow if we've found the person causing you havoc. We need to find the culprit, then be certain Bryce is the one behind the stalking."

She pushed herself from the chair and stood. "I'm certain, why aren't you?" Her eyes flashed with ire.

He rose to stand by her. "Look, we don't have everything we need. I have a lead, but it takes time to get the solid evidence together."

She picked up her purse and crossed her arms. "Can I get in the cottage yet?"

Joel scratched his head. "Yes. Levi didn't tell you we finished?"

"No."

He stepped in front of her and wrapped his hand around her upper arm in a soft caress. Her tense stance eased. "I'm sorry. Levi should've told you. I'll talk to him about it. You go ahead and clean and do whatever you need to do. Please change the locks on both cottages."

He drew her into a hug. "We'll figure this out."

A soft lavender scent wafted from her hair as she nodded and lay her head on his shoulder. He longed to hold her forever.

# CHAPTER TWENTY-NINE

Joel's smart phone dinged with a notice alert. He put the car in park, shut off the engine, then checked the email message. The subject line advertised car insurance. Not the one he hoped to see. When would forensics send the DNA information? He banged his fist on the steering wheel, climbed out of the cruiser, and trooped into the police station.

The brisk walk smoothed the edges of Joel's anger as he approached his coworker's desk. "Levi, why didn't you tell Sadie we finished the search in the cottage?"

The young man stood as if at attention. "I wasn't sure we were. I'm sorry."

Joel jingled the keys in his pocket, his patience as thin as the thread he'd secured a button with this morning. "She came to me last night and asked, and I told her to go ahead. Next time, listen to what I tell you."

Levi dropped to his chair. "Sorry, man. Guess I didn't hear you."

"I guess not." Joel rubbed his temples. "Here's the deal: we need to figure out who's hounding Sadie. The long red hair you found might belong to the girl who delivered the roses, the same one who applied to work for Lucy. I want to question her. If she's on the island, I'll bump into her and see if we can chat about her activity in the past month or so."

Levi nodded. "Sounds good. What do you want me to do?"

Joel retrieved a photo from his phone. "This is her. Find out where she lives. Lucy saw her on the mainland, but I've seen her on the east side of the island. Start there."

Levi grabbed his cap and jacket. "Will do."

An hour later his radio alerted him. "Hey, Levi. What you got?"

The connection crackled. "I think I found where she lives. There's a small blue house on Woodruff Street with an older, gray Civic parked in front. I spotted her at her mailbox. Want me to hang around?"

Joel studied the map on the office wall. "Yeah, stay for at least an hour and see if she leaves. It's Saturday and close to lunch. Maybe she'll go out."

"You got it." The radio clicked off.

Head in his hands, Joel rested his elbows on the desk. "God, I need Your help. I know I don't talk to you much. I'm asking for Sadie, not me. Help me protect her and find the jerk who's causing her grief." A nudge of confidence pushed him to attack the case and dig in for answers.

When Levi waltzed into the police station, Joel caught the smug look on his face. "Have you got news?"

Levi placed his hands on the desk and leaned in Joel's direction. "You'll never guess who stopped by the redhead's house."

The young man's nonchalant attitude irked him. "You going to tell me?" The yellow pencil in Joel's grasp snapped in two.

"Emmet's grandson, Derrick parked at the house, and Red hurried out to meet him. She gave him an envelope, they chatted and smooched, then he left. I waited a few minutes, then figured I'd better let you know."

He tossed the two pencil pieces in the trash. "Good work, Levi. Now to have a chat."

Before Joel left the office, his email message beeped an alert. DNA results flashed across his phone's screen, but no match had shown in the database. No choice now but to bump into the suspect and have a talk, if she'd be willing.

In the cruiser, he drove to Woodruff Street and located the young woman's home. The Civic, parked in front, wore rust and salt from the streets. He parked in a gravel lot. Might as well eat the blueberry muffin Lucy baked this morning. He downed the sweet treat as he monitored the house.

Paint chips fluttered from the worn door when Red stepped out onto her porch. She rubbed her arms as if the chill caught her. No coat, a scarf, and sandals on her feet, she trotted to the car. Joel tailed her a few blocks. When she parked, he waited for the opportunity to talk.

In front of the General Store, Joel approached her. "Excuse me, Miss, I'm Officer Grayson. I'd like to speak to you a minute."

She turned to him, shoulders stiff, back straight, and eyes wide. "What do you want?"

"I'd like to chat with you about a few things that happened on the island." He nodded to the entrance of the store. "This is my sister's shop. She's got an office inside. What do you say we talk there?"

She twisted the ends of her purple scarf. "Um… I don't think I have to talk to you."

"You're correct. You don't, but I'd rather talk to you here than at the station." Joel stood feet apart, arms crossed.

She cleared her throat and choked out a response. "Do I need a lawyer?"

He softened his stance. "Up to you."

The redhead blinked away unshed tears. "I told Derrick we'd get caught. He said no way."

Joel stepped to her side. "Want to tell me about it?"

She nodded. Shoulders slumped, she trudged into the store.

Bagged pinecones emitted a strong cinnamon fragrance. With the holiday near, he longed to close the case and be free to date Sadie.

He spotted Lucy in the apparel section. She straightened a shirt on a hanger, then looked at her brother. "Hi. What's going on?"

He nodded at the redhead. "Looks quiet today. Do you mind if I use your office?"

Lucy strode to the store's entrance and flipped the open sign to closed. "I'm taking a lunch break, so help yourself."

"Thanks. We won't be long." His sister stepped into a workroom where she kept a small refrigerator and microwave for her staff.

The redhead followed him to the office. Their footsteps clicked against the hard wood floors. The sweet smell of gingerbread cookies emitted from a freshener near the dressing rooms.

He left the door open. "Have a seat. May I record our conversation?"

"Yeah." Her voice quivered. "Am I being arrested?"

"No. We're having a conversation."

He pressed the record button on his phone. "Please, state your name and date of birth."

"Rayann Price, June 2, 1999." She blurted. "He paid me to do it."

"Who paid you to do what?" Joel stared at the young woman.

She wrapped the scarf around her hand. "A man my dad owed money to found me outside my house one day. He offered to pay me to do stuff to the new woman on the island, to get her to leave. He waved big bucks in front of me, enough to help my dad."

Joel sat on the edge of Lucy's desk. "Can you tell me the name of the man who paid you?"

She paused and closed her eyes. "He hasn't given me all the money, yet. Says I haven't finished the job. And if I tell you his name, he'll go after my dad. Dad's not in good shape, and I'm afraid he'll have a heart attack."

Thin as the pencil Joel held, the girl shook. She was scared, and he needed her to talk. "You mentioned Derrick. Is he Emmet's grandson?"

Rayann pushed her copper tresses behind her shoulder. "Yes. Derrick's my boyfriend and when he heard about the money I'd make, he wanted a cut. So he helped me. He made a couple of phone calls to the lady."

"What about the fire, Rayann? Did you start it?"

Tears glistened in her eyes. "Derrick helped me. I didn't want to do it, but the man told me I'd have to do something drastic to get the lady's attention. He convinced me it was a bunch of junk in the shed nobody needed. I'm so sorry." She sobbed.

Joel took notes as he recorded her voice. "Did you tear up the cottage?"

"No, Derrick did. I couldn't destroy her stuff. The quilt was so pretty." Rayann's far off look focused on the wall behind him.

"Rayann, I have to take you to the police station. You've broken the law, and you're under arrest for menacing." He spoke the Miranda rights to her. "You'll spend the night in the cell. If you share the name of the person who's paying you, it will help your case."

Her gaze dropped and focused on the wood floor.

Joel gestured for her to approach him. "You need to follow me."

Without handcuffs, she lifted herself from the seat and followed him to the cruiser. Her timid manner reminded him of Sadie the first summer she visited the island. She'd responded to his teasing like a frightened puppy. Once she met Lucy, she shook free of her inhibitions and conquered her fears. His sister's adventurous spirit led all three of them to fun times and some trouble.

Rayann's eyes met his in the rearview mirror. "Are you going to arrest Derrick, too?"

After he drove a block to the station, he climbed out and opened her door. "I plan to talk to him as soon as I secure you in the holding cell."

Inside the jail, Joel clicked the metal bars shut, and Rayann curled up on the cot.

His heart hurt for Rayann, because the young woman got involved with a scumbag. Yet as an officer, he had to do his job. When he found Derrick, he planned to interrogate him and dig into who paid the big money for the crimes. He pictured Sadie's face filled with anger. She blamed Bryce. He understood her misery and frustration, but his job made him responsible to follow the evidence.

Joel rubbed his forehead where a headache threatened to build. "Levi, have you talked to Chief Jansen this afternoon?"

Levi looked up from the papers he studied. "I think he went to the mainland today to check leads on the damage to the docked boats. The ones with the slashed covers."

"Yeah, I know the case." He kneeled to pet Griff. "If you see him, catch him up on the woman in the cell and tell him I went to find Derrick. She confessed to the fire at Sadie's shed." Joel secured his cap on his head, then patted his leg. "Griff, come with me."

~~~~~

Parked along the gravel road by Emmet's cabin, Joel studied the woods. No one lurked in the shadows, no sound but the squirrels scampering over dried leaves. Time to find Derrick.

Stones crunched under Joel and Griff's feet as they crossed to the woods. With no car, Emmet never installed a driveway, only a path to hike in from. In the woods, snow clung to the shadowed ditches and dips. When they paused, a deafening quiet hung over the bare trees.

Along the path, Griff stopped to do his business. While Joel waited, he took in the look of the cabin, some yards away. In the daylight, the place appeared desolate, with no movement or sound. Smoke from the woodstove curled above the house, and the pungent odor permeated the air.

When he bent to adjust Griff's collar, something whizzed past his ear. "Griff, get over here." The dog trailed him to a thick tree. "What on earth?" Joel peered around the old oak and spied Derrick on the porch with a shotgun.

"Derrick, it's me, Joel. I want to talk to you."

Emmet's grandson pointed the barrel of the gun to the ground. "What do you want?"

"To talk."

Emmet stepped out the door and removed the gun from his grandson's hands. He called into the woods. "Come on, Joel."

On the porch, Joel sat in a rickety, paint-chipped rocker, and faced Emmet and Derrick perched on a weathered pine bench.

Emmet had moved the gun from his grandson's grip and propped it against the wall. "What do you want?"

With his gaze on the shotgun, Joel rested his hand on Griff. "I came to talk to Derrick."

Derrick shook his head. "What now?"

Joel stared at the young man. "I heard you helped start the fire at Sadie Stewart's home."

His eyes darted to the side, then rose to meet Joel's. "I don't know no Sadie."

With a pause and a look of disdain, he ventured deeper into the questioning. "You know Rayann, right?"

Anger darkened Derrick's face as he clenched his fists. "What about her?"

A rush of wind blew dried leaves across the porch floor. Joel stood. Griff followed him to stand in front of the men. "She said you helped her light the fire to Sadie's shed, and you made a few phone calls. Is that true?"

Before he asked another question, Emmet raised his hand and smacked his grandson in the back of the head. "If you did those things, you tell Joel the truth. I won't have you lollygagging around here with guilt on your conscience."

"Settle down, Gramps. Yeah, I helped her. She's the one who made the deal for the money from the city slicker, hot-shot."

Joel tugged his handcuffs out of his pocket. "Derrick, you're under arrest." He gave him his rights as he cuffed him, trekked Derrick through the woods to the road, then loaded him in the car. Griff jumped in the front seat.

Emmet had tagged behind, head hung low. He bent to the back seat window and looked his grandson in the eye. "I can't believe you, boy. I'd hoped you'd amount to more than your dad."

With a nod, Joel climbed into the cruiser, pressed the button to roll up the windows, and drove away from the old man. When he glanced in the rearview mirror and saw Emmet stand by the road with slumped shoulders, a lump formed in Joel's throat. He hoped the disappointment in his grandson's behavior didn't affect Emmet's health. Nevertheless, he sucked up any ounce of empathy and focused on finding the truth.

# CHAPTER THIRTY

The green and red star quilt added a festive touch to the cottage. Sadie smoothed the wrinkles of the cover, then placed a petite Christmas tree decked in miniature bulbs on the side table and plugged in a gingerbread air freshener. Satisfied the Old Ben cottage offered an invitation to relax, her anxiety seeped away.

A tap on the door drew her from her dream of satisfied customers. She lifted the latch and pulled the door open.

"Joel, you're here." Sadie smoothed her shirt as her heart fluttered. His recent absence from her everyday life triggered her desire to spend more time with him. She'd let go of her anger and wanted to hear what he'd learned about the case. Now she yearned for the man, and longed to hold his hand and be protected, with a hug from those muscular arms.

He removed his hat. "I am. Sorry it's taken me so long to get with you. I've... we've been busy at the station tracking the people who've harassed you."

"I'm happy you're here. Come in." Sadie backed to the bed. She gestured to the chair in the corner. "Have a seat." Her heart thumped in anticipation of the news they might have caught the stalker. Not sure whether to laugh or cry, she tapped her foot on the floor. "Tell me what's going on."

Police cap in hand, he twisted the rim with his fingers. "I've arrested Rayann Price and Emmet's grandson, Derrick. They're both in custody. No doubt they'll get out on bail, then we'll take them to trial on menacing charges."

Rayann's name didn't match anyone she had met on the island. "Who is Rayann Price? I've never heard of her." She shook her head and twined her fingers in and out. Bryce had manipulated or threatened another woman into doing his dirty work.

Joel scrubbed his hand over his hair, then stood and paced the small space. "You remember the redhead who brought you the roses?"

"Yes. Lucy and I saw her when we shopped in Sandusky."

Joel carried the chair to a spot closer to her. He settled in, rested his arms on his knees and faced her. "Rayann, AKA the red-haired girl, confessed to the fire and phone calls, and she sobbed when she admitted to kidnapping Rosie. Her Rottweiler attacked Rosie as soon as Rayann opened the door to her house. Rosie lashed out and bit a hunk out of Rayann's jacket, which we have as evidence. By the time she'd torn the dogs apart, they'd both suffered injuries. Before anything else happened, she shoved

Rosie in the car and dropped her off by your house. We're lucky Rayann loves dogs. Whoever paid her wanted her to hurt Rosie to the point of ... well, you don't want to know."

"Unbelievable." Sadie shook her head, then stood and walked to the window. "Poor Rosie. Thank goodness this girl didn't follow through. I heard you say 'whoever paid her.' Didn't she tell you who hired her to harass me?"

Joel walked behind Sadie and rested his hands on her shoulders. "No, she won't share the name because he's made threats to her dad. Derrick admitted he helped Rayann for the money."

The sun shone through the window but didn't warm the cold shivers his news gave her. He had caught the two who caused the trouble, but Bryce, or whoever aimed to scare her, still lurked in the shadows. She turned to Joel, the man her heart belonged to. However, with her life a mess, why would he want anything to do with her?

His arms reached to hug her, but she moved away. "I'm thankful you caught them, and pray they reveal who paid them. I hope with them in custody, the harassment will stop." Doubt filled her as she spoke, because she knew better. Bryce would continue to threaten her until she ran to him.

~~~~~

A few days later, after a restless night, Sadie rose early and worked in the kitchen. She stirred the second batch of her gram's cranberry muffin recipe with the items Joel picked up on the mainland yesterday. He'd supplied her with fresh cranberries and walnuts, and now she relished the smell as the first batch plumped in the oven. Perfect for a holiday treat for her guests, she'd freeze most of them and add them to the welcome baskets. She'd share the rest with Joel and Lucy.

She lingered by the kitchen window, while she waited for the timer to tell her to take the muffins from the oven. The waves of the lake ebbed and flowed as a chill rose along her spine. The relentless cold water splashed the shore and beat the rocks. Persistent and ruthless like Bryce. With his helpers caught, she prayed he would disappear from her life.

~~~~~

Sadie wished to relax and celebrate Christmas with her friends, but fear and stress painted everything she tried to enjoy. She had settled guests into the cottages yesterday. Even though the visitors admired the cottages and complimented her on the decorations and muffins, she worried they wouldn't be satisfied.

Joel and Lucy had invited her to watch *It's a Wonderful Life*. She'd offered to bring the ingredients for her gram's hot chocolate. Joel planned to pop popcorn, the old-fashioned way, with a pan and oil. He detested microwave popcorn.

With a basket of muffins and hot chocolate fixings, Sadie tapped on their front door. A spray of white poinsettias mixed with greenery adorned with red berries hung from a hook. She rubbed the petals, not real, yet pretty.

The door opened, "Come in." Joel's smile brightened the night. He removed her coat, then hung it in the closet and led her toward the kitchen.

"Where's Lucy?" She peered around him into the kitchen.

Joel lifted the basket from her arms and placed it on the island. Sadie pivoted in a circle. Walking into Joel's house lifted her spirits and calmed her nerves. They had had a lot of fun there.

"I'd forgotten this amazing kitchen. We used to perch at the counter and pour Kool-Aid into Popsicle molds. Remember those huge pizzas we made? They dripped all over the oven."

"They tasted great. Mom about had a fit when she saw the mess." He stilled, then stepped beside her. "Sadie, we need to talk."

Lucy blew in with the wind. "Hey guys, am I late to the party?"

"No, not at all." Sadie hugged Lucy.

She scrunched her face and set her gaze on her brother. "Did I interrupt something?"

"Nope." Joel turned to the stove and set a pan on the front burner. He poured oil in the bottom, then waited for it to heat.

"Okay, then." She raised her eyebrows at Sadie.

Sadie took a pan Joel handed her, placed it on the stove, mixed the hot chocolate ingredients, then turned on the heat.

Joel added popcorn kernels to the hot oil and, after the last kernel popped, he dumped the popcorn into a large bowl and carried it to the living room. Sadie trailed him with mugs of steaming hot chocolate.

Lucy handed out smaller bowls, and the three of them settled on the couch, Sadie in the middle.

"I love this movie." Lucy dipped a small bowl of popcorn from the bigger container.

Sadie gripped the big bowl Lucy passed her. "Me, too."

Joel bumped Sadie's elbow and a few puffs of corn flew in the air. "The hot chocolate is perfect as usual."

"Thanks. I've made plenty of it this year." She set the popcorn bowl on the coffee table and stirred marshmallows into her drink. "I think I've got the recipe memorized."

~~~~~

At the end of the movie, Joel clicked the remote to turn off the television. Year after year, he suffered through this movie with Lucy. Every time George wondered what life for the people around him might have been like without him, Joel pummeled himself over what might have happened if he'd made better choices.

"I love a satisfying ending, with Jimmy Stewart as the hero." Lucy leaned her head on Sadie's shoulder. "I wish I'd been born in an earlier century." She stretched and yawned. "I think I'll head to bed, if no one cares."

Sadie hugged Lucy. "Night."

"Night, sis." Joel cleared the remnants of popcorn and carried the bowls to the kitchen.

Cups in hand, Sadie followed. "I had fun."

He loaded the dishes into the dishwasher. "Me too. Every time Clarence helps George Bailey, I'm more thankful for my family." He hung his head.

"You okay?" She touched Joel's arm.

"No. I need to talk to you." He bit his lip.

Sadie nodded. "Is now a good time?"

He dried his hands on a dishtowel. "Good as any. How about I follow you home, so we can chat in private? Besides, I don't want you out by yourself this late at night."

~~~~~

When they reached her house, Joel parked behind the Mini-Cooper. When Sadie opened the front door, Rosie met her with a yelp.

"Hey girl, I'm home." She knelt and hugged her pet. "I'm going to make us some coffee, all right?" She stepped into the kitchen.

"Sure. How about we talk on the couch?" Joel tossed their coats on Grandpa's recliner.

"What's going on?" she asked as she returned from the kitchen. "News about my stalker? I haven't heard from him in several days."

Her serious expression halted him. The burden he carried pressed on him. He'd been forgiven, freed of responsibility, but he'd still caused his family unimaginable grief. Would the confession repulse Sadie?

Tempted to hold her hand, Joel scooted to the cushion farthest from her. He faced her, his stomach rolled, but he pushed out the words. "This isn't about the man menacing you, I have to tell you something else. I care about you, and I hope you feel the same, but this might change your mind." He pushed his fingers through his hair. "I'm the reason my mom's in a wheelchair."

Sadie blinked. "What?"

"Let me start at the beginning. After you left the island, I went to college. I did decent in my studies, even though I never settled on a major. I finished an associate's degree in liberal arts, then moved home. Mom and Dad didn't say much, but they weren't happy with me."

He stood and paced across the room. "I wasn't in a hurry to get a permanent job, so Lucy hired me to help at the store, and I did odd jobs for people. Then, one night Dad told me I needed to get a full-time job, or I'd have to move out." He rubbed his chin. "I'd turned into a smart aleck jerk. I yelled at Dad, then escaped to my buddy's house."

Sadie rose to stand by him. "What did your dad do?"

"He let me go." Joel shook his head. "I think he thought I'd come home later in the night. I didn't. I was frustrated and a little lost."

"I understand." She led him to the couch. "Let me get that coffee."

Steam rose from the mug Sadie handed him moments later. "I added cream the way you did at the festival."

"Thanks, Sadie. Sweet of you to notice." He sipped the brew, then dove into the story he prayed wouldn't run her off. "A couple nights later, we went to the bar. I was twenty-one and full of myself. Dan, too. He liked to drink. Not me so much, but I bought him a few, you know, to repay him for sleeping on his couch." He rested his drink on the coffee table. "Before the evening ended, Dan got drunk and accused me of mooching off him. Then he got in my face and accused me of taking advantage of him and being a jerk to my dad." He lifted the coffee to his lips, took a long drink, then returned the mug to the table. "Let's say, we came close to punches. Before I could stop him, Dan grabbed his keys to his motorcycle and took off."

Joel's voice caught. "I tried to stop him, Sadie. I tried."

He bent over and placed his elbows on his knees, head in his hands. "It was too late."

Her hand rested on his back. He raised his head and met her gaze. Pure warmth emitted from her green eyes. He pushed himself to croak out the rest of the story.

"You know how much Mom loves... loved to ride her bicycle? Dan's taillights sailed around the curve. By the time I wound around the road, the scene in front of me made me sick. Dan's bike lay on the side of the road. He sat on the berm, bleeding. A bystander called 911. Mom lay twisted in the ditch... she looked so bad." Tears wet his face. "I'm the reason she's in a wheelchair." Joel sobbed.

Sadie wrapped her arm around his shoulders. "Oh, Joel." She held him for a while. He lifted his head and looked at her. With a soft touch, she dabbed away the tears. "Your fault? I don't think so."

"Don't you get it? I bought Dan the liquor. I'm the reason he drove drunk."

"Dan decided to drink and drive. Not you. He made the choice to drink too much." Sadie rubbed small circles on his back.

He shook his head. "I knew he had a problem with alcohol."

Sadie's hand wrapped around his.

Her touch warmed him. "Truth is, Mom's forgiven me. She and Dad wanted our family to heal. Mom trusted God to take care of her, and He has." He cleared his throat. "I stayed in one of your gram's cottages until I could go home and face them. When I did move back home, Mom and Dad welcomed me." He swallowed a deep breath. "Mom and Dad forgave me. God's forgiven me, but I can't forgive myself."

Sadie grasped his hand tighter. "My friend Anne once told me, the hardest person to forgive is yourself. She helped me understand I didn't hold responsibility for what Bryce did. I didn't need to hang a ball of guilt around my neck like a scarlet letter. God loves us, Joel. You've shown me more than anyone."

"I'm not so sure."

She squeezed his hand. "I am. You've shown me the kind of love my grandparents poured over me. You sacrifice for everyone, and you're a great man. I'm happy you're in my life."

"Wow. I pour out my story of sorrow, and you turn it around to tell me I'm great." He tangled his fingers with hers.

"Because you are." A rosy glow reached her cheeks. "I love you, Joel. Always have, always will."

"I love you too, Sadie." He caressed her face and ran his thumbs over her soft skin. He pressed his lips on hers and sealed their love.

His heart raced as he committed to not only love this amazing woman, but protect her, too. He'd track Bryce and stop him, no matter what.

# CHAPTER THIRTY-ONE

Sunshine spilled through the kitchen window and escalated the joy in Joel's heart. He poured a bowl of cereal and whistled *Hark the Herald Angels Sing,* his favorite Christmas hymn. At the table, he doused the cereal with milk, then bowed his head.

*Thank You, God, for second chances with Sadie and with my life.*

If he stood, his feet would dance across the tile.

Lucy peeked around the kitchen door, then scurried to Joel's side. "Somebody's happy this morning. What happened after I went to bed?"

"I bet you'd like to know." He shoveled the last spoonful of Raisin Bran into his mouth and chewed.

She opened the bagel bag and popped a blueberry one in the toaster. "Did you kiss her?"

"None of your business." He rinsed his bowl, then gave his sister a peck on the cheek. "Got to go." Before Lucy bombarded him with more questions, he grabbed his coat and hustled out the back door.

In the pickup truck, Sadie's words from last night confirmed his mood. Sadie, a beautiful, kind, caring woman, loved him despite his flaws and imperfections, and she trusted him to love her back. She'd struggled after the pain her parents caused and the humiliation of her relationship with Bryce. The thought of that man lit fury in Joel. How could he manipulate and abuse a woman the way he did? Thanks to her friend, Anne, she'd escaped his cruelty.

He vowed to track him down and nail him. For today, he focused on Sadie.

Dressed in khakis, a green and blue plaid shirt, and a navy dress jacket, Joel stood on her porch. When she opened the door, his jaw dropped. "Wow, you look gorgeous."

Her dark hair gleamed in the sunlight, and her green eyes sparkled. He admired how the red dress clung in all the right places.

Her cheeks pinked. "Thank you. Come in."

"Ready for church?"

Joel lifted her coat from the chair and held it as she slid her arms into the sleeves. Then, she tucked her hand into the crook of his elbow, and they walked side-by-side to the truck.

Before she climbed in, she ran her hands along the lapel of his jacket. "You look handsome today." She kissed his cheek. "I'm so thankful I came back to the island."

His knees quaked as he savored her sweet scent. "Me too."

~~~~~

Seated in the pew next to Marigold and Lucy, Sadie twined her fingers with Joel's. He'd asked her to help him let go of his guilt. Anne had prayed with her, now she sought God's ear for Joel.

*Lord, help this man let go of the past and move on to a new future. I praise You for his mom and dad's kindness and gracious spirit. Pour your grace over this man I love so much.* Sadie tightened her grasp.

God rained peace over her as she sat beside the man she loved. She'd imagined her return to the island as an escape, a place to hide and heal. Even better, God opened the door to the future. She'd launched her cottage business, rekindled a relationship with Joel and friendships with Lucy and Marigold, and realized a broken life could be mended.

*O Come All Ye Faithful* echoed through the tiny church, with a choir of eight who raised their voices and led the congregation. Light shimmered through the stained-glass window featuring the Holy Family and gave a golden glow to baby Jesus. The minister preached on the hope of the season and how to hold on to joy in times of busyness and stress. Mesmerized by the flicker of candles on the communion table, Sadie tucked a nugget the preacher shared into her heart. "Jesus gives a peace beyond understanding."

She'd lit a Christmas candle for her grandparents when she arrived, a sweet remembrance of pure love and faith. Her Gram and Grandpa had understood Jesus' peace. When Marigold revealed Gram's story and how Jesus' love comforted her after Marcus died, Sadie longed for the same assurance.

For the first time, Sadie embraced the island as a place where she fit in and people accepted her as herself. Good friends surrounded her, and harmony filled her soul as gratitude spun into joy.

With Joel by her side and dear friends in her court, she trusted God to give them the wisdom to rid her of the one black mark on her life, Bryce. *Protect us from evil, God. Please help Joel capture my stalker. May Your will be done.*

~~~~~

*I'll be Home for Christmas* streamed from the restaurant speakers. Silver garland and blue bulbs embellished a tall, skinny evergreen. Joel dined with Sadie at a table decked in a lacy white cloth. Johnny, the restaurant owner, decorated with his best holiday touches for the annual Christmas feast. The chef loaded festive plates with roast beef, mashed potatoes, and green beans. The cinnamon scent of stewed apples and the smell of fresh yeast rolls rounded out a perfect meal.

Joel unfolded the cloth napkin and placed it on his lap. "I enjoyed the service today. The preacher's words about hope encouraged me to give my guilt to God. Thanks for praying for me. Your faith in me means more than I can say."

Sadie rested her hand on his. "You're welcome. Soon God will whisper in your ear to let go, and I know you'll obey. Is it easy? No. Yet I have all confidence, you'll be able to give the burden to Him."

He took her hand in his. "I've not felt this free in a long time. Now I can move forward with my life and let God work in me. Thanks for believing in me."

A joy-filled glow reflected in her eyes. "Of course I believe in you. I love you, more than ever."

Joel squeezed her hand. "I love you, you know. After you left to go to college, I missed you, and I asked God to bring you home. It took a while, but I'm so thankful He did."

Sadie flashed a smile. "Me too." Then she released his hand. "I guess we'd better eat before our food gets cold."

"Save room for a slice of Johnny's Italian cream cake."

"I haven't eaten Johnny's cake in years. I'd like to take my piece home to enjoy this evening."

"Good idea." Joel paused after a few bites. "Do you still have guests?"

She nodded and placed her fork on the edge of her plate. "The most recent group leaves this afternoon, a man and woman from Toledo on their way to Pittsburg. They wanted a few days to themselves before they visited family." She dabbed her mouth with a napkin. "I have one more booking before Christmas. A single guy who arrives on Tuesday and leaves Thursday. His personal assistant reserved the cottage. Said her boss needed a quick break. She paid ahead, too."

He scooped more mashed potatoes. "Sounds like you'll be cleaning tomorrow, eh?"

"Yep, that's the plan. I want to close the Julia for winter and spruce up Old Ben for the last guest. With Christmas close, I need to finish personal errands, too."

He had business to take care of as well. He'd keep his eyes open for Bryce, who might visit the island since his accomplices were in custody, and Joel had an important Christmas gift to secure.

~~~~~

Monday morning, Sadie tossed the last load of laundry into the dryer. "Rosie girl, all I have to do is make the bed, replenish the towels, and straighten a few things in the Julia cottage. Then I can ready Old Ben for the new occupant."

While she waited on the sheets to dry, she retrieved the few gifts she'd purchased for Christmas. She cut squares from the wrapping paper she'd found in the attic. With tissue paper, she tucked Lucy's light blue mittens, with a tiny cardinal embroidered on the front, into the bright red paper. With a flourish of tape and a big gaudy bow, she admired her work. Gram would be proud. For Joel, she placed the plaid scarf in a box. Something to keep him warm while he patrolled the island, and her grandpa's gold pocket watch. He had helped Grandpa so much, she wanted him to have the timepiece as a remembrance. Gram had the jeweler engrave Proverbs 3:5-6 on the back. When she searched for the verse in Grandpa's Bible, she knew Joel would appreciate the sentiment. *Trust in the Lord with all your heart and lean not on your own understanding, in all your ways submit to him, and he will make your paths straight.*

She loved Joel. She'd dreamed of a man who would respect and cherish her. Bryce had shattered those aspirations to the point she almost missed out.

Like the patchwork quilts her gram had created from the scrap basket, Sadie had pieced together a life on Abbott Island. Gram had taught her to snip the worn fabric away from the salvageable pieces and stitch them into a brand-new quilt. Now, God replaced her heartbreak with the patches of Joel's love and bound the edges with hope, as He stitched together a mosaic of peace.

With the last gift wrapped, Sadie knelt by the Christmas tree and positioned the packages underneath. She scooted away from the tree, sat cross-legged, and watched the lights twinkle. Rosie snuggled into her lap.

"You are too big to be a lap dog." The retriever rested her head on her owner's arm, then licked her. "We're home, girl. We're home."

~~~~~

Why didn't the imbecile answer her phone? Bryce punched in the number for the third time. Voicemail, again. Red must have assumed she'd earned her money. He slammed the desk. She'd not scared Sadie into leaving the little island or the pathetic new boyfriend. Good thing he planned a visit. If Red failed to convince her to go home, he'd take on the task himself. He'd force her to beg him to take her back. He imagined her on her knees. Oh, how he'd love to see her grovel.

After one more failed attempt to reach the woman, he shoved his cell into his pocket and opened a small travel bag. A quick trip called for fewer clothes. His insides quivered at the idea of a visit to her quaint little cottages. Maybe she'd leave cheap mints on the pillow, or smelly flowers in a vase. If her police friend showed his face ... Bryce tucked a small pistol into his case and zipped the closure. Ready or not, he planned to rescue his most important possession... his Sadie. She'd belong to him, along with her dad's company. He rubbed his hands in anticipation. Once his lawyer assured him Daddy's girl stood to inherit the money, he'd dispose of the old man.

# CHAPTER THIRTY-TWO

"Rosie, stay in the house while I spruce up the cottage. I don't want to trip over you while I clean." Sadie loaded a wicker laundry basket with fresh bedding and cleaning supplies. She added her hammer to straighten a shelf and then tossed in a few scented pinecones for holiday cheer.

At the Old Ben cottage, she unlocked the door and nudged it open. She toted the basket to the small table beside the window, then reviewed the work needed to ready the cottage for the next guest. She spied a white envelope, addressed to her, propped on the kitchenette's sink.

*Sadie, thanks so much for a wonderful stay. We'll be back in the summer.*

*The Johnsons.*

She held the card to her chest and spun around. "Yes." Another positive review. Her future looked brighter than she'd imagined. Yet doubt overshadowed her, and fear gnawed at her heart. So many positives surrounded her, but the one huge negative, the whale in the bathtub, threatened to smother her joy.

Joel had arrested Rayann. Sadie prayed the girl would identify Bryce as the one who'd hired her, in spite of his threats. She understood he frightened the poor young woman into breaking the law, and Rayann feared her father might suffer. Even as Sadie empathized, he still lurked somewhere in the shadows. She shivered and rubbed the goosebumps on her arms.

*Lord, give me the courage to move forward and the strength to accomplish my tasks. My joy is in You.*

Sadie tucked the card into the bottom of the laundry basket. With an orange-scented cleaner, she wiped out the sink, then scrubbed the bathroom. With all the surfaces disinfected, she changed the bedding. The evergreen coverlet she placed at the end of the bed created a pleasing contrast to her gram's poinsettia quilt. With her hands, she smoothed the wrinkles out. Perfect. She hoped her new guest enjoyed Christmas.

The assistant who booked the cottage revealed her guest needed a few days off work, but she didn't disclose anything else. She hadn't shared where they traveled from or why they booked at the last minute. When someone called, Sadie tried to guess their age by their voice. Two out of three, she'd guessed right. Since the assistant sounded young, she imagined the boss might be too. Perhaps the mystery guest needed a day or two to put their feet up and relax before the Christmas rush.

Two more items on the to do list and she'd finish the refresh. With the hammer, she pounded in nails to set the shelf straight. She dropped the hammer, one of the few tools she'd rescued from the shed, onto the bed. Satisfied with her work, Sadie lifted the pinecones from the basket.

With a smile, she settled on the floor to add the last touch.

~~~~~

Gravel crunched and the sound of an engine shut off outside the cottage. Must be Joel or Lucy. If her friends knocked on the door at the house and didn't find her, they'd know to check the cottage. Sadie sat cross-legged on Old Ben's floor as she sorted and arranged the scented pinecones in a small basket, with green and red Christmas bulbs. On top of the basket, she secured a red plaid bow for a perfect touch. Before she got up from the floor, a knock thumped on the door.

Certain her friends dropped by to visit, she remained seated. "Come in."

A man's shadow poured across the hardwood. When no one called out a greeting, she turned to look.

"Bryce. What are you doing here?" Sadie's stomach twisted and her hands shook. No one else seared her with fear the way he did.

She scooted to the edge of the bed and reached to steady herself. With a push, she stood. A ball of angst stirred in her gut as his heavy cologne nauseated her.

His gaze darted around the room. "Nice little place my assistant rented for me." The evil in his eyes glimmered, and sarcasm dripped.

He stalked in and closed the door with a thud. The sound of the lock's click shot terror through Sadie. She steadied herself and positioned her body in front of the bed where she'd left the hammer. With slow, deliberate movements, she grasped the tool and tucked it in the back of her waistband.

"What do you want?"

"The pine smell's a nice touch. Look at all this you've done. For me." A wicked grin crossed his face.

She straightened her spine to stand her full height. "I didn't know you rented the cottage, so don't flatter yourself."

He lurched for her and grabbed her wrist. "Now Sadie, I know you love me. You got scared and ran away." He twisted the skin on her forearm. "How about you pack your things and we'll head home. Where you belong. With me." His voice raised in volume as he loomed over her. His breath wreaked of alcohol.

Sadie shoved herself into him. He let go of her arm, then she jerked the hammer from her pants and swung. He ducked, but stumbled. She kicked his shin, then ran for the door. With a twist and yank, she wrenched the door open. As she vaulted out the door, he grabbed her leg. He tumbled on top of her as she landed in the grass.

"I forgot how feisty you are. Makes me want you more."

"No!" She shoved hard. He clung to her. Her hammer soared as she swung and hit his back.

He yowled and rolled off her. "You little--"

"You aren't ruining my life. I'm sick of this and of you," she yelled as she leaped to her feet and darted for the house.

Bryce lunged at her, then fell on his face and sprawled in the grass.

Sadie jumped the porch steps, grabbed and twisted the door's knob, and pushed. Rosie bounded to her owner's side and barked. Sadie clicked the lock, then dropped to her knees on the floor and hugged Rosie. After taking a breath, she found her cell phone, and called Joel. Out the window, she watched as Bryce held his side and tried to stand. He stumbled to the ground, then flattened on his back. His intoxication saved her.

Ten minutes later, a siren squealed outside, while Rosie barked from inside the house. Sadie staggered to the couch and collapsed.

~~~~~

The police cruiser flew into Sadie's driveway, sirens blaring and lights flashing. Joel and Levi stepped out and surveyed the yard. A man slumped in the grass.

"Levi, he might have a weapon, get behind the car." Joel joined him, then called to the man. "Show us your hands."

The man sat up and tugged something from his pocket. With a shaky hand, he aimed a pistol at the squad car.

Joel squatted beside Levi and shouted to the man. "Put the gun down."

The man raised the pistol to the sky and fired a shot. "You want to be next, copper boy?" His words were slurred.

Levi edged his way to the back of the car. With precise movements and his gun in front of him, Joel tested how close he could get to the lowlife. A few feet in front of him, Joel yelled a command.

"Drop it now, or I will shoot."

With a grunt, the man threw the weapon at Joel. The gun discharged and planted a bullet into a nearby tree.

"Face down on the ground. Now!"

The drunken man rolled over and lay sprawled in the yard.

Joel secured the pistol, and Levi cuffed the guy and read him his rights. This man resembled the description Sadie gave him of Bryce. Fury filled his mind, but his self-control kicked in. He inhaled, exhaled, and whispered a prayer of thanks.

Now to check on Sadie and to assure himself she fled this maniac unharmed. Joel tapped on her door. She flew out and threw her arms around him. He pulled her close and buried his face in her hair.

After a minute, he stepped away, brushed a strand of loose hair behind her ear, and met her gaze. "Are you okay?"

"I'm shook up, and I think I have a few bruises, but I'm all right." She nodded at the squad car. "That's Bryce. His assistant rented the cottage, and he had the audacity to think I'd go with him, and it wasn't happening. I had my hammer with me, and I hit him in the back. Gave me enough time to get in the house."

Joel placed a hand on each side of her face. "Remind me to be careful when you're swinging a hammer." A smile crossed his lips. "I'll be back later to get your statement. Do you want me to send Lucy over?"

"Yes, if she's not busy."

Sadie stood in her yard as the police cruiser raced around the bend and carried her stalker away. Arms folded around her middle, the peace God promised washed her soul.

~~~~~

When Lucy tapped on the front door's glass, Sadie's chest tightened. Not okay. Every nerve in her body tingled and her head pounded. Lucy pecked again and Sadie waved for her to come in.

They met at the front door, and Lucy wrapped her in a bear hug. Sadie scooted away and eyed her friend.

"You about made me wet my pants. I didn't expect you so soon."

"Sorry. I tried to get your attention by waving." Lucy led her to the couch. "You okay?"

She leaned on the cushion of the couch. "I'm not sure. I'm not afraid anymore, and I have peace." She held her hands in her lap to keep them from shaking. "He came after me. Demanded I go with him." Rosie rested her head in her owner's lap. "I'm scared to think what he might have done to me. No way I was getting in a car with him." She ran her hand over the retriever's coat.

"Joel's got him now. He'll take him to the mainland, via the airport. They'll lock him up."

Lucy went to the kitchen, filled the kettle and set it on the burner for tea. "I hope this nightmare is about over."

From the cupboard, Lucy grabbed two mugs. She placed a tea bag in each one, then washed the plate, fork, and cup she found in the sink.

When the kettle whistled, Lucy poured the piping hot water over the tea bags. "Here you go. Peppermint tea should help."

The sweet-scented steam floated across Sadie's face. "Thanks." She twisted sideways on the couch and faced her. "I can't believe he chased me and tried to scare me. I'm praying he's retained for a while, and Dad realizes what a jerk he is."

Lucy's eyes rounded. "You wouldn't go to work for your dad with Bryce gone, would you?"

Sadie closed her eyes and sipped her tea. The waft of peppermint relaxed her nerves. "No, I plan to stay put." She returned the mug to the table. "I'm an island girl, and I'm not leaving." She rubbed her forehead. "I wonder how much Dad knows about Bryce."

# CHAPTER THIRTY-THREE

*Bryce's relentless pursuit pushed Sadie into the depths of the thick woods.*
*"I have to find Rosie."*
*Her legs throbbed and her head ached. A few more yards.*
*"Rosie."*

Sadie shot straight up in bed, her heart pounding. Rosie nosed her face under her owner's arm.

"You're okay." She ran her hand over the dog's soft fur. "What a horrible dream." She patted the bed for her pet to join her, and she wrapped her arms around Rosie's neck.

With the actual nightmare over, the realization that she once again had freedom to run the trails brought joy to her soul. No more worries about Bryce or his accomplices.

"What do you say, Rosie, ready to run?"

Once she was dressed in leggings and a fleece sweatshirt, Sadie stretched and then took off to the nature sanctuary. The forty-degree weather encouraged her to push herself to run faster. Rosie loped beside her master. In the woods, she listened to the wind rustle through the bare branches. She inhaled the fresh scent of cedar. A deer peered at her from behind a tree, and cardinals twittered above her. Filled with the peace she'd longed for, she pumped her arms and moved her legs to the rhythm of joy. Fear diminished in the face of sweet release, and with each step anxiety gave way to peace, fear to freedom.

Her new-found hope dimmed as she returned home and rounded the corner to see she had a visitor. A silver Lexus parked in her driveway meant one thing. *Dad.* Why was he on the island? Two days before Christmas, no less.

Sadie slowed to a walk, in no hurry to get berated by the man who called her daughter. He'd arrived to convince her to return to work. Or he wanted to yell at her for getting Bryce thrown into jail. Either way, she prayed to God for strength. She squared her shoulders and stood as tall as her frame stretched.

The Lexus door swung open, and her father stepped out. His long, midnight black, wool coat draped over pressed slacks. He dressed for business… always.

"Dad?" She walked to him as she tugged her sweatshirt over her hips.

He opened his arms.

She stilled and tilted her head in question. The last hug he'd given away was at Mom's funeral. *What's up?*

"Can we talk?" His dark brown eyes glinted in the sun.

Sadie nodded. She patted Rosie, then walked to the porch. He stepped ahead of her and pulled the door open for her to go inside.

"Do you mind if I change? I need to shower after my run." She stared at the man she called Dad.

He stood as if at attention. "That's fine. I'll wait here."

"Dad, you can sit. Take off your coat and hang it on the hook, here. I'll be back." Sadie sprinted to the loft. *Now what?* Her dreams of a peaceful day faded.

Her hands trembled as she tugged off her running clothes. What did Dad want? *God, I need wisdom and strength. Can You pour those over me? Sorry if I'm begging. I don't trust him. Thank You and Amen.* After a quick shower, she tugged on jeans and a red sweater, then put her hair into a ponytail.

At the bottom of the steps, Sadie paused and studied her dad. His face held more wrinkles than she remembered, and more gray strands mixed through his dark hair. He'd aged. He looked older than his fifty-nine years. As usual, he wore an expensive suit and leather shoes. All business, all the time.

She walked into the living room and stood in front of him. "Dad, you want a drink? Tea, coffee, bottled water?"

"Coffee. Black, please."

She brewed a K-cup with bottled water and hoped it tasted good enough for his discerning palate. He made no effort to help. His staff waited on him like he reigned as king.

"Here you go." She placed the mug on one of Gram's crocheted coasters and held her teacup in hopes the warmth penetrated her shivers.

With him on one end of the long couch, she perched on the other, as far away as she could. As much as she wanted to ask why he came, she waited.

He took a sip of coffee, then rested the mug on the table. "Sadie, are you okay?"

She about spilled her tea. Shock permeated her heart as her mouth gaped. Dad never asked about her feelings. He barked orders.

"Did you know your friend came to visit me? Marigold." He unbuttoned his suit coat and stretched his legs in front of him. "Why anyone named their child such a hippie name is beyond me."

There was the dad she remembered. Critical as usual.

"She mentioned it. Yes."

He stood and removed his jacket. Then he folded the sleeves of the navy-blue fabric under the coat and laid it across the couch, as if it might break.

Frank paced behind the couch as he unfastened and rolled his shirt sleeves. "Her visit made me curious."

Curious? Marigold's rant about Bryce made him curious. How about angry? Defensive?

With his hands on his hips, he faced her. "I've noticed errors in my accounts. Money missing. I've suspected someone funneled funds to a bogus account. You left, so I didn't have your expertise to find the errors. I'd hired another forensic accountant, but then I got to wondering if she'd stolen the money."

Sadie angled away from the cushion and sat straight. "Someone embezzled from the company?"

"Appears so." Frank lowered himself near her on the couch. "I hired another company to look at my accounts. They found the person responsible."

"Dad. Who?" She'd twisted around to face him. "You know it wasn't me."

"Of course not," he barked. "I ..." His head dropped. He stared at his manicured hands.

"What?" She touched her dad's arm. He didn't pull away. A first for them. Sadie carried no memory of affection from her father. No hugs, no pats on the back. If she cried or teared up, he'd declare her tears fake and manipulative. The room's silence asked a roar of questions. The strong aroma of Dad's coffee reminded her of his ever-present power.

"I'm trying to say..." His head dropped.

"Dad?" Sadie ducked her head to look at him. Her ponytail swished against his arm. The rhythm of Rosie's soft snore calmed Sadie's breathing and slowed the quick pace of her heart.

He raised his gaze to her. "I'm sorry." His eyes glistened.

Sadie raised from the couch, then crouched in front of the man. Her brows scrunched together. Her heart fluttered. "Dad, I'm not following. Who embezzled, and why are you sorry?"

Frank grabbed her hands. He clung to his daughter as if he might fall. A deep rumble came from his throat. "Sit by me."

She planted herself beside the man she had feared for years. Empathy filled her. "Tell me, please."

He swiveled to face her. "Bryce did it. He embezzled thousands of dollars over four years. The accountants said he'd paid off a few of my people to help him. They found the money, and I'll get most of it back."

"Dad, I'm ... "

"No, don't say you're sorry. You recognized his deceit. I didn't listen." A tear fell on his cheek. He blinked away the rest. "I'm so sorry."

Sadie wrapped an arm around her dad's shoulders. She rested her head against his. He leaned into her, and the two sat for several minutes. Rosie lifted her head, then stood and nudged her hand.

"It's okay, girl. We're okay."

~~~~~

Sadie dished chili for her dad, Joel, Lucy, and Marigold. "I have cheese, crackers, and sour cream on the counter if you want it. Come grab a bowl and help yourselves." She'd laid out a vintage holiday tablecloth with sleighs and snow, and people laughing around a tree. In the center, Lucy had arranged a bouquet of holly mixed with red and white chrysanthemums. Sadie had hesitated to dream of a Christmas Eve with family and friends. Yet here they were, gathered around her table. Her eyes drank in the people she loved, while her heart smiled with joy.

Joel turned to Frank, who had relinquished his tie and unfastened his top button. "Not to mention a sour topic, but with the embezzlement charges, stalking, and aggravated assault, Bryce should be in jail for a long time."

"He deserves to rot there. Joel, thank you for keeping Sadie safe."

"You're welcome, sir. Sadie did a pretty good job keeping herself out of danger." Joel cast a smile at her.

Frank pursed his lips. "I wish I hadn't been so bullheaded."

Marigold elbowed him. Frank jerked his head to face her. "What? If you hadn't barged into my office, I still wouldn't believe Bryce was such a cad." He glared at her. "I suppose I should say thank you. So, thank you."

"You bet you should." Marigold nodded and passed the bowl of crackers.

Sadie looked at Lucy. Both of them bubbled with laughter.

"What's so funny?" Frank's gaze rested on Sadie. She bit her lip, then grinned. The corner of his mouth raised. "I guess your old man's getting soft in his old age."

Sadie walked around the table and wrapped her arms around him from the back. "I can hope, Dad. Soft is okay with me."

~~~~~

After dinner and a rambunctious game of Uno, Joel put the cards back into the box and cleared the table of napkins and silverware.

Frank excused himself to go to the downstairs bedroom. "Night all."

"Good night," they each called to him.

Marigold and Lucy gathered cups and dessert plates, then washed and dried dishes. When they finished, Lucy went to the hooks where their coats hung.

"What a fun night." She wrapped a green and blue crocheted scarf around her neck. "Marigold and I are heading home. Thanks for supper, Sadie."

"You're welcome. I appreciate you cleaning the mess." She hugged her friends. "Enjoy the rest of your evening."

Lucy wiggled her eyebrows, then looked from her brother to Sadie. "You, too."

Sadie closed the door, then faced Joel. "This is the first Christmas Eve I remember with Dad. Most years he sequestered himself in his office. I know he'll never be warm and fuzzy, but at least he appears to care."

Joel twined his fingers with Sadie's. "Yeah, he enjoyed himself."

With her free hand, she patted her chest. "It makes my heart so happy to have all my favorite people together tonight."

"Makes mine happy to do this." He placed a gentle kiss on her lips.

"Mmm... I like your happy."

From the couch, Joel lifted a quilt and wrapped the soft fabric around Sadie's shoulders. "Care to join me on the porch?"

He took her hand and tugged her to the swing, as it creaked in the breeze. They snuggled on the wooden seat. The faint smell of burnt wood lingered in the air, and fresh fallen snow glistened under the full moon.

He stretched his arm across the swing and rocked the wooden seat. Sadie tucked in and placed her head on his shoulder. Her long brown braid hung in front of her.

Joel touched her chin. "What are you thinking?" He inhaled the scent of lavender in her hair.

She turned her face to his. "I'm thinking, I'm blessed beyond anything I could imagine. When I arrived on the island in October, I had a tiny drizzle of hope for my future." Her eyes brightened. "Now look. I have my dad, my friends, and you."

"I love you, Sadie." Joel ran his thumb along her jaw, then his finger across her lips. She breathed in and out in soft wisps. His lips covered hers. The cherry flavor of the pie they'd shared lingered on their lips. With both hands, he framed her face and deepened the kiss. He wanted her to know she was his one and only, his island girl.

He pulled back, then kissed her forehead before he rested his head on hers.

For the first time in a long time, he saw the dazzling smile Sadie wore in her teens, her "I've got this" grin.

"I love you too, Joel."

He rose, lifted her from the swing, and wrapped his arms around her. She tightened her hug. A sign she'd be there for always.

"I better go. I'll see you tomorrow. Mom and Dad are coming over to celebrate Christmas with us."

"Rosie and I will be there."

Joel left a goodbye kiss on her lips, then headed to his car. Tomorrow could be a big day.

# CHAPTER THIRTY-FOUR

"Dad, are you positive you can't stay? Joel invited you." Sadie scrambled eggs with cheese and green and red peppers. She toasted thick wheat bread and buttered the slices, then slathered it with blueberry-lemon jam from the farmer's market.

"No, I need to get back and finish investigating the mess at work." He stood in the kitchen. "I enjoyed the little party last night. You have good friends."

"I do. They've been great to me." She plated the food and placed the dishes on the table. "Let's eat."

Frank pulled out Grandpa's chair and sat. She relaxed in the seat across from him.

"Can I pray, Dad?"

"If you want." He bowed his head. Sadie thanked God for another chance with her father. *God, how about a new start at life and a chance to find genuine love?* Out loud, she asked God to bless the food and give Dad safe travels.

He lifted his fork and sampled the holiday eggs. "These are outstanding. I bet you'd win Joel's heart with these." He winked and laughed. Another first for Sadie.

"You're funny, Dad." The road might be long to repair the hurt, but she intended to give him grace as they fumbled along. In her heart, she'd forgiven him, now she'd strive to keep the lines of communication open.

~~~~~

A Christmas filled with fun, love, and peace ignited Sadie's heart with joy. In Joel and Lucy's living room, along with their parents, the group opened gifts around the tree. Lucy squealed when she ripped the wrapping from her present.

"I love these, Sadie. Where did you find such cute mittens?" She jumped from her seat on the floor and hugged her friend.

"The day we went shopping on the mainland. You admired them, so I bought them." Sadie lifted another box from under the tree and passed it to Joel.

"For me?" He tore off the tape, then unfolded the snowman paper. A green plaid wool scarf and a pair of all-weather gloves spilled from the package. "These are great. Thank you."

She patted his leg. "I hope they'll keep you warm while you're on patrol."

He rested the box on the arm of the couch and refolded the scarf. "They will." Before he tucked the winter wear in the box, a square wrapped in tissue paper caught his attention. "What's this?" He lifted his gaze to Sadie's.

"Something I found in Gram's recipe box." She shrugged.

Joel tore off the layers of tissue paper. He stared at the framed photo and a smile crossed his face. "How old were we?"

"Fourteen or so. I've no idea why she kept photos in with her recipes, but she did." Sadie scooted a few inches to lean over Joel's shoulder. "I was looking for the fruit cocktail cake recipe the other day, because I wanted to bake it for today, and behind it I found us."

He held the frame for his mom, dad, and Lucy to see. Then gave it to Mom.

"I remember when you two ran all over the island. Lucy, too. The three Musketeers." Amy shook her head. "These old photos were the best."

Joel studied the framed memory. "Look at those skinny legs and buck teeth."

Sadie stood and propped her hands on her hips. "Who are you calling skinny?"

"Me." He laughed as he set the gift on the mantel. They stood side by side and admired the photo. He twined his fingers with hers as the fire popped and crackled.

"We're going to get dinner ready. You two lovebirds stay here." Lucy, her mom, and dad hustled to the kitchen.

"Time alone." Joel snatched a kiss.

Sadie led him to the tree. "I have one more gift for you." She lifted a small package from the branches. "I hid it there when I came in."

Joel tore off the paper. Grandpa Ben's pocket watch rested inside a square box. "I've seen this before."

"For as long as I can remember, Grandpa Ben kept time with it."

He turned the timepiece in his hand and ran his thumb over the ship engraved on the cover. "I don't know what to say... Thank you."

"You did so much to help him, I want you to have it." Sadie wrapped a hand around his. "Grandpa carried the watch in his pocket, a gift from Gram. I thought I'd pass on the gesture."

"I'll carry this beauty every day."

"I'm so glad you like it."

The delicious aroma of pineapple-trimmed ham and cheddar potato casserole floated in from the kitchen. "Smells like Lucy has the food out of the oven." Sadie nodded to the kitchen.

"Come on, guys. Dinner's ready," Lucy called.

Amy glowed as she rolled around the table to her spot. "I'm so proud of you, dear. This is Lucy's first Christmas dinner, you know."

A blush rose to her cheeks. "Mom, it wasn't a big deal."

Joel rubbed his hands together. "Let's decide after we eat, Sis."

Lucy frowned at him. "You're so funny."

"Here you go." Joel pulled out Sadie's chair for her, then Lucy's.
Dad grabbed Lucy and Amy's hands. "Let's bow our heads."

~~~~~

Joel pushed away from the table. "Delicious, Lucy. Almost as good as Mom's." He stretched his arm over Sadie's chair. "I'm stuffed."

Sadie folded her napkin. "Me too. Thank you so much for inviting me. This has been the best Christmas I've had since I was a little girl." She stood and started stacking plates.

Lucy rose. "I'll get those."

Sadie held out her hand. "No. You did all the cooking. The least we can do is wash the dishes. Right, Joel?" Her eyes met his.

"Sounds fair." He carried plates and glasses to the kitchen.

~~~~~

At the sink, his elbows submerged in suds, Joel scrubbed the last pan. "You want to walk on the beach when we finish?"

"Isn't it chilly outside?" Sadie dried the plates and stacked them in the cabinet.

He drained the sink and dried his hands on a Christmas towel. "Don't worry, I won't let you freeze." He caught her hands in his. "Let's go."

~~~~~

"I haven't walked on this beach this winter." Sadie snuggled into Joel after he'd wrapped his arm around her waist and pulled her to him. She tugged the hood of her red parka to her head.

"Do I look like a cardinal in all this snow?"

"You're more beautiful than any bird." He planted a soft kiss on her cheek.

Cuddled together, he led her to a bench. He let go of her and snatched a kitchen towel from his pocket. The snow fell to the ground as he brushed the towel over the seat. "Join me." He gestured to the clean seat.

"I'd love to." A giggle escaped her. "It's so quiet tonight. I love the solitude of the island." She reflected on the waves as they rolled in and out and listened to the water swish over the sand. A bird squawked in the distance, as fireplace smoke drifted overhead. With her mittened hand wrapped in Joel's, Sadie's heart swelled with peace and joy. She'd found her place.

He leaned into her. "Do you remember the last time we sat here? In this exact spot?" He peered at her.

She bent her head back and considered the stars. "Of course I do." A grin spread across her face. Her dimples deepened. Her gaze landed on the man she loved. "We were so young. What? Seventeen or eighteen? You followed me on my bike, then we ran along the beach, playing a version of teenage tag."

"More like catch and kiss." Joel chuckled. "I chased you for a reason." He wrapped his arm around her shoulders and faced her. "I had a gut feeling you'd never be back, and I wanted you to know I cared." He brushed a loose strand of hair from her face, then cleared his throat. "The best way I knew to show you was my awkward kiss."

She studied his eyes, the blue of a summer sky and so sincere. The love in her heart swelled as she tugged her mitten off and ran her fingers along his chin. "I think I knew, too." She cupped his jaw with her hand. "I'm so thankful God brought me home." Sadie memorized his kind eyes and glimpsed the boy who grew into the man she loved. Her lips touched his, then he drew her closer and returned her tender kiss.

When Joel leaned away, his gaze met hers. He stood, then bent over and removed her other mitten. With one swift move, he embraced her hands in his and knelt on one knee.

"Sadie, I've loved you since the day we met. You're as beautiful inside as out. I love your infectious smile and hopeful way of thinking. You make me a better man."

Her eyes rounded, as she let out a gasp. Happy tears burned her eyes in anticipation.

He squeezed her fingers. "Sadie, will you marry me?"

Sadie's laughter woke the quiet, and with one quick tug she pulled Joel closer and embraced him. "Yes. Of course I will. I love you."

From the pocket of his coat, he pulled a small box. He held it out to her and flipped the lid open.

Warmth radiated from her head to her feet. "Is this Gram's?"

"Yes." He placed the blue princess-cut diamond, shouldered with Celtic knots, on Sadie's finger. The diamond glistened in the moonlight.

"Where did you find it?" She shook her head. "I thought it was gone forever."

A grin spread across Joel's face. "The pawn shop in Sandusky called a few weeks after I'd given them the description of the ring. I bought it back. Forensics released it from evidence last week."

Sadie held her left hand out and admired the diamond. "With all the craziness, I'd given up hope of ever seeing it again." She grinned. You've given me the best Christmas gift I could ever want. You."

She wrapped her arms around his neck. He gathered her to him and caressed her lips with his. Her heart beat a steady rhythm as the kiss deepened and her future brightened.

He whispered into her ear. "I love you, Island Girl."

"Love you, too." She rested her head against his chest. "I'm thankful I found my way back to the place I belong, with you."

# CHAPTER THIRTY-FIVE

*Four months later ...*

On a warm April morning, Sadie and Marigold walked on the pebbled path to the tiny chapel. Sadie admired the tulips flourishing in shades of pink, red, lavender, and yellow. A clump of golden daffodils nodded in the breeze. Songbirds tweeted in the redbud trees, and the sun shone on this extraordinary day.

Sadie held the door open for Marigold, who toted a bag of wedding paraphernalia. "Mrs. Sadie Grayson sounds wonderful, don't you think?"

"Yes, it does." Marigold peered at the garment bag Sadie carried over her arm. "Be careful not to wrinkle your wedding dress."

She patted the bag. "I am, Mari. I worked too hard to be careless now."

Down the aisles of the small sanctuary, Lucy and two of her employees had dressed the ends of the pews with cone-shaped, paper and lace May baskets. Greenery and pale pink and lavender flowers spilled from each one. On the low-rise stage, Joel had installed an arch he'd built from birch branches and draped with sheer white organza. Three glass canisters stood on a table, two filled with sand from the island beaches and an empty one for Joel and Sadie to combine the sand as one.

"So pretty." She revolved in a circle to soak in all the beauty, as delight filled her soul. "I can't believe I'm marrying Joel today."

"Lucy did a fantastic job decorating. Now, we'd best get you ready." Marigold hurried her to a room in the back.

She wove pink, lavender, and white freesia into Sadie's dark hair. With the tail of a comb, she wound the hair into a chignon and secured the style with a few bobby pins and a delicate butterfly clip. "You chose a flattering hairstyle, and the flowers add the essence of the season."

At the mirror, Sadie applied lip gloss and mascara, the only makeup she wore. "I'm not sure why, but I'm trembling." The mascara wand shook in her hand.

Marigold plucked the wand from her. "You're excited, my dear. Let me finish for you."

"You know what you're doing, right?" She opened her eyes wide.

The older lady brushed the deep brown coloring on with gentle wisps. "I wore makeup once upon a time. I haven't forgotten how to apply the stuff."

The door to the dressing room flew open. Lucy twirled into the room in a candy pink, knee-length, chiffon dress. Ruffles cascaded along the Vneck. "What do you think?" She placed a box on a corner table.

Sadie's hands flew to her mouth. "When you tried it on at the store, you looked beautiful. With the cute shoes and your hair curled, you are gorgeous."

"Thanks for not picking a fluffy dress I'd never wear again." Her soon-to-be sister-in-law admired herself in the full-length mirror.

Behind her, Sadie unfurled a ruffle on Lucy's dress. "The sanctuary looks amazing. Thank you for organizing the decor." She sat and slipped on her lace-embellished flats.

"One more surprise." Lucy joined the bride in the chairs and flipped the lid open on the box she'd carried in. "Take a look."

A small gasp escaped Sadie. She lifted a bouquet of pink, yellow, and lavender tulips tied together with her gram's handkerchief. Tears threatened to smear her mascara. After she buried her face in them to smell the sweetness, she rested the flowers in the box and hugged Lucy's neck. "They're perfect."

"Mom picked the flowers in her garden this morning."

Tears threatened to ruin Sadie's makeup. Lucy dabbed her eyes with a tissue. "She wanted you to have them."

"I'm marrying into the most wonderful family."

Lucy placed her hands on Sadie's shoulders. "We're blessed to have you. Now, turn around and let me see what Marigold did with your hair."

Sadie spun.

"I love it."

In the mirror, she checked her mascara. "How much longer do I have?"

"Thirty minutes, sweetie." Marigold blinked tears away. "Your Gram and Grandpa would be proud."

"I wish they were here. It's comforting to know how much they loved Joel." From a padded hanger, she lifted her dream dress. "Has anyone seen Dad, yet?"

~~~~~

On the opposite side of the chapel, Joel paced. Anxiety and joy vied for a place in his head and heart. He'd waited so long for Sadie, what if he failed as a husband?

*Son, you're going to soar. Together, you and Sadie will face life head on and accomplish great things.* Sadie's grandpa had held on to the belief she'd return to the island and to Joel. Grandpa Ben's simple faith had given him hope.

He fumbled with the pink tie. "Levi, can you help me with this? I'm all thumbs."

"Calm down, man. I'll get it." Levi wound the fabric together to make a Windsor knot. "At least we aren't stuck in a cummerbund and tux."

Joel ran his hand over his slacks. "Yep. Buying a new suit made more sense."

A wooden bench lined one wall. "Sit for a minute, Joel." Levi patted the seat. "You've got like thirty minutes before we go on stage."

He tugged his new watch out of his pocket and opened the face. "I guess wearing a hole in the floor won't make the time move any faster."

"Nope. Sure doesn't."

A knock sounded on the door, then opened. The pastor peered at Joel. "You doing okay? Any cold feet?"

He stood and shook the man's hand. "No, sir. I'm good."

"Great. I'll tap on the door when we're ready for you."

"Thanks."

The door closed and Levi patted his friend's back. "Have you heard any more about Bryce and his accomplices?"

"They go to trial soon. He has a lot against him. You know he embezzled from the company he worked at before, plus the embezzlement at her dad's business. Sadie's dad told her women have pressed sexual harassment charges against him. Piled on top of all the other charges, he should be put away for a long time." Joel tugged on his tie.

Levi grasped his arm. "I don't want to have to redo the knot." He flashed a grin. "Good to hear he'll be out of your lives, and you two can live in peace."

"Thanks. I'm looking forward to a long, happy marriage to Sadie."

Levi punched Joel in the arm, like a brother might. "You've waited long enough."

A knock on the door echoed through the room.

"This is it." Joel donned his charcoal gray suit jacket, sucked in a deep breath, and strode to the sanctuary.

~~~~~

Sadie studied the tea-length ivory gown she'd sewn with Marigold's help. Lace overlaid silk charmeuse, and the boat neck complimented the sheer lace sleeves. Lucy fastened Gram's silver rose necklace around her neck, and Sadie put in the earrings.

Marigold fluffed out Sadie's full skirt. "You look stunning."

"I couldn't have made it without your help." She'd oiled Gram's sewing machine and discovered the vintage pattern in her files. With Marigold's guidance and Sadie's determination, she'd mastered the dress. "I found the photo of Gram and Grandpa's wedding day and copied her dress in as much detail as possible. Do you think she'd approve?"

"Oh honey, she'd be thrilled." Marigold kissed Sadie's cheek. "I'd better head to the sanctuary. Johnny's waiting on me."

As she left, Sadie's father strolled in. He paused and cleared his throat. "Sadie, you are a beautiful bride."

Her arms out, she hugged him. "Thanks, Dad."

He straightened. "Um ... well, we'd better get out there."

Music floated from the sanctuary as Lucy led the way.

~~~~~

Vivaldi's *Spring* flowed from the piano. The pastor raised his hands for all in attendance to stand. Lucy strolled down the aisle runner, carrying spring flowers, as Joel struggled to stand still and not rock on his toes. Instead, he glued his gaze to the sanctuary's archway in anticipation of his bride.

At the sight of Sadie, the corners of his mouth curved into a grateful smile. His bride clung to her father's arm and graceful step after graceful step, walked to him.

When they reached the front of the sanctuary, Frank nodded to the minister and placed Sadie's hand in Joel's. The bride and groom recited heartfelt promises and combined the sand from their beaches into one.

"You can kiss her now, Joel."

The crowd cheered at their passionate kiss, as he hugged Sadie to him.

"I've waited so long for you. I love you, Sadie."

She whispered back, "You're my best friend, Joel, and I love you, too."

**THE END**

# About the Author

If Penny Frost McGinnis could live in a lighthouse or on an island, she would. Instead, she and her husband are content to live in southwest Ohio and visit Lake Erie every chance they get. Blessed with five children, their spouses, and a passel of grandchildren, she adores her family, indulges in dark chocolate, enjoys fiber arts, and grows flowers and herbs in her tiny garden. Penny has been published in Chicken Soup, and The Upper Room. She blogs at Hope for Today's Heart and believes God has called her to bring hope to people's lives through the written word.

Contact Penny at penny.frost.mcginnis@gmail.com or visit her website at www.pennyfrostmcginnis.com.